The White Buffalo's Feather

Rita K. Kasinskas

Rita K. Kasinskas

Dedicated to my children:

Phillip for his inspiration and support.

Rachel for her artistic talent, which was instrumental in the creation of the cover.

Valerie for planting the seed that grew into this book.

To my sister, Lindalee, for spurring me on to book's completion.

Contents

Preface

Our world consists of many cultures, with vast and rich histories. Understanding the way of life of other cultures, enriches our own, as we explore the beautiful variey our world has to offer.

Chapter One – Making Wishes

A lone white buffalo, silhouetted against the vast horizon of Montana's great open skies, leads a massive herd of buffalo, their powerful hooves striking the ground with thunderous fiery. The air was thick with clouds of dust and the buffalo's hot, steamy breath.

An elevated sense of adventure and daring surged through Deseray's body, as she sat perched proudly upon the back of the great white buffalo; her fingers clung tightly to the thick tuff of white fur at the back of his neck. The fur felt course and wiry, clenched between her fingers. Her fingers ached as she held on tightly.

The white buffalo's proud majesty radiated with each stride of his powerful hooves, as he led the ever-moving waves of brown across the vast, golden prairies. With symbolic purpose, the great white buffalo fashioned the herd into a thundering circle, around and around, the circle of life. Enclosed within this living circle, an impressive warrior stood, solemn and alone.

The moment she saw him, Deseray's heart leapt with admiration and joy. Her excitement grew as she looked upon this ultimately handsome and majestic figure of a man. He was so perfect in his solitude and prayer. He stood with his hands lifted upward, slightly above his waist, his palms up toward the heavens. His bronzed body barely covered, his dark ebony black hair hanging loosely about his shoulders and trailing down his muscular back, except for two long braids the framed either side of his handsome face.

An eagle feather hung from each braid. An elaborate breastplate covered his strong chest, while fine leather ties dangled against his bronzed thighs, securing a breechcloth that covered him front and back.

From her perch upon the white buffalo's back, Deseray intently gazed upon his solemn physique, encircled in the center of the massive herd. He radiated an intense sense of serenity. The clouds of dust came nowhere near him, as he stood proudly under the endless sky.

His eyes fixed upon the heavens, speaking silently to the Great Spirit. The sight of him overwhelmed Deseray with desire. Her heart whispered, "I am here. Look at me!" As if in reply to her plea, the handsome warrior's eyes left the heavens and bonded with hers. It was for only a moment.

His momentary gaze affected Deseray so intensely, that her heart quickened, and she found it difficult to breathe. She felt the blood rushed to her face and claimed the moment as hers. Then, as suddenly as his eyes had found hers, they returned to the heavens.

The buzzing of the alarm startled Deseray from her dream. "Not now!" She moaned. Reluctantly she reached over and taped a button, the buzzing stopped. She buried her face in her fluffy soft pillow as she thought, "Only a few more minutes would have been nice." Being wakened by the alarm and ending her dream was such a disappointment. She sighed, "Oh well, time to get up anyway."

She had mixed feelings about her dreams. She enjoyed them because of the adventure she felt while riding the white buffalo. She also enjoyed the vision of the handsome warrior who visited her in her dream world.

The frequency of the dreams had increased and had always been similar, except this time. This time, instead of a hazy, shadowy image of the warrior's face, she had seen it clearly. Their eyes had met. In a sense, they had finally met. The strong feelings of affection and desire she already felt for the handsome warrior who lived in her dream world, intensified.

How calmly he stood in the center of the powerful, circling herd. She sighed. Oh, he is handsome, she thought. The image of his high cheek bones, firm, square jaw and dark, passionate eyes remained embedded in her thoughts.

The clean scent of the sheets against her face were alluring as she stretched her arms, billowing the sheets over her head as she snuggled deeply amongst them. If she could have gone back to sleep to return to her dream world, she would have. Yet, the pounding on her door kept her from doing so.

The pounding on the door accompanied Angelia's high-pitched voice.

"Hey, it's time to get up. You can't sleep all day!"

"I could if someone would stop beating on my door!"

"That's fine, except you have an appointment with your professor in about two hours!"

"Damn, I forgot!"

Deseray flew out of bed, as her roommate, Angelia, appeared through the now opened door.

A tan blouse flopped into Deseray's face by the time her feet hit the floor.

"I took this out of the dryer for you and there's coffee on, so get your butt moving."

"Angie, what would I do without you? You're like my mom away from my mom."

"Yeah, right and you're like the kid I never had."

Their laughter mingled with the new days early morning sun that quickly filled the room.

"I don't know why my professor insisted on an 8:00 a.m. meeting. I really wanted to sleep for just a little while longer." Deseray was thinking about how nice it would have been to stay in her fantasy world with the young warrior.

"I'm making a bagel, want one?" Angelia asked, as she headed toward the door, her long red hair flowing about her shoulders.

"Sure, I'll be down as soon as I take my shower."

As she sat in front of the mirror, brushing her long dark, brown hair, memories of her dream once again invaded her thoughts. She had had the dream many times yet pondered on the fact that this time there had been such a dramatic difference. This time she had clearly seen the young warrior's face. While in her dream world, she felt as though she was a part of his life. She wondered how it was possible for her to be so infatuated with someone she had never met.

Her heart pounded with excitement as she thought of him. If only, she thought, if only he were real. Deseray noticed the quickening of her heart as she thought of him. When she gazed into the mirror, she was surprised to see, she was blushing.

She had heard that dreams could have meaning within the life of the dreamer, especially frequently repeated ones. Deseray wondered what premonition or significance her dream could possibly have for her. It was difficult for her to imagine what meaning riding a white buffalo across the plains of Montana, or the growing desire for a man who did not exist, could have to do with her life.

She enjoyed having the dream, though, and the thrill of riding the great white buffalo. It gave her a sense of total freedom. During her waking hours, she loved to fantasize about the handsome warrior, who began to dominate her daily thoughts as often as her dreams.

Even though college life was filled with excitement and challenges, deep inside there was a yearning for something more fulfilling.

She had been unable to discover what instigated this yearning or what she was looking for. Was it simply fulfillment of life, or was it something else? Presently, it remained unanswered and beyond her comprehension. By allowing fantasy to play a role in her life, she found an oasis of peace and contentment outside her everyday life. Deep inside she felt a temporary fulfillment within her undefined fantasy.

The lives of the early America Indians, when they seemed wild and mysterious awakened a desire to learn more about their nomadic lives. She often wondered if history actually reflected their lives, customs and beliefs. Many times, she yearned to have been born in the past. She yearned to have been born an American Indian and to have experienced their lives as it had been. The addition of the warrior in fantasy dreams just made it even more desirable.

Deseray began to braid her long hair, but as she began to twist the hair over itself to form the first braid, she decided against it, and once again brushed it so it hung loosely about her shoulders.

She glanced about her room for a moment. It was truly of reflection of who she was and also reflected her interests with many Native American items and decorations.

On one wall hung a large Navaho Mandala decorated with fleece and feathers. Mandala means "circle" which symbolizes that all life moves in a circle. They are decorated with objects from natural surroundings. It was a gift from her Uncle John, of which he had sent to her while he was on a trip to New Mexico. Traditionally, the Navaho believed that hanging a Mandela in one's home would bring happiness and prosperity. Deseray knew her Mandela was working, for her life had prosperity through her education and happiness through her encounters with wonderful people she met each day.

The fall would bring her to the beginning of her final year of college. As an archaeology major with an anthropology minor, her studies were concentrated on cultural spiritualism and customs. Her studies proved to heighten her interest and fascination about the early American Indian culture, an interest she had nurtured since childhood.

As a young girl, one of her life's ambitions was to grow up and marry an Indian, a mountain man or a cowboy. As she matured, the little girl ambition blossomed into that of an adult. It served to open up her interest in the west, nature, and Native American customs. Occasionally, her studies would feed her fantasy world, as she made new discoveries about various cultures, spiritualism, and romantic customs the different cultures practiced.

As she continued to gaze about her room, she realized she had carried this childhood ambition into her adult life.

Over her bed, hanging from the ceiling was a dream catcher. It's circular spider webbing held colorful beads, polished stones and a black feather dangling from a piece of leather string attached to the center of the web. A dreamcatcher is also a type of mandala. It was the first dreamcatcher that she had made herself using an Ojibwa pattern. Her skills in this area had greatly improved, but the dream-catcher's sentimental value kept her from replacing it with one of better quality.

The Ojibwa and Sioux believed that the night air is full of dreams, good ones, and bad ones. As the dreams float about the air, they are caught in the dream web. The good dreams know the way down the feather, travel to the dreamer, while the bad dreams entangled in the web, and become destroyed with the first light of the dawn.

A variation of the traditional Ojibwa pattern was adopted by their neighbors, the
Sioux. The Ojibwa pattern depicted the spider web while the Sioux pattern depicted the spider.

Good dreams truly knew their way for Deseray, especially after she woke from her dream of the white buffalo and the handsome brave.

Enough dawdling thought Deseray as she draped the tan blouse over a chair as she reached into her top drawer for some fresh underwear and a bra. She walked into the bathroom, turned on the shower and while waiting for the water to be just the right temperature; she slipped her nightgown to the floor. A few moments later, she stepped into the shower.

As the hot water splashed down over her body, she imagined herself and the young brave together, standing beneath a cascading waterfall, entwined in each other's arms. As the water spilled over their naked bodies, their lips found each other's through the deliciousness of the water and each other's taste. Their arms gently held each other, pressing tightly against each other's bodies.

14

The thought of him made her shiver, even though the hot water warmed her body.

Deseray was reluctant to leave the seclusion of her shower. She could have stayed there forever and imagine being with him, leaving the whole world of reality outside.

If I stay here to long, thought Deseray, my skin will shrivel up so gruesome, that even my young brave would not want me, no matter how hard I imagined.

She reached for a towel and patted herself dry. As she wrapped a terry cloth robe around her freshly cleaned body, she walked over to the bed.

The cotton blouse felt soft and smooth as she put it on. She was excited to start her day.

As Deseray entered the kitchen, the tantalizing smell of freshly toasted bagel permeated her nostrils. Her stomach responded with a faint but distinctive growl.

"You're up and moving!" Echoed Angelia, placing a cream cheese laden bagel on the table next to a cup of Hazelnut flavored coffee.

"You are so good to me!" Deseray replied as she positioned herself squarely in front to the treat she was about to eat.

"I promised your mom I would take care of you while we were away at college. I'm just keeping my promise."

"High school is so far away, isn't it?" Deseray voiced somberly.

"It seems like only a few months have gone by since we took off to college together."

Angelia sat across the table from Deseray.

"It sure does. Just think, we have only one year to go and we are free of books and classes and professors. We have been through a lot together, ever since kindergarten."

"Yes we have, but I'm glad we decided to go to college together. I think it helps so we don't miss our families so much while we're away."

Smiling, Deseray reached over and squeezed Angelia's hand as her bright red hair tumbled about her face.

"So what are you talking to your professor about this morning?" Angelia asked, as she was about to take a big bite out of her bagel.

"We're discussing my trip this summer to Montana. I'm using the research from the trip for my senior thesis and he wants to see my synopsis."

Angelia began to laugh.

"What's so funny?"

"You sound like you're reciting a poem. Discuss, research, thesis, synopsis. I just found it funny."

"I guess it's a mouthful," laughed Deseray.

Angelia warmed Deseray's coffee.

"I thought you were heading home today?"

Deseray took a sip of the freshened coffee.

"I am. The car is loaded, and I am taking off for home straight from campus. I'll be home for about a week and I'll take the train out west."

Excitement grew within Deseray as she realized the trip she had been waiting for, was about to become a reality.

"I'll be taking the train to Whitefish first and then my uncle John will meet me at the train station. I cannot believe how excited I am. I haven't seen my uncle for a few years, and we have a lot of catching up to do."

Angelia smiled, "You have a good time and stay safe. I guess I am like your mom when it comes to those expeditions you go on. That digging and stuff can get dangerous if you're not careful."

"Don't get so worried. I will be with my Uncle John. You know he would not let anything happened to me. If it did, he would have to answer to my mother."

Deseray credited her uncle John for much of her interest in Native American culture. As an archeologist and geologist, many of his expeditions were throughout the United States. The discovery of interesting artifacts that revealed many aspects of the early lives of Native Americans were some of his accomplishments. As he shared much of his stories with her

16

family when she was a child, Deseray's interest grew. Her barrage of constant questions about what he did had flattered him so much that he began to share much of it with her on a regular basis. This not only fed Deseray's desire to know more, it also nurtured a strong and unique friendship they retain.

As she recalled her memories of her uncle, her thoughts drifted to home. She was excited to be going home even if it would be a short visit.

"So, Angelia, when are you heading home?"

"I have a few things to take care at school and then I'm out of here."

Deseray paused before she took another bite of her bagel. She wondered if she should discuss her silly dream with Angela. After all, she was a psych major.

"Angelia, I have a question for you."

"Oh, dear, you're going to strain my brain this early in the morning?" Angela twisted her lips as she smiled.

"Do you believe that dreams have meaning or may even be premonitions of things to come?"

Angelia paused before answering.

"I look at dreams from purely a physiological function, so I do limit my ideas about them as a bodily function."

"What are you talking about?" Deseray's eyes were wide with confusion.

"It's simple. I do not believe that dreams are premonitions. I know you believe in visions that come in the form of dreams, but I believe that dreams are our way of sorting our daily life. For example, last night I had a dream with many strange things in it. Nevertheless, as I recalled all my activities from yesterday, I was able to relate all the things in my dream, no matter how obscure they seemed, with things throughout my day. My brain was just sorting and filing all the information that I took in yesterday."

"But what if the dream is either the same or similar time after time?"

"It simply means that you have unresolved issues that

you have to sort out and deal with during you waking hours."

Deseray sat thoughtful.

Angelia could see that Deseray was not satisfied with the explanation she had provided.

"I tell you what; keep a journal of your dreams and also you daily activities. At the end of summer, we will sit down, go over all the information, and see if we can make some sense of your dreams. Does that sound fair?"

Deseray smiled. "That will work out just perfect. I have to keep a daily journal for my summer project, so I will just include personal footnotes about my dreams as I journal."

"Great. Now the clock on the wall tells me you are going to be late if you don't hurry."

Deseray popped the last morsel of bagel into her mouth, sipped her coffee and began a search for her pack-back.

After securing the bag, she walked over to Angelia and gave her a hug.

"Thanks for the info. I am leaving straight from campus. If I don't see you before I leave on my trip, I'll give you a call after I get home."

"Drive careful home and don't take any crap from your professor."

"I'm not worried. He'll love my synopsis and the project."

Deseray was satisfied with spending her summer on an archeological expedition. A vast and wide-open classroom setting in Montana was more appealing to Deseray than a classroom with four walls, no matter what the subject matter.

Campus seemed strangely empty as Deseray made her way to her professor's office. The crowed walkways were deserted, and normally congested halls were empty. Most of the students had already left for the summer. The few remaining students were staying for summer classes, which would begin in two weeks.

As Deseray approached her professor's office, the silence of the empty halls had given way to the distinct sound of rock and roll music roaring throughout the building. Somewhere within the building, a stereo, cranked up full blast, were causing the walls and the windows to vibrate to the beat.

The "rock and roll" radiated from her professor's office.

As soon as her professor noticed Deseray standing in the doorway, he calmly flipped the volume to off.

"It's my end of the school year ritual. It helps me put finality to the year's end. Besides, it just seems to sound better without the headphones." A pair of headphones lay crumpled in a twist of wire on his desk. His music and player seemed so old school, but then, so was her professor. His go-t suited him.

"Come in and sit down." He had a big grin on his face.

"So, tell me about your senior thesis."

"I've decided to concentrate on the elements needed to determine whether a site is worth the time and effort for archeological exploration. This summer I am going on a dig with my uncle in Montana. An assortment of arrows heads was discovered in southeastern Montana, which may prove that a small tribe of Sioux Indians, possible Hunk Papa, lived in the area."

"There is evidence that the Sioux visited the area in Montana called Medicine Rock, but none that they lived in the southern part of Montana. The Sioux did not have a strong presence in Montana until they were forced onto reservations in that state. The direction my thesis will be in a documentary style based on a daily journal, interviews with other members on the team and photographs when possible."

Deseray paused to take a breath.

"So, the expedition you will be going on is based on the finding of arrowheads which is believed to be Hunk Papa Sioux? Do you feel this is enough evidence to justify a dig?"

"Yes, I do. Any little thing that may help to provide a bet-ter picture of our country's history is worth pursuing, at least to the point when it becomes evident that the digging is a waste of time. That is what I am basing my thesis on."

Deseray handed a copy of her synopsis to her professor.

The paper outlined what Deseray had been saying thus far and included the details of her record keeping plans and documentation.

He examined the paper's contents carefully.

"I see you plan to provide time-lines, schedules and some graphs to demonstrate the dig's progress and findings."

Deseray nodded as she confirmed this with him.

He smiled at her as he handed back the paper.

"Out of curiosity, who is financing the expedition?"

"Part of it will be financed by an association my uncle belongs to, but the bulk of it is from an unknown contributor. The contributor is working through an attorney and wants to remain anonymous. The results and process of the expedition is to be given to the attorney."

"That sounds like a mystery in itself." He gently rubbed the hair that covered chin.

"Overall, I am looking forward to reading your findings when they are done. I hope you do find evidence to support your ideas and I would personally be interested to read your findings even though I have to read it anyway. It should prove to be educational."

Deseray took the paper from him as she said, "I'm hoping we find something as well."

"You have a good trip and I'll be looking forward to seeing you this fall."

His brief smile and silence indicated to Deseray that her thesis plan was accepted and that their meeting had ended.

With the flip of the on button and the resumption of the rock and roll, Deseray knew that it was her clue to depart.

She was excited he had accepted her plans and was looking forward to her summer in Montana more than ever.

As she descended the stairs, the sound of rock and roll began to fade. She chuckled as she thought about her conservative professor being rebellious and letting his hair down. It was healthy for him, she thought.

Looking at her watch, she noticed it was shortly after

nine o'clock and was pleased that the meeting did not take as long as she had thought it would. She was anxious to be on her way home.

The combination of the bright summer sun, large cups of coffee and great music made the four-hour trip from Madison to Baldwin go by quickly.

An overwhelming sensation of regeneration overcame Deseray as she steered her car onto the 700-foot tree-lined driveway that guided her longingly toward her house and family.

Her short visit at Easter seemed so much longer ago then just ten weeks, to her, it seemed like several months. Deseray felt an even stronger sense of rejuvenation overcome her as she saw her mother standing on the porch.

Almost as soon as the car door shut, her mother was standing beside her ready to embrace Deseray with a warm hug.

"I missed you so much!"

Her mother's embrace was like the answer to a prayer of reassurance and support.

"Mom, you look wonderful!" Deseray exclaimed as she returned the embrace.

"Have you had lunch?" her mother asked, not wanting to release her daughter.

"No, I haven't. Lunch sounds good. Do you have some made?"

Her mother lovingly swatted her daughter on the shoulder.

"You know I do!"

It felt good to be home!

There is no other smell as welcoming as the smell of home. Mother's perfume mingled with the smell of her favorite furniture polish and the fragrance of lunch, chow mien, thought Deseray.

The 16-foot vaulted ceiling of the living room hosted south facing clearstory windows, allowing the warmth of the southern sun to gently caress the plants, walls and anyone who entered the room.

Deseray tossed her purse on the couch as she spotted the kitchen table already set.

As she sat down, her mother placed the food on the table and then joined her.

"This is really good, mom. I miss eating home cooked meals."

"You mean meals you don't have to cook yourself!"

"You're right. Thanks."

Her mother had a dark complexion much like Deseray. Her hair was short but retained its rich dark color.

"So how were finals? Do you know any of your grades yet?"

"Tests went fine. I will not know my grades until they come in the mail, but I feel good that they will all be high. I will not be here when they arrive, so you can open it and let me know how I did. I can call you from Montana."

As her mother removed the dishes from the table, Deseray noticed her long delicate fingers. That is where I got my slender fingers from, thought Deseray. She never noticed her mother's hands before. Strange she noticed them now.

As Deseray was about to speak, a sharp, high-pitched whinny broke the silence.

Her mother laughed. "You'd better get out there or the two of them will break down the fence to see you."

"Do you want help with the dishes first?"

"No, you go out and see them. I can handle it."

Deseray opened the back door and stepped onto the porch. She took a deep breath. The cooling breeze skipping across the lake filled the air with the scent summer leaves, refreshing her in the hot, afternoon air.

At that moment, she felt as though she were in a world of her own. The twenty acres that surrounded the house provided a greatly appreciated seclusion, of which Deseray treasured.

Having spent so much time in the city while attending college, Deseray developed a new appreciation for her country home.

A well-worn, packed dirt path guided her way to the pasture. As she approached, hoof beats prodded the ground as her two horses, Licorice and Diamond, quickly made their way toward the fence and the master they loved.

The faint humming radiating from the fence, warned Deseray that the electric fence was functioning. Walking into the small stable, she flipped a switch and the humming silenced. The electric fence had become necessary after Licorice displayed her keen abilities of attempted escapes on a regular basis, even though she managed only an escape or two. The call of fenceless freedom was stronger than any electric fence.

As Deseray nuzzled her nose deep into the fur on Licorice's neck, she lovingly inhaled the smell she had missed. Deseray enjoyed nothing on earth as much as the warm smell of a horse's hair!

The two of them were happy to see their master. Licorice was reddish brown with an almost black-brown tail and mane. She got her name, Licorice, because her mane and tail reminded Deseray of black candy licorice whips. She had a white blaze on her forehead and two white rings around each hind foot. Diamond was a marbling of light brown, tan and white with a golden mane and tail. Diamond received her name because the center of each eye looked like a multi-faceted diamond.

As Deseray vigorously scuffed up Licorice's mane, a few scanty strands of black hair tumbled to the ground.

"How are you girl? I missed you!" She snickered affectionately, happy to see her master once again.

"Tell you what. When Mathew is home tomorrow, we can all go riding. Would you like that?'

Abruptly, Diamond began forcing herself between Deseray and Licorice, not wanting to miss the affection and attention.

"I love you too, silly," Deseray told Diamond as she nearly stepped on Deseray's toes trying to get her fair share.

Deseray walked to the stable, with both horses following

close behind, almost going over the top of her. She took two brushes from a shelf.

"Is this what you want?"

Walking out to the pasture, she began brushing one and then the other, alternating frequently so a shoving match would not result. Their snickering sounds of affection showed their appreciation of Deseray's tender loving care.

Deseray's attention turned towards the driveway. The car coming up the road belonged to her brother Mathew.

Deseray was surprised to see him a day early.

"I've got to go now, you guys, but I'll be back to feed and water you after I say hi to Mathew."

With that, she tossed the brushes back onto the shelf and hurried up toward the house.

Mathew was tall and well built. This was result of his physical training in the Marine Corp. He had sandy colored hair and blue eyes, taking after their father.

"Well hello bro. How have you been? You're home early!"

"I've been good," Mathew said as he hugged his little sister. "It worked out so I could leave base sooner than I had thought."

"That's good; it will give us a little more time before I leave."

"So, are you home for a while?"

"For about a week then I'm off to Montana."

"Oh yeah, you're going sightseeing with Uncle John." He chuckled.

He put his arm on her shoulder as they walked into the house.

As they entered the house, their mother quickly greeted them.

"Well, hi Mathew. I did not hear your car. You are home early. I'm glad you could make it home to say hi to your sister." She reached over and patted his shoulder. She wanted to give him a big bear hung and a motherly kiss, but she figured a big Marine like him would not care too much for it.

She was wrong as she found herself locked inside two big arms and Mathew picked her up and whirled her around the room.

"What's the matter? Am I too big to hug?"

"I didn't know if Marines liked that kind of stuff." She said while blushing.

"Always from their mothers'." He replied as he placed his mother back on the floor. "I wouldn't miss it for the world."

His Marine uniform fit him well.

"It's good to be here. As luck would have it, my CO said I could take my leave before I head out for my new base."

"It's good timing, we just don't get together often enough. It seems like the whole family is never in the same place at the same time anymore. It is even tough at the holidays. It's good to have you home. You look so handsome in your uniform."

"Why does everyone keep saying that?"

"We keep saying it because it's true."

She gave him a motherly pat on the arm.

Mathew sat comfortably at the kitchen table.

"I stopped at Karen's on my way out here. She liked the uniform too. Her and Paul and the little rug rats will be here in about an hour."

Karen was the oldest. She got married right after high school graduation since she had no desire to go to college. Her whole life, all she ever wanted was to be a mother and raise some children. They had four, with no plans of making any additions to their family. She firmly decided that four were enough.

"What time will dad be home?" asked Deseray.

"He should be here in about an hour or so."

"Good, that will give me time to change my clothes and help you get supper on."

Big brother interrupted.

"Go relax. I'll help mom with the food."

To Deseray surprised, he was serious.

"That sounds good to me." With that, Deseray almost flew up the stairs to her room.

Except for some light cleaning and dusting, her mother had done nothing else to her room. It was just as she had left it. When she first left for college, she had heard horror stories where parents rented out their children's room to make extra money while they were away to college.

It was comforting for her to know that the stories were not always true.

As she entered the room, a figurine of a brave sitting upon a painted pinto pony warmly greeted her. He wore leggings, a breastplate, and a full headdress. He held his feather-laden lance high in the air as though he were letting the world know that he feared no man.

The statue reminded her of the brave in her dreams. Since it symbolized her fantasy world, she had left it home. This part of her remained an intense secret, even from her best friend Angelia.

Many White buffalo figures, made from a variety of materials such as carved wood, marble, glass, and white fur, stood near the statue of the brave. She had become fascinated with the white buffalo after she had studied the legend of the white buffalo calf women.

As the legend went, one day a beautiful woman appeared before two braves while they were out hunting. One brave looked upon her with lust and the wind blew so hot that he burned to ashes and his ashes swept away by the same wind. The other brave honored her and invited her to come to their village. She told him she would visit his village, but he was to send runners to many villages and have them gather, as she had a message for all the people.

He did as she had asked and, in a few days, she appeared in the village carrying something wrapped in a bundle of white rabbit fur.

As she un-wrapped the bundle, inside was a pipe made of stone as red as blood. She told the people that the pipestone came from a sacred place on the other side of the mighty river. (Now known as the Mississippi and the place now known as

Pipestone Minnesota.) It was the only place they could get this sacred stone and this ground was looked upon as a sacred place where no tribes may war upon it. It is a ground of peace. The pipe is one of peace.

She stayed with the people for many days teaching the scared words to use when praying with the red peace pipe. She told them to carry the scared pipe wrapped in white fur, to keep it pure and honored.

One day she told the people it was time for her to go. They begged her to stay, but she told them it was her time to leave. The people followed her to a large prairie opening where herds of brown bison were grazing. She smiled to the people and began to walk into the herd of buffalo.

Slowly, before their eyes, she began to change into a white buffalo calf, disappearing into the herd. The legend says that one day the white buffalo will return with another message for the people.

The legend was very meaningful to Deseray. It symbolized much of the culture of the American Indians and added to her fascination with their strong spiritualism and customs.

She pondered about the origin of the name "buffalo". Scientist proclaimed the American bison to "bison bison" rather than buffalo since the American bison was not a buffalo. The Sioux called them Tatanka, translating to "buffalo or buffalo bull" so they prefer to call them - buffalo.

Amongst the white buffalo figures she had, there was also a variety of brown ones. For early Native Americans, the buffalo strongly symbolized livelihood, food, clothing, and shelter.

Contentment overcame her as she sat at the foot of her own bed reflecting upon her chosen profession. With an archaeology major and an anthropology minor, she felt confident that she had covered at the areas of interest to her.

Her deep-rooted drive to learn as much about the first people of America went beyond career enhancement. She felt compelled. She often wondered if her life was a reincarnation from a past life, possibly a life as a Native American. Perhaps she had not completed her life's journey, and this was her opportunity to do so. This was the best explanation she could give herself as to why she, a non-Native American, had such a passion about early Indians that consumed her.

She could not answer these questions. Answers she may never find.

She was certain however that in less than a week she was actually taking a trip to Montana. The idea of finally stepping her feet on Montana soil alone, heighten her excitement. Being part of an exploration searching for historical Sioux territory, possibly offering artifacts that would bring this early culture to life, was like a dream come true.

The sound of her mother's voice calling to her interrupted her thoughts.

"Deseray, dinner is on!"

She rushed downstairs to see her whole family sitting at the table.

It felt good to be home.

Chapter Two - The White Buffalo

The rays of the rising sun warmed Deseray's face as she woke from a dreamless sleep. She was excited to spend the morning with her beloved horses. She quickly dressed and went downstairs.

Her mother, an early riser, had breakfast ready as she entered the kitchen.

"It feels good to be home," Deseray said as she gave her mother an affectionate hug.

"It is good to have you home." Her mother smiled.

Deseray finished her breakfast and placed the dishes in the sink.

As she stepped off the back porch, the magnitude of her natural surroundings embraced her, filled with the sounds of its inhabitants and the smell of country freshness.

It was a perfect setting for attracting and keeping a wide variety of wildlife. She enjoyed the study of wildlife habitats. It complemented her college studies, but in her heart, it was just pure enjoyment.

Deseray's skin quickly absorbed the heat from early morning summer sun. With confident footing, she walked down a small hill that led to the pond near her house. She was quickly reassured at how beautiful it was.

A rich green circle of trees nearly surrounded the small pond, making it appear like a small, green cave, filled with water. As she neared the pond, she heard a loud, solid slap on the water.

Deseray had to laugh. The beavers' tail flap upon the water signaled danger to the colony. She found it humorous that the beaver perceived her as a danger. She valued animals almost as much as she valued people. She could never harm any one of them. There was no way the beaver could they know that, thought Deseray. The beaver's instinct told him danger was near and he reacted. She did not blame him for that.

A huge boulder surrounded by piles of smaller rocks lured Deseray to take perch upon its broad leveled surface. It was her selected personal haven, quiet and alone. It was remarkably close to the partially enclosed north end of the lake, creating a quiet advantage point from where she could watch the nature that surrounded her. From her perch upon the huge boulder, she could watch the beaver work and play. If she sat quiet, long enough, the colony would go about their daily business, unconcerned.

A once open and flowing canal between the lake and the north end of the lake was now a dam of which the colony of beaver had built. This entrance intertwined with branches, sticks and mud, creating a private habitat for the colony. They had built their lodge further down the lake where the depth was sufficient for the underwater opening. The construction of the dam between the north and south end of the lake resulted in the "pond" becoming covered with green algae, making the water appear as though a velvety green carpet covered it. The area waterfowl, such as ducks, geese and cranes, loved the pond this way, providing a banquet with enough variety to satisfy them all.

Deseray often saw deer, raccoon, beaver, snapping turtles and an occasional skunk in her backyard. She could feel the peace and serenity that radiated about her, begin to fill her soul.

She laid back on the large flat rock, carefully balancing herself, and closed her eyes as she continued to absorb the early morning sun. She imagined herself once again riding upon the great while buffalo. She often imagined how wonderful it would have been to live in the past. In a time when the buffalo ran free and all of nature lived together. How magical it would be to meet the young brave and to share thoughts and feelings with him. How serene it would be to have his arms around her, keeping her safe and content.

The fresh air and warming sunshine lulled Deseray into a peaceful light sleep. Thoughts of the young brave met her as she entered her dream world.

The herd of buffalo slowly came to a stop. From the encirclement of bison, the young brave gently lowered his eyes from the heavens and sought out the glance of Deseray's longing eyes.

As their eyes met, he began to walk toward the edge of the great herd. Mysteriously, the herd reverently parted as he neared, creating an opening for him to pass thorough. Slowly, his eyes never leaving hers, he walked nearer to Deseray.

His firm square jaw was relaxed as he approached. His dark eyes were inviting. Deseray's heart began to pound wildly within her chest. It was challenging to breath. Slowly he raised his hand, reaching toward her, as though inviting her to come with him.

Deseray sat up on the rock so suddenly she almost fell off. A wet nibbling on her arm gave her a start.

"How did you get out?" she said as she reached up to pet Licorice's muzzle.

She already knew the answer. She had forgotten to turn the fence back on yesterday in her excitement to see her brother, Mathew.

Licorice was the escape artist. She was brave enough and stubborn enough to test the electrical fence that stood between her and the open meadows. Sometimes it was on and sometimes it was not. Licorice knew this and took advantage of the times it when it was not.

Deseray carefully climbed down from her perch, pressing her hand against Licorice's chest, pushing her backward to give herself space to place her feet on the ground.

"I guess I'm going to have to leave that fence on all the time, aren't I?"

With Licorice following like a little puppy, they made their way up the small hill toward the stable. A pleading whinny greeted them, as they got closer to the fence. Diamond was expressing her jealousy because Licorice was on the other side of the fence and she was not.

Diamond never followed Licorice on her little adventures. She was content to remain within the fencing in familiar territory. As Deseray and Licorice approached the fence, Diamond trotted along the inside as they made their way to the gate. Once the gate opened, Licorice quickly trotted in. She took her place next to Diamond who began sniffing her to see if she was all in one piece.

"I see she got out again. I noticed her from the house." Mathew, looking as though he had just woken up, came meandering toward the fence.

"Good morning Mathew! You look bright eyed and bushy tailed this morning, "she laughed.

He reached out his large hand, rubbing his little sister on the head, mussing up her hair.

"I'll help you fix the fence," he said as he entered the stable to get some electrical tape and tools.

"Thanks," Deseray chimed. "I was hoping to go for a ride yet today."

"You need a riding partner? These guys don't get nearly enough exercise with everyone so busy lately," Mathew added.

"Sure, that would be great. Have you had breakfast yet?" She asked.

"Yeah, mom made me eat as soon as I got up. I'm ready if you are."

A short walk along the fence line revealed the broken wire of which Licorice had made her escape. Mathew unrolled a section of electrical tape and connected either end to the existing wire to make a new connection. After a few more twist, the connection was complete.

"This should hold you for a while," Mathew said as he looked at Licorice. Then, looking at Deseray, he said, "You need to remember to turn on the fence." Then he chuckled.

Deseray ducked under the newly repaired fence and entered the stable with Mathew close behind her, with the two horses closely behind him. Upon entering the stable, Deseray stuck her hand into a small bucket and put some of its contents into her pocket.

She lifted Licorice's saddle and saddle blanket from a rack, resting the bulk of the saddle's weight on her hip as she carried it. With her free hand, she reached for Licorice's split bit and bridle, which were hanging on a hook just above where the saddle had been. With Licorice almost walking on her heels, made her way back to the pasture. Diamond waited patiently as Mathew grab the other saddle, blanket, and Diamond's straight bit and bridle.

The four of them met in the paddock area of the pasture. Mathew saddled Diamond while Deseray saddled Licorice. Deseray walked over to the gate and swung it open. She skillfully slid herself up onto Licorice, who was anticipating the pleasure of the ride, and off they rode with Mathew close behind.

The joy of riding again filled Deseray with joyful energy as she felt Licorice's body move beneath her. Since she started college, she had little time to enjoy what used to be a daily ritual. A shelf in the family room lined with first place trophies displayed the hard work she and Licorice had dedicated to being a barrel riding team.

Licorice's mane flopped freely in the wind, as did Deseray's unbounded hair. The acres around their house provided many hours of trails and beautiful scenery to enjoy as they rode. It was nice to spend time with Mathew, allowing them to catch up on all the things each had been doing.

"So Mathew how is the army life?" She chuckled since she knew Mathew hated it when anyone labeled him as 'being in the Army'. He was a Marine.

"It got better after I got out of boot. The sergeant was rough but becoming a Marine "is earned" he said. I'm going to be stationed in North Carolina after my leave is over." He paused and said, "So you are finally going to Montana?"

"I'm leaving next week. I am anxious to see Uncle John.

It has been a long time. I am eager to go on the expedition and start digging. I envision us finding some very authentic and historical artifacts. That would be just great!"

"Mom said you are taking the train. Why are you? Flying is faster."

"I want to see the countryside." Deseray replied. "I know the plane is faster and I'm anxious to get there, but I want to see some scenery and other things along the way."

The sun was climbing higher into the sky, as Deseray looked at her watch.

"I guess we should be getting back. I am taking a drive to Menomonie this afternoon. I have a friend I have not seen for a few months, and I want to visit before I leave on my trip."

With that, they turned the horses toward the stable at a nice easy trot.

Mathew helped removed the saddles.

"Hey sis, I got to get going. I have a few things to do this morning. You ok with brushing down the horses?"

"Sure, I will see you later."

After removing the saddles, both horses received a vigorous brushing. As the brushing proceeded, Deseray reached into her pocket and gave each of them their well-deserved treat. The homemade horse cookies which were made of molasses and they loved them.

Deseray tried to create a brushing routine for them, but they both wanted her attention at the same time. Normally, she would rotate brushing one and then the other. Just like little children, each one wanted to be first.

As soon as the brushing session ended, Licorice proceeded to roll around in the dirt, kicking her legs up into the air so she could gain some momentum and movement in the dry dirt. Diamond too, proceeded to roll in the dirt, not wanting to left out of anything. Dust encircled them both creating their own private dust bowl. They enjoyed rolling around in the dirt and sand, especially Licorice because of her dark coat. The new coat of dirt cooled her, and the rolling scratched where it itched from gnats and flies. They were just like little children. Deseray did enjoy her horses!

When both horses were satisfied with the attention they had received, the wandered off to do some serious grazing. They are wonderful friends, thought Deseray.

Deseray brushed the dust from her clothes and walked to the house.

After a quick shower, Deseray walked over to the closet, steadfastly looking for a particular blouse. A beautifully decorated turquoise blouse adorned with intricate beadwork hung from a hanger.

The beadwork had taken Deseray several weeks to complete. She ran her slender fingers softly along the delicate beadwork of thunderbirds and clouds that adorned the front of the blouse. The pattern complimented a variety of Native American symbols that represented mother earth such as a small turtle enclosed in a blue circle.

She had chosen turquoise blue, as it was her favorite color. It reminded her of the stone, which in turn reminded her of the Native American culture. The brilliantly rich pastel color accented her dark skin.

After a quick shower, she carefully removed it from the hanger. The cotton blouse felt soft and smooth as she put it on. The intricate beadwork added an unexpected weight to the otherwise lightweight fabric. Once it sat comfortably upon her shoulders and against her chest, the carefully crafted beadwork was quite attractive.

A pair of black shorts and her black moccasins completed her attire, and she was on her way to Menomonie and an old friend, who happened to live at the nature refuge located there.

Deseray had discovered the nature refuge in Menomonie one day while considering attending the University of Wisconsin Stout. It was close to home but did not offer her the volume of studies she required.

While college classes were in session, Menomonie was teaming with students everywhere. During the summer, it became a peaceful and relaxed place to visit. Easy exits off from the freeway lead to a single lane road that wound its way past the lake and continued for another half of a mile. She was excited but feeling a little silly at the same time. After all, she was going to visit an animal. She would never dare to tell anyone and so she never had.

The park was quite rustic and simple, not anything like the elaborate zoos in the nearby metro cities of St. Paul and Minneapolis. Trees grew thickly, offering cover for the animals from the sun and rain. The park divided into several areas by fencing, giving the different types of animals their own spaces in which to live.

The right side of the park housed the elk. Elk were much larger than a deer with dark brown upper bodies and tan running from under their chins all the way under their bodies to just below their tails. Their tails were an off-white color underneath and dark brown on top.

Similar to deer, except the males are bulls instead of bucks and the females called cows instead of does. The bulls fascinated her most due to the size and shape of their antlers, Deseray enjoyed just staring at them. Like the deer, the bulls lose their horns each year and grow new ones.

"Hello Helena," she exclaimed to a very petite young cow. She named her Helena, the capital of Montana, because she liked the way it sounded.

Carefully making her way along a rough, dirt path, she ambled her way around the elk pen toward the rest of the park. The two small lakes on either side of the path had subjected it to years of water erosions, narrowing the path with each passing year.

Swamps would be a better description of the two lakes. She proceeded with caution, as she knew snakes like the swampy environment. Her eyes darted from one side of the path to the other, as she walked along, just in case. One of her biggest fears was that of snakes.

Having safely made it to the other side, she enjoyed the

birds and the deer as she passed by. All the while though, she kept her eyes opened, looking, as she neared the buffalo pens. The special friend she had come to visit was an old white buffalo.

The white buffalo had been at the nature park for as long as Deseray had been coming. He was unlike any other animal she had ever seen. His seemingly mystical powers mesmerized Deseray whenever she was near him, convincing herself that he understood her thoughts and feelings. She liked to pretend that he was the white buffalo she rode in her dreams.

Upon nearing the fence, she was unable to see him. She looked down the well-traveled path the buffalo took to get near the fence. He was not there. She glanced over at the buffalo barn, only to see two brown buffalo, stamping their feet to discourage flies from biting them when they landed. She looked all around but could not see the white buffalo. Sadness began to creep over her as she imagined that he might have died. She had no idea how long buffalo lived.

Double fencing surrounded the entire buffalo yard. This type of fencing was for the safety of visitors. Buffalo could sometimes get mean and aggressive. It was also to keep the buffalo in, of which Deseray always thought would be happier if they were free.

Where the fence turned a corner in a low ravine, it had not been doubled fenced. Since she could get close enough to touch, this is the area where she always visited the white buffalo.

After scanning the buffalo yard one more time, she finally saw him. He was standing under some thick trees, cooling himself in the early afternoon heat. As soon as he saw her, he began to lumber her way. He was the biggest buffalo there, and like the rest of them, all shaggy with scattered patches of long hair. He had not yet shed his entire winter coat, leaving him looking pathetically ragged.

Deseray thought he looked beautiful.

His chest was broad, and his sturdy legs carried his large

frame and massive body with grace and dignity.

She was thrilled that he was still alive. She called him White One because he was the only white buffalo she had ever seen. The earth seemed to vibrate as he lumbered toward her. He came right up to the single fenced area as Deseray reached out and pet him. She learned long ago to ignore the warnings about not touching the buffalo. He radiated such peace and contentment toward her; she never experienced any concern about touching the huge creature.

The fur on his head was thick and springy as she rubbed it. It was longer than the hair on the rest of his body and surprisingly soft. She made a gentle fist and rubbed her knuckles against his head with quick, firm movements. Deseray felt sure that if a buffalo could purr, White One would.

"How are you big fella?" she said softly, "I missed you."

While standing alone with the white buffalo, she seemed transcended into a private world of their own. Suddenly a voice caused her to jerk her hand suddenly against White One's head. White One pulled back for a moment. Then he relaxed and waited for Deseray to resume petting his massive head.

"He doesn't let just anyone pet him, you know."

The voice came from a figure standing a few feet to the right of White One. Where did he come from, thought Deseray? She had not noticed him earlier.

The person who had been speaking stepped out from behind the huge buffalo. Deseray noticed he was tall and dark skinned, with thick, long black hair. In a small section of braided, a feather entwined amongst the braid. He wore the remainder of his hair in a loose ponytail that trailed down his back.

"I'm sure it's ok," said Deseray. "He seems to like it and it makes him happy."

"How do you know it makes him happy?" he asked.

"I just know," she said. She brushed her long hair away from her eyes so she could get a better look at the person who was speaking to her.

His laugh was kind and friendly as he replied, "I think you're right, he does like it. He likes you also."

"How do you know?" she asked.

"I just know," he said with a smile. His rich, black hair glistened in the sun as he moved about.

Deseray blushed as she smiled.

He walked over to the fence, taking his place next to White One. He had no fear of this great creature that could easily destroy him. He put his hand through the fence, offering it to Deseray.

"My name is Reg."

He stretched his muscular arm toward her, offering his hand in an act of friendship.

As she shook his hand, she noticed that his grip was firm, but gentle. She also noticed that he was Native American.

"My name is Deseray. It's nice to meet you."

"That's a very beautiful name," Reg replied.

"Thank you." Deseray felt her cheeks flush.

She paused thoughtfully for a moment a little hesitant to ask her next question.

"You're Native American, aren't you?

"I'm Sioux. My family name is Goldentrees."

Reg began to finger the beaded leather cord that was hanging from White One's right horn.

"This is very nice." Reg said. "Did you make it?"

"Yes, I gave it to White One as a token of our friendship."

"It's very nice and well made."

"White One?" he continued, "It is a fitting name."

"He's a wonderful creature," Reg continued, "and I can tell you feel the same way. You honor him by giving him a name. You have shown him great respect by doing so. Now I understand why he likes you so much. You understand him."

His voice was gentle but contained a lot of strength. His eyes were kind and understanding. He awakened within Deseray a longing that was new to her soul.

Deseray found herself drawn to this person she had just

met. There was no smile on his face, but his eyes told Deseray that he was pleased with her sincerity and compassion for the magnificent white buffalo. The respect contained within his eyes made Deseray suddenly feel special, as though she were a part of something greater than she was.

Silently he continued to gaze affectionately at Deseray. The gentleness in his eyes alleviated any discomfort Deseray would normally have felt during such silence. It was as though he had not come to her as a stranger. It was as though they had been friends for a long time.

"I come here to talk to White One as often as I can. Animals can be good listeners and I can tell him things I would never share with anyone else."

"Is there some special reason you come to see just him?"

"Yes, but I would rather not say. It's personal."

"You have been visiting White One for some time now. You speak to him often. I have sensed this from him. You have many wonderful thoughts to share. I have also sensed from him that you have many questions you would like answered. White One has let me know this."

"Does he talk to you like we are talking?" she asked.

"No. He talks to me much the same way as he talks to you. No words, just a sense of knowing."

In an effort to change the subject, Deseray decided to ask him a few questions.

"How long have you worked here? I've never seen you before."

"I've been here for only a short time. This guy," he patted White One affectionately on the head, "is the main reason I am here."

"Is he ill or something?"

"No, nothing like that,' Reg assured her, "He has some special needs right now and I am here to meet those needs."

"I guess I am here for you as well," he added with a smile.

His words caught Deseray off guard. What did he mean for me as well?

"I don't understand," she replied.

"I know you have been coming to see the great white one for some time. I feel as though you are here for a reason. I cannot tell you why I feel this way, but you will have to trust me."

Deseray looked into White One's eyes. He seemed to be assuring her that she could trust him.

Reg skillfully slipped his body through the fence and stood next to Deseray. She noticed that he was a few inches taller than she was.

As she stood near him, his height reminder her that she likes taller men. Something about having to look up as a man was romantic to her. Gently cupping his hand under Deseray's elbow, he motioned her to sit down on the grass beneath a nearby oak tree. The newly leaf laden branches created a shady refuge from the scorching sun.

The cool breeze skipping its way across the hillside where the tree stood felt refreshing as Deseray sat down. The cool grass felt good against her bare legs offering a soothing relief against the day's heat.

As Reg sat down, seemingly in one smooth motion, crossing his legs as he lowered himself to the grass, close to Deseray.

She liked how his closeness affected her. She could feel her heart quicken and a feeling of anticipation overcame her. The longer she spent time with him, the more she imagined he was the brave of her dreams. Could this be, she wondered?

She took a cleansing breathe, allowing all her inhibitions to drift away from her with the gentle wind. All her fears and self-consciousness disappeared as well.

She felt as though she had known Reg for as long as she had known White One and trusted him as much also, even though they had just met.

Deseray looked at Reg as he spoke.

"Sometimes," Reg began, "people need another person to talk to. Animals are great listeners, and if the spirits are willing, the answers come from them. But this is not always so."

He was quiet for a moment.

"You are seeking answers to many questions. White One has let me know this."

Deseray gently threw her hands up in the air.

"This is bizarre. How could you know that I tell my deepest secrets to White One? No one could possibly know that."

"Do you believe in powers greater than we are, such as the Spiritual powers that come from the spirit world?"

"I have studied many instances of spirituality and unexplainable things that have occurred in people's lives, but I have never experienced anything like it in my own life."

Reg smiled, "My tribe depends upon the spirits and the wisdom of the holy man for its survival. I have undergone my vision quest when I became a man. I have also taken part in a sun dance. It is because of these experiences and my openness to the spirit world that I have been brought to you. Do you understand what I am saying?"

She sat quietly, letting everything he had said filter through her thoughts. She had always wanted to believe in the spiritual events that were the basis of the Native American culture, but since she had never had any, it was difficult for her to understand fully what he was actually saying.

"I think I understand what you are saying. When things happen to me that I do not understand, I need tangible things to help put it into perspective. If there is not a logical answer to events, it makes me feel unaccomplished. An example of this is a reoccurring dream I have been having. Could this be related to the spirit world you are talking about?"

Once again, his smile was reassuring.

"My people believe certain types of dreams are visions. Visions come from the spirit world. It is a great privilege to have a vision. Visions foretell future events or serve as a guide for ones' future. Understanding a vision is important to learn."

Deseray took a gentle breather before she began.

"I don't understand my dream. I know that when I awaken from this dream, I feel refreshed and find a little peace about who I am, even if it is only for a little while. However, the dream leaves me wanting more. I am not sure if it is to find answers or just to find something in my life that leaves me with the peace I feel when I wake. The dreams transcend me to a time hundreds of years ago, during the time when your people walked upon an earth unspoiled by the white man and modern society. This is something I have secretly longed for."

"I guess it all started when I was a little girl. Why and how I have no idea, yet I am compelled to learn and understand as much about your culture as I possibly can. It is more than an interest. It is as though it is a part of me. It seems as though I am looking for answers about my heritage, yet it is not mine."

When her eyes met his, any remaining fears she had been keeping inside, disappeared. His eyes had so much trust and compassion in them that the whole world about them seemed to fade away.

It was at that moment that she realized his closeness and his handsomeness.

She had been so concerned about sharing her true feelings with someone she had just met, that she had not taken the time to notice him.

His high cheeks and dark eyes awakened an attraction toward him that Deseray could not deny.

In spite of these feelings, she did not feel the evasiveness that usually accompanied first time meetings. Even though they had just met, an essence of a long-time friendship was present, bringing with it a true insight of trust and respect.

The chatter of the birds and the whisper of the wind all seemed to silence themselves in a form of respect for the conversation that was to ensue.

Deseray twiddled with a stand of hair as she carefully chose the words she would use.

"I've always had a special sense toward animals, all animals of every kind. This includes the things of nature also, such as the trees and the grass. I made the mistake once of telling someone I could talk to trees. They thought I was crazy. It was not like the trees and I had a conversation, you know. It was like

I could put my hands near the tree, not touching though and feel the tree's life radiate into my hands."

Shyly she looked into Reg's face to see his reaction. There was neither laughter nor criticism. He sat calmly and listened.

"I understand that the early American Indians held a strong regard for all of nature. It made me wonder if they had the same type of power or insight such as I felt I might have. I wondered if it is all connected somehow. This is primarily what drives my desire to learn more."

Deseray sat quietly, uncertain as to whether she should continue or not.

Reg gently placed his hand upon hers. Sensations like no other she had ever felt raced through her body. They were both stimulating and exhilarating.

She felt herself blush slightly, hoping Reg had not noticed.

"Your differences are what make you so special," he said.

As Deseray listened to him speak, the soothing gentleness of his voice was unexpectedly alluring.

"Many of my people believe we have more than one life. We are returned to mother earth either to finish things we did not accomplish or to bring a message to the people."

"I believe you have lived once before," he added, "As one of the people. I believe you lived among my people and hunted the great buffalo. My people consider the four-leggeds as their brothers and showed respect for them, much like you do."

Her sense of joy peaked as she realized that sitting next to her was someone who actually understood the true feelings of her heart. The things she had shared with no one else except White One had been revealed to another, and he understood!

"If the spirits are willing," he said softly, "I will teach you the ways of my people."

Deseray could hardly contain her joy and without realizing it, she leaped toward Reg and threw her arms around him. Her sudden movement sent them both tumbling over onto the grass.

Deseray felt embarrassed by her boldness.

Reg laughed freely.

"I wish all my student had the same enthusiasm as you!"

"I'm sorry," pleaded Deseray, recovering from her embarrassment.

"Don't be," Reg said with a smile. "I rather liked it."

Deseray's embarrassment quickly changed to shyness. She could feel the warmth slowly covering her cheeks.

Reg untangled himself from Deseray and slowly rose to his feet. He reached out his hand to help Deseray.

"I'm going to enjoy being your teacher." Smiling he added, "the beadwork on your blouse shows great skill. You would be honored among my people with such skill. Beadwork is one area I could tell you about, but not teach you, as I do not have such skill. The women of my tribe do this type of work. Have you ever used porcupine quills? That is the traditional way of my people."

"I've tried, but it takes a lot of patience and I'm not sure if I am supposed to dye the quills first and then make my pattern or make my pattern and then dye them."

"Most often you should dye them first. It helps you plan your design more easily."

"I must go now, "he added. "We'll see each other again."

The thought of seeing Reg again was exciting and she was looking forward to it.

"I'd like that," she said. "I'm anxious to start learning more about your people."

Without taking his eyes from Deseray's, he quickly slipped back through the fence. White One was at his side almost immediately.

"You're right," he said, "about my people. It is all connected us two-leggeds, the four-leggeds, and all the earth. Do not be afraid to feel what you feel. These are good things to hold dear."

White One understood that a great friendship had formed. He edged himself close to the fence between the two young people as a display of approval.

The serenity had lingered in the air was ended by the pawing of White One's hoof upon the ground. As they looked down upon the ground, lying only a few inches from White One's hoof was a large, brown and white feather.

As Deseray bent down and picked it up, a powerful force such as she had never felt before, surge throughout her body. Her first instinct was to cast the feather immediately to the ground, but the sensation within her caused her to continue holding onto it.

She softly ran her fingers along the silky strands that gave the feather its full and graceful shape. It was white from the quill to within a few inches of the end, where it blended into a brilliant, rich, blackish-brown color to the tip.

"It's beautiful," exclaimed Deseray. "I think it's an eagle feather."

"A Bald Eagle," replied Reg solemnly. "Like the white buffalo, eagles are highly respected among my people and held in great reverence."

Her eyes glowed with great admiration as she carefully turned the feather over in her hand.

"I've never held an eagle feather before."

Then an expression of sadness came over her face.

"Why does this make you sad?" Reg asked with concern.

"Because more than anything I'd love to keep it, but the laws say it is illegal to own any feathers from birds of prey. This includes most of all, the bald eagle."

She reluctantly, but gently placed the feather back on the ground.

Reg stood silently as he watched White One once again paw the ground near the feather, only this time with a great boldness.

Reg lightly laughed, "I think he is determined that you have the feather."

"Do you really think so?" Deseray looked at White One.

"I think your right," she said to Reg.

The look in White One's eyes convinced her that he

wanted her to have the feather, so she bent down, once again carefully picking the feather up.

As Deseray held the feather in her hand, White One seemed pleased. He stepped back a short distance and watched. She then slipped the feather under her blouse and carefully patted it to make sure it was safety tucked away.

"I wonder why he wants me to have this feather." Deseray looked at Reg.

"Someday," Reg said softly, "He will ask for it back."

Deseray was about to ask him what he meant when he cut her question short.

"I have to go now."

He smiled at Deseray.

At that moment, more than anything, she did not want to see him go. By this time, his attractiveness was overpowering to her. Was it his handsomeness or the fact that he understood her deepest thoughts? Was it her infatuation that he was the brave of her dreams, or that he understood her heart?

She lightly touched her blouse to make sure the feather was still securely in place. As she did, she remembered the necklace she had been wearing.

"Wait, I want you to have something."

She reached up to her neck and took it off. The necklace was a smooth round stone attached to a leather braid, secured with a silver bead. Upon the stone, she had painted an eagle with authentic Sioux symbolisms. She handed it to Reg.

"I'd like you to have this," she said, "as a token of our friendship. I made it myself."

"I will value it always," he replied as he took it from her and slipped it over his head.

"When will I see you again?" she asked.

He smiled at her, sensing her longing for their newly formed friendship.

"Keep the feather safe and a secret," he instructed. "There are a lot of powers at work in our world. One of them has brought us together and may bring us together again. But you must be sensitive to the world around us, so when the right time comes, we will not miss each other."

His words confused Deseray. By now, she had learned that he said things in little riddles, and she decided she would figure out what he meant later.

"I guess that means we will then," she replied. "I can't begin to tell you how important meeting you is to me."

Deseray turned and looked at White One who stood almost motionless.

"And thank you for the feather. I will take good care of it. It's a wonderful gift."

"I'll see you again," she said as she began to follow the path that led her back to the park's entrance.

Reg affectionately watched Deseray as the thick trees engulfed her and she soon disappeared from his sight.

He put his hand on White One's head, his fingers almost disappearing in the thickness of his fur.

"Well, Great One," Reg said to White One, "I hope the spirits are right about choosing her. She is very special. I pray she will be perceptive to the signs that she will be shown and will respond when the spirits are ready for her journey."

Skillfully and swiftly, Reg swung his strong body up onto White One's back. White One quickly turned and strode toward the thick trees where Deseray had first seen him that day. As he neared the trees, he began to hurry his speed, until he was in a full run. Almost as soon as they entered the trees, they vanished from sight, as though into the sky and were gone.

Chapter Three - The Feather

That night, as she lay on her bed holding the eagle feather, she thought about Reg, White One, and the feather. She gently turned the feather over, allowing its softness to caress her skin with each movement.

Her mind flooded with both excitement and confusion as she recalled the words Reg had used about the feather and about them meeting again. If I am 'sensitive to the world around us', she wondered. He had also said, "When the right time comes, so we will not miss each other."

Strange words, thought Deseray.

She was looking forward to seeing him again. His mannerism and even the way he spoke were like no other person she had ever met. His handsomeness was like no other man she had ever met either. She anticipated new the things she knew were to come.

As she drifted off to sleep, she remembered the smell of his closeness and longed even more to see him again. Sleep came to Deseray, full of wonderful dreams of a day that would indeed bring many new things.

When Deseray woke the next morning, the first thing she realized was that she had not had her dream about the White Buffalo and the young brave. She did however have a dream about a magnificent feather that allowed her to fly.

She jolted up in bed. Was there really a feather or had she just dreamed it. She looked all over the bed and to her comfort, saw the feather lying near her.

She picked it up, realigning the separated feathering so it was once again smooth and streamlined like a feather should be. Her next task was to find a safe and secretive place to keep the feather.

Reg had said to keep it safe and a secret. As she looked around the room for a special place for the feather, she also remembered that Reg had said that someday White One would ask for it back.

While sitting on the floor next to her bed, Deseray reached underneath it and pulled out a small, wooden box. The box was made of a fine aromatic cedar with a desert scene carved on the top lid. It was a gift to her from her brother Mathew. He made it in shop class. He had told her that her name reminded him of a warm, peaceful desert.

As she opened the cover, along with the sweet smell of cedar, warm feelings rose up to greet her. The things she kept inside were as special as the box itself. Each item stimulated specific remembrances and feelings.

Within the box were magazine and newspaper articles about Native American events that she found especially interesting. In addition, Native American artifacts, and jewelry she collected over the years surrounded these.

She carefully and lovingly began to take some items from the box, remembering where or whom she had received them.

In a small-hinged wicker case, she kept four stone arrowheads. Her uncle John sent them to her. He had discovered them on one of his digs in South Dakota. He felt she would enjoy owning them. These were symbolic of a culture and a way of life.

Within the same case, she kept her totem stone. Her totem or power animal was the buffalo. There was a white buffalo painted on her stone. Native Americans believe that certain animals give special powers to a person to help them throughout life. They carried their stone with them in a special leather bag called a medicine pouch.

Deseray felt that the buffalo was her power animal and believed it even more since she met White One. She did not carry her stone with her because she did not have a medicine pouch, even though she wanted to get one someday.

The bundle of rabbit fur that she took out next contained

a very special gift. It was a peace pipe carved from red stone. It was a gift from her uncle John. He had made the pipe himself, using the red stone found only in Pipestone, Minnesota.

A smile of pure affection covered Deseray's face as she thought of her uncle John. He was her mother's brother and lived in Montana. He actively shared Deseray's interest and enjoyment of the Native American culture and its rich history. He knew more about the Native American culture than anyone else Deseray knew.

He had included a letter with the gift, of which Deseray kept with the pipe.

Dear Deseray,

I know you will appreciate and value the gift I have made for you. When I was in Pipestone, Minnesota, I bought the red stone, which is still used by Native Americans, to make their peace pipes.

If you do not have the peace pipe out for display, keep it stored in the rabbit fur as reverence to the sacredness of the pipe. Peace pipes are used in religious ceremonies and should never be abused.

We are all looking forward to your visit with us this summer.

Love, Uncle John

Deseray smiled as she read the last line. She read it repeatedly when she got the letter. She anxiously anticipated a vacation out west.

The thought of her vacation made her suddenly realized that she had not even starting her packing and she was supposed to leave in a few days.

As she put everything back into the box, she imagined all the wonderful places she was going to see. The expedition would be covering some rough terrain and would require horseback entrance into some of the areas. Cars and trucks would be left behind and most other modern conveniences. That seemed exciting to Deseray, as it would be as though she were living in a time before the invention of mechanical and electronic devises.

In preparation for her trip, her uncle had sent her maps of the area where they would start the dig. It was located northeast of the Little Big Horn battle sight. If they are able to determine the location where the arrows were found was an established village, they would excavate. If the evidence did not support this theory, another one would have to be determined. Since it would be an archeological dig, the thought of discovering things that had not been touched by human hands for hundreds of years, peeked her interests even more.

When everything was safely back in her box, she gently placed the Eagle feather on top. She closed the lid and slid the box back under her bed.

Nestling the back of her head against the headboard of her bed, she thought how wonderful her life was and how good she felt about it.

Seeing Reg again was foremost in her mind as well. He is so handsome, she thought. She was impressed that he shared much of the same interests that she enjoyed. Even more, he was willing to teach her many things about his Native American culture that she felt no one else could.

Staring at her ceiling, she decided it would be great to share all the adventures from her trip with him. As she thought about this, she realized that she had forgotten to tell him she would be gone for most of the summer.

Just being around him made her mind whirl, making her feel forgetful. When she was near him, her only thoughts were to stare into his eyes.

She would have to make some time to go back to the park before she left so she could tell him. Her excitement grew as she began to look in her dresser drawers, deciding on the perfect clothes to pack. Her summer in Montana would be a summer she would always remember.

The next few days flew by and it was time for Deseray to leave for her trip. Mathew took Deseray to the train station. Deseray realized the Mathew would be shipping out in few days so she hugged him exceptionally tight.

"Whoa, you're going to break me," he exclaimed.

"Sorry, but I know it is going to be a while before I will see you against and I already miss you."

Mathew waited with Deseray until she boarded the train. The train reminded her of a large bus. The seats were comfortable, and she decided on one by the window. As she watched the people boarding, she wondered where they were going. She knew where she was going. She was going to Montana.

The train slowly began to move as it pulled out of the station. Shortly, the train gained momentum as it began to move along the tracks. The clanking of the train's wheels against the steel tracks soothed Deseray and helped her to sleep. The last days before her departure had been busy ones and she had gotten very little sleep.

Making time to return to the refuge to see Reg had put her off schedule and behind. To top it off, when she got to the park, she could not find Reg or White One anywhere. This left her feeling depressed and lonely. She knew no other way to contact Reg.

The night filled with stars, but the fast movements of the train made them seem as though they were merely blurs of light against the black sky.

As luck would have it, the only train west left late at night. She would miss most of the scenery in Minnesota but would be able to see some of North Dakota the next day.

As she sat comfortably in her seat on the train, she clutched a small, soft-bodied jewelry case against her side. The case contained a very precious item. It contained the eagle feather she had gotten from White One. Many times, she was tempted to open the box and hold the feather, but knew it was not a good idea, just in case someone may see it.

Instead, she affectionately ran her fingers over the case from time to time, thinking about how special the feather was. Thoughts of the feather and White One made her miss Reg. She was disappointed she had not seen him before she had left. She was afraid he might think she lost interest in her Native American studies and possibly lose any future interest he may have developed in her.

She wondered if she should show the feather to her Uncle but decided against it since Reg had told her to keep it a secret.

Deseray slept for a few hours but wakened as passengers got on the train.

A young woman with two children was sitting in the seats across the aisle from her. Deseray leaned over to get nearer to her.

"Excuse me," she whispered softly so not to wake her sleeping children, "Do you know where we are?"

"Sure. We are in Fargo."

"Thank you."

At least she knew how far they had traveled. The beginning of North Dakota was not nearly far enough to suit her, as she was anxious to reach Montana.

As the train stopped in Bismarck, the woman with the two small children were getting off. The children were sleepy eyed and tired from the trip. As the woman was leaving, she smiled at Deseray.

"Enjoy the rest of your trip."

"Thank you, I will."

A man with a suitcase sat in the seat the woman and her children had just vacated.

The train rumbled and screeched as it pulled out of the station. It jerked from side to side as it gained momentum and was soon racing on its way.

Once again, the clanking sound and rocking movement of the train made Deseray sleepy. She took her jacket and rolling it into a ball, stuffed it under her head and soon fell asleep.

When she woke a short time later, the sun had begun to climb above the eastern horizon. How beautiful, Deseray thought, as she watched the earth transfer from darkness to a wispy gray giving way to the brightness of the new day.

Almost miraculously, during the night, the landscape outside her window had changed dramatically. Flat land was evident for as far as she could see except for an occasional development of small peaks and a few low valleys. The land was almost barren of trees, dominated by the tight, round shapes of the sagebrush blowing freely across the open prairies.

Also roaming freely across the open prairies was a variety of animals Deseray had never seen. One such animal was similar to the deer in Wisconsin, but much smaller with unique markings she had never seen.

Their bodies were light tan with the full underside all white. Black markings on their faces made them look as those it they were wearing a burglar's mask. Two round, black horns rose up from the top of their heads and formed a small y-shape at the top. One tip of the y-shape was much larger than the other tip, forming the ends of the horns.

She saw them more frequently as they traveled further across North Dakota.

The only other people near her on the train, was the man with the suitcase. He did not look like he was too friendly. Deseray thought he looked a little sad.

His clothes were clean, but quite worn. His thick dark hair was speckled with wisp of grey as was his thick beard, which was neatly trimmed. His dark hair complemented his dark skin. Deseray suspected he might even be good looking but could not tell due to the thick hair on his face. His dark hair rested gently on his shoulders. He seemed as though he would prefer to be left alone. For some unknown reason, Deseray was drawn to him.

As the scenery went by outside her window, she noticed a grumbling in her stomach. She had not eaten since she had gotten on the train the night before. As she stood up to get her backpack from the overhead compartment, she noticed how good it felt to stretch her legs.

"You kin walk around these trains, ya know," echoed a somber sounding voice.

As she looked toward the direction of the voice, to her surprise, it was the man with the suitcase.

He was smiling. One of his front lower teeth had a small chip in it, but the rest of them were as white and bright as pearls on a necklace.

"It makes fer a long trip," he continued, "if ya sit all the time. Besides," he added in a whisper, "you'll probably need to use the ladies necessary room." His smile was friendly and sincere.

The necessary room, thought Deseray, and realized that she did need to use it.

"I wondered about that."

"It's that way," he said as he pointed toward the front of the train car.

Deseray laid her backpack onto her seat and moved into the isle. As the train swayed slightly back and forth, she had to adjust her movements as well to keep from losing her balance as she walked.

Making her way back to her seat was much easier.

"I think I'm getting the hang of it," she told the man as she sat down.

He laughed and then looked out the window.

She picked up her backpack and dropped it into her lap as she sat down.

Her mother had packed her a "good lunch" so she "wouldn't starve" before she got to Uncle John's.

Nestled inside her pack were four egg salad sandwiches, apples, cheese and crackers and some bottles of water. Deseray was surprised to feel that everything was still cold and then discovered the cold pack tucked in the bottom of the pack.

Deseray looked at her large lunch and then at the helpful man sitting alone.

She leaned across the aisle and asked, "Would you like to share my lunch with me?"

"Oh," he replied, looking thoughtful, "they have a dining car on this train."

"Oh. I guess you'll be eating there then?"

"No, I don't like the food they serve. I'll git somethin ta

eat when I git off the train."

Deseray smiled, "I have lots of food here. My mom over packed. She must have thought I was going to be on the train twenty-four days instead of twenty-four hours. I know I won't be able to eat all of it."

Deseray waited patiently as she looked at him for a response and then added, "Besides, I've always hated to eat alone."

"In that case, I'll be happy ta share yer lunch with ya."

Deseray picked up her pack and sat in the seat next to the man.

She held out her hand. "My name is Deseray."

"My name is Jingles," he said in that somber sounding voice.

"Well, it's good to meet you, Jingles."

She handed a sandwich and a bottle of water to Jingles.

A sound of tasty enjoyment reverberated from his mouth as he took the first bite.

"This is a perty good sandwich. Yer mom is a good cook."

"I guess she is. I only cook a little. I have had to learn to cook for myself since I left home to go to college. She's trying to teach me how."

"Ya want be a cook, huh? I'm a fair cook myself. At least that's what I've bin told." He chuckled to himself.

"I used to be a rodeo rider. I rode bucking broncos, but after my injury, I couldn't ride no more. Tried being a clown, that didn't work out, so I became the rodeo cook. So, that's what I am, a cook. I'm heading to my new job as a cook as we speak."

"That's great! Where is your new job?"

"Montana," he said, "On the west side of the divide."

"How did you get your name, Jingles?" she asked.

"When I was a tad younger, I used ta wear a necklace with small bells and silver feathers and such on it. Ever time I moved the necklace jingled. When people saw, or should I say, heard me comin', they'd say 'here comes Jingles'. I guess the name just stuck."

That is all the information he offered about himself, where he was going or about his new job.

They sat quietly for a while and then Deseray broke the silence.

"What is a divide?"

Jingles laughed.

"The divide is the 'great divide'. It's the biggest mountain range in this here country. It runs clean down from Canada til it reaches Mexico. It divides our country the whole long ways."

"How tall is it?"

"As tall as the sky," he laughed as he raised his hand high above his head.

Deseray swallowed hard.

"Will we fall off?" She asked, not knowing what a mountain range was like or how one goes over a mountain.

Jingles chuckled.

"It's a tall mountain range all right, but the train tracks and road are on what they call passes. We don't go over the mountain. Just hug onto the side of it. Some of the roads are even built right through the mountain itself."

Jingles seemed to have wondered off into a world of his own thoughts as he gazed out the window.

"Imagine," he finally continued, "Tons and tons of rocks and trees right over yer head as the train passes through a huge mountain that was blasted open."

"Pretty impressive, huh?" he asked as he wink his eye.

Deseray's throat felt dry. The idea of driving through a mountain made her nervous. She could not imagine how tall a mountain was and never dreamed that people drove through the inside of one.

Jingles winked again, "Relax, you'll love it."

Deseray leaned back on her chair and tried to relax when she noticed some of the unusual deer-like animals she had been seeing.

"Jingles, what kind of animals are those." She pointed out the window.

"Those are antelope, pronghorn antelope to be exact. They're perty common in the western states."

He reached into his pocket and took out a piece of paper.

"Here's a traveling brochure. There's some perty good pictures in it of the pronghorn."

He handed it to Deseray.

"They look more interesting close up," Deseray replied as she looked at the brochure. "I did not realize their horns had two very distinct horns on the ends. It would be great fun to see them up close."

She handed the brochure back to Jingles.

As he took the brochure from Deseray he asked, "Where're ya from?" he asked.

"I'm from Wisconsin," she replied. "We don't have antelope there. We do have deer though," she added.

"How fer ya go'in?"

"I'm going as far as White Fish, Montana. I am going to my uncle's house for the summer. He lives in Kalispell."

"I guess we'll be travelin' together fer a while cause that's where I'm gitten' off too. Thank ya fer lunch."

Jingles then leaned back in his seat and closed his eyes. Deseray took that as a hint that he had enough company for a while and wanted to be alone.

As Deseray returned to her original seat she took the jewelry case from underneath her jacket where she had hidden it. She ran her fingers over the soft case. The trip seemed long, but she knew it would be worth it once she got to her uncle's house. Her main concerned was surviving the ride through the mountain passes and the tunnels. Jingles did not seem too concerned, so it must be safe.

As the train left North Dakota, the scenery began to transform from a vastly grass covered prairie to a diversified mixture of rolling hills and deep valleys. Tumbleweed bushes were exchanged for small pine trees and occasional hardwood trees.

As they came closer to Havre, Montana, Deseray noticed the rolling hills had gradually begun to increase in size. The further west they traveled the larger the hills became.

Jingles was looking out the window as well.

"Jingles," she said as she pointed out the window, "Are those the mountains?"

Jingles chuckled.

"Not yet little lady. Those are just foothills. The big uns are yet to come."

Deseray gasped.

"Foothills! Those are the biggest hills I have ever seen. We don't have hills that big in Wisconsin."

Jingles laughed again.

Deseray could not take her eyes away from the window. The train began to climb higher and higher getting ever closer to the mountain range. The tracks for the train appeared to cut along the side of the mountain.

Deseray stretched her neck to look at the top of the mountain they were ascending. Thick trees were along the mountainside of the train while the valley got deeper and deeper on the other side.

Deseray's fingers dug tighter and tighter into the arm of her seat as the train confidently followed its pre-designated path along the tracks, seemingly clinging to the side of the mountain. The sky was getting dusky and gray and the sun began to take its leave behind the mountains.

Jingles pointed toward the setting sun.

"The sun sets earlier in the mountains than anywhere else. But it sure is perty."

The setting sun cast a brilliant glow behind the mountain peaks, giving them the look of fiery silhouettes against the glowing red backdrop.

It was breath taking. Deseray was so impressed with the beauty of the mountains, she lost her fear of them and found them enchanting and majestic.

"I know I'm going to love the mountains!"

"Aren't afraid of fallin' off no more?"

Deseray blushed, "I wasn't sure what to expect," she replied, "but now it's great."

The train continued to climb the mountainside and traveled along with no mishaps. As Deseray looked down the mountainside into the valleys below she noticed everything become smaller and smaller, as they went higher. Soon night crept over the entire valley and the mountain blanketed with darkness.

"We'll be in Whitefish in an hour or so, little lady. You should git some rest so you'll be fresh when yer uncle comes to git you at the station."

"Good idea," agreed Deseray.

Deseray tried to rest, but her excitement grew as the train neared Whitefish. She was more anxious to see her uncle than she had realized.

With her jacket once again tucked under her head and the feather within its case nestled under her arm, she closed her eyes and drifted off to sleep.

The clouds over head seemed closer and bigger as Deseray soared high above the earth. She was flying upon the currents of the wind. This must be how it feels to soar like an eagle, she thought. How wonderful.

She had no control over the direction the wind was taking her. Unconcerned, she allowed herself to be carried by the winds wherever they depicted. In her hand was the eagle feather.

Chapter Four - Uncle John's Family

A faint voice interrupted Deseray's deep sleep. "Wake up little lady." The faraway voice was saying. "Wake up, we're in Whitefish."

As she sat up, Deseray tried to focus on the voice, wondering where she was.

"Where are we?"

"Whitefish," Jingles replied.

"Oh yes, Whitefish." The sleepiness disappeared as she realized she had arrived.

Jingles motioned Deseray to leave the train in front of him as he waited patiently for her to gather her belongings.

"You go first. I wouldn't wanta be run over in yer excitement to see yer relatives."

She made her way to the door, stepping carefully onto the uneven platform where the two train cars were connected. She had to step carefully as the two cars had not stopped at the same level. While descending the metal steps, she continually looked around the station, hoping to find a familiar face.

She was concerned that Uncle John would not recognize her since it had been five years since he had seen her last. She was wrong, as a booming voice sounded above the small group of people milling about the station.

"Deseray, Deseray," boomed the voice, "We're right here."

Uncle John was standing a few feet away from her. He shared the same dark complexion as Deseray and her mother, but the brawny build was all his.

Before Deseray's foot could touch the ground, he had grabbed her up in his arm, embracing her affectionately.

"Oh, my!" gasped Deseray. "You've grown a beard!"

He set her back onto the ground. Rubbing his hand on either side of his face, he asked, "Do you like it?"

"It'll take some getting used to, but it's a nice beard as far as beards go."

Waiting patiently nearby were three children and a lovely looking woman.

The woman was on the short side, Deseray thought, with light brown hair. She had a tan completion with soft features, which made her look friendly and kind. Deseray liked her already.

"Deseray, I want you to meet my wife. This is Elisha, who is now your new aunt."

Deseray gave her a gentle hug.

"I'm sorry it took me five years to finally meet you."

Elisha smiled. "Don't worry about it. We understand you could not make it for the wedding. We all have busy lives."

"Well, it's nice to meet you." Deseray replied.

Uncle John motioned the children to come closer.

"These are our children, Curtis, Kachina and Louis."

Two of the three children were his wife's and the youngest one was theirs.

She had seen pictures of Curtis and Kachina, which had been taken at the wedding. Elisha looked much the same now as she had in the wedding pictures, but the two children had changed quite a bit. Then of course, the children had over five years to change.

Louis had not even been thought of yet.

Curtis was tall with light hair like his mother and seemed to be about twenty years old. Kachina seemed a few years younger than Curtis's age, with long strawberry blonde hair of which she had braided. She was tall and slender, like Deseray, and had a welcoming smile.

Louis looked so much like her uncle John that it was not hard to figure who he was. He was big for four years old and had the same dark hair and dark complexion as his father.

Uncle John put his arm around Deseray's shoulder and

began to walk.

"Curtis is studying paleontology and is coming on the excavation with us.

"Hi everyone, it's nice to meet you all."

Curtis shyly gave Deseray a quick hug.

"Nice to meet you."

Kachina hugged Deseray so hard she thought she would stop breathing.

Her enthusiasm was almost overwhelming.

"I'm so happy to finally meet you. It will be great fun having another girl to talk to on the excavation."

Uncle John smiled.

"Oh yes, she's going also."

When Deseray tried to greet Louis, he hid behind his sister, wanting nothing to do with Deseray.

"I guess he's a little shy right now," explained Uncle John, "but once he gets to know you, he'll drive you crazy for attention."

Deseray looked around the train station for Jingles. She could not find him.

"Did you lose something?" John asked.

"No," Deseray replied. "I was looking for the nice man who kept me company on the train. I wanted to wish him good luck at his new job."

With a degree of regret for having missed saying goodbye to Jingles, the excitement of the moment took all her attention.

"Sorry we missed your friend," Uncle John said. "We should get your luggage and get on our way. Kalispell isn't very far."

Uncle John put his arm around Deseray's shoulder and began to walk toward the luggage claim area.

Very few people had gotten off in Whitefish, so it was easy to find her luggage. Her luggage was the only four suitcases remaining.

John lifted two large suitcases from the luggage rack.

"Packed a little on the heavy side, didn't you?" he

laughed, as he winked at Curtis, who took the remaining two suitcases in tow.

Deseray blushed. "I wasn't sure what to bring, so I guess I must have brought it all."

Everyone laughed as Uncle John and Curtis dragged the luggage out the door of the station.

"It feels a little chilly for a summer night," exclaimed Deseray as she shivered, putting on her jacket.

"You'll find the summer nights are a bit cooler here," Elisha said, "Once the sun goes down behind the mountains."

While rearranging the luggage he was carrying and attempting to point, Uncle John motioned everyone to follow his lead.

"The truck is over this way."

After putting the luggage in the back of the truck, everyone piled inside. Within fifteen minutes, the small group had reached Kalispell.

"This is Kalispell, and the ranch is a little north of here toward the mountain range," explained Uncle John.

The night was so black that Deseray could not even see a single mountain, let alone a whole range.

After a short ride from Kalispell, John stopped the truck in front of a two-story house. The porch was as long as the front of the house. Lit oil lamps hung from the eves, spaced evenly apart every few feet, along the full length of the porch. Deseray found the view to have a wonderful storybook effect.

As soon as Uncle John closed the truck door, he began giving directions to everyone.

"Kachina, show Deseray where your room is so she can get some sleep. Curtis, you help carry in her luggage."

"It'll take a couple of trips," he chuckled. With his muscular build and long arms, Curtis had no problem carrying all four suitcases.

Elisha was carrying the now sleeping Louis into the house. She paused, "I'm really glad you could come for a visit. John is very excited."

"So am I." Deseray replied with a smile.

Kachina's room was toward the back of the house. Her window faced the mountain, of which Deseray still could not see.

"John put an extra bed in here for your stay. I'll sleep on it and you can have mine."

"Oh, no," protested Deseray. "I wouldn't be comfortable sleeping in your bed. I'll like this one fine," she said as she took off her jacket and laid it on the spare bed.

"I suppose you're pretty tired after your long trip. You can put your things in the top two drawers of the dresser if you want to."

"I think I'll wait until tomorrow to do that, if that's ok."

"That's even better. I have chores to do early so I guess we both had better get some sleep. It's nice to have you here."

"The train was exciting, but all the sitting seems to have tired me out." Deseray yawned.

The warmth of the bed felt good as Deseray lay there recalling the events of the day. Soon everything seemed to fade away and she quickly fell asleep.

The next morning soft talking from another room awakened Deseray.

"Don't wake her up," someone whispered, "She's probably still pretty tired."

It was Elisha's voice.

Deseray sat up in bed. Kachina was gone, leaving her bed neatly made.

Anxious to see the mountain she was unable to see the previous night due to the darkness, she got out of bed and walked over to the window. As she pulled the curtain back, she gasped.

Right there, in front of her as wide as she could view, was a huge mountain. It appeared to rise up from the earth and go on forever. Even straining her neck to look above its peak, she could not. The house was nestled near the mountain's base and seemed as though the house and the mountain were the same.

The view was more than she had expected and was in awe of the fantastic beauty and massiveness.

She had no doubt in her mind that she was falling in love with the mountains.

Dressing quickly, she entered the kitchen.

"You're awake. Are you hungry?" Elisha cheerfully asked.

Elisha was just putting away the last of the dishes that Deseray assumed was from everyone else's breakfast.

"Yes, thank you," Deseray replied as she sat at the table where one lone place setting had remained.

As she sat quietly waiting, she observantly looked around the quaint but sizable kitchen.

The walls were painted sunshine yellow with pictures of fields and country scenes such as horses running freely about. Basketry and weavings of Native American designs accented the pictures, giving the whole room a comfortable homey atmosphere.

Elisha set a plate of eggs, bacon and toast in front of her.

"Where is everyone?" Deseray inquired.

"They're out doing their chores. You can join them when you're done."

Deseray wondered what type of chores they were doing. The chores she had before she left for college, consisted of washing the dishes, helping to clean the house, and keeping her room neat. She also took care of her two horses, Licorice and Diamond, but she had never considered this a chore.

Elisha sat down to keep Deseray company as she ate.

"How was your trip? Did you enjoy the train?" She asked.

"It was fine. A little long to be on a train, but I was able to see some countryside and animals as I traveled. I also met some nice people." She was thinking of Jingles.

Elisha gently squeezed Deseray's hand.

"Just wait. There are quite a few animals here in Montana you may not have seen. We have mountain goats and mountain sheep. And of course, there is moose and elk."

As the last mouthful past Deseray's lips, she picked up her

dish and placed it on the counter.

"Can I help with anything?" Deseray offered.

"No. I just have to do the last of the dishes and start some laundry. Why don't you go outside and look around? Kachina is in the barn."

"Thank you for breakfast."

The crisp morning air greeted her as bright sunshine began to change the coolness of the nighttime air to pleasant morning warmth.

Looking around, she noticed Curtis carrying bales of hay from a wagon into the hay barn.

Off in the horizon the mountain range stretched on further than Deseray could see. Gracefully raising out of the ground the mountains captured the sky as they reached seemingly to the clouds.

"Finally decided to get up?" Curtis chimed.

"It's really nice here." Deseray replied.

Curtis was much taller than she was, with a muscular build and pleasant looking eyes.

"Grab a few bales and help me out, would you?"

He laughed as he hoisted another bale from the wagon.

Deseray looked the large size bales and smiled. "Yeah, right, but I don't think so."

Curtis laughed as he lifted another bale and disappeared into the hay barn to reappear a few moments later.

"Can you ride a horse"? he asked.

Deseray hesitated to answer.

He asked again.

"Think a city girl like you can handle it?"

"I'm not a city girl. I live in the country." Deseray protested.

A girl's voice entered the conversation.

"Don't let him bother you. He still lives in the dark ages where men were men and women were thought of as wimps."

It was Kachina. She was leading a small calf as she approached them.

"Where is its mother?" Deseray asked as she pet the calf.

"She's out on the range. The calf was weak when she was born and the herd left her behind. I brought her back here and have been hand feeding her ever since. She thinks I'm her mother."

"She seems pretty strong now." Deseray said as she continued petting the calf.

Kachinas pat the calf on her head.

"She is doing great now. We are going to let her go on the range early tomorrow. She has to be return before we leave on our trip. She'll have to learn to make her own way."

"So you guys raise cows?" Deseray asked.

"Cattle," acknowledged Curtis.

"OK, cattle," conceded Deseray.

"Our father did," added Kachina, "before he died. Our mother wanted to keep the ranch going and so did Curtis and I."

"We managed on our own for a while, but after mom and John got married, things seemed to go much better. John has been wonderful for mom and we all like him too. He's a very special person."

Deseray smiled in approval that her uncle was indeed a special person.

"My dad died about eight years ago. Curtis was old enough to handle a lot of the work. I did my best and mom managed the hands and the business end of it. But we could tell she missed dad a lot."

Curtis stopped lifting the bales of hay.

"John and my dad were good friends. We all got along back then so when mom started dating John and decided to get married, it was easy to accept. He brought back the sparkle in our mom's eyes."

Kachina continued, "Then little Louis came along and it seemed to bring us closer as a family. He's a pretty good little kid and has a lot of John's humor and our mother's charm. Curtis started college last year which was possible with John as part of our family."

"Enough of this gabbing," Curtis piped in, "we have to get a lot done before we leave this operation in the keeping of the hands."

"Kachina, Uncle John said you are going on the trip as well?"

"I wouldn't miss it for the world." She smiled.

Curtis reiterated his earlier statement.

"I hope you can ride a horse. That's how we will be doing most of our traveling."

"Can you ride?" asked Kachina.

"A little," replied Deseray with a sheepish smile.

Deseray's mind was contemplating a joke to play on Curtis, so she reserved letting anyone know that she was indeed a skilled rider.

John arrived home about suppertime later that day.

"Well, everything is set. I worked out the diameter of the area we want to explore with the Department of Natural Resources and got the permits we were required to have. Both the guide and the cook should be here by tomorrow."

He was beaming from ear to ear. It has been a long time since Deseray had seen an adult so excited. It was almost childlike.

"I almost forgot," he said as he looked at Deseray. "You do know how to ride a horse, don't you?"

Curtis was the first to answer. "A little," he replied.

Kachina tapped him on the shoulder. "Be nice."

"I am nice. But that's what she said."

John interrupted.

"The first thing we'll do tomorrow is to get you on a horse and see how well you can ride. Our horses are bred for mountain riding and are very sure footed, but it helps if you're a good rider."

Everyone spent the remainder of the day including verifying checklists, packing and planning. Lunch was a quaint meal enjoyed on the magnificent front porch. Almost before the last morsels were swallowed, bodies took off in many directions to complete the "necessity" lists each one had.

Deseray helped Kachina with her chores while Uncle John spent the day giving instructions to the foreman of the ranch.

As the sun took its place peacefully behind its mountain refuge, everyone gathered for the evening meal. John stretched his long arms over his head.

"I do believe we accomplished quite a bit today."

Everyone nodded in agreement, as food was place into their eager mouths.

As the late evening meal ended John announced, "We've got a lot to do tomorrow so why don't we call it a day and get some sleep."

Deseray hugged her uncle.

"Thank you for inviting me along. I love being in Montana and I'm having a wonderful time."

"I'm glad you're here too." He returned the hug.

Deseray slept dreamlessly and peacefully.

The next morning Deseray woke Kachina early.

"Can you help me? I want to see the horse I am going to be riding. I have an idea. I want to play a joke on Curtis."

The two of them giggled and laughed like little girls as they quietly snuck out of the house.

Deseray loved the smell of the stables. Warmth radiated for the horses body heat making the stable warm in contrast to the cool morning air.

"I can't get over how clean your stable is."

"Thanks. We work hard at it. You can ride, can't you? I mean more than just a 'little'."

"Sure, I can ride. I have two horses at home, and I compete in barrel riding all the time."

Kachina laughed loudly. "I can't wait to see Curtis's face when he sees you on a horse. Do you want to make it a really good joke on Curtis, because I have an idea?"

"Why not, it should be fun."

"You'll probably be riding Molly."

Kachina walked over to a stall and stopped.

"This is Molly. She's a good horse and rides easy."

Molly was tan, white and brown with a salt and pepper muzzle.

"When John asks you to try her, pretend you don't know much about riding. That will make Curtis just gloat. Won't he feel silly when you show him how well you can ride?"

Deseray petted Molly gently on her muzzle.

"She seems real sweet."

Molly made a soft whinny and Deseray moved close to her side.

"She likes you!"

Deseray gave Molly one more pet as she motioned to Kachina.

"If we're going to make this work, we'd better get back into the house before someone notices we're gone."

Deseray and Kachina snuck back into the house chatting and planning all the way.

After breakfast, everyone gathered at the coral to determine who would ride which horse.

Curtis led a large buckskin from the stable. A look of pride shown on his face, as bright as a star against the black night sky, as he walked alongside his horse. He briskly rubbed the horse's ears as he spoke.

"This noble beast is Rocky. He is the most sure-footed horse in these parts. I think he could out-climb a mountain goat."

"He's beautiful!" exclaimed Deseray.

Rocky nuzzled Curtis with affection as Deseray thought how well they looked together. Uncle John came out of the stable leading Molly.

"This is Molly. She is sure footed and has enough stamina and spirit to make her a good riding companion. She isn't spooked by cars or sudden noises and is gently spirited. She's been on trails several times and knows what she is doing."

"Even if the person who's riding her doesn't know what she's doing," Curtis snickered.

John cleared his throat as he looked directly at Curtis. Curtis took the hint and decided to keep his comments to himself.

"I've saddled her, but before we go, I want you to be able to saddle her as well as anyone."

He led Molly up to Deseray who pet her on the neck and spoke to her softly.

"Go ahead," coaxed Uncle John, "let's see how well you can handle her."

Deseray stood next to Molly and put her hand on the saddle horn. She stood there for a moment and then put her right foot into the stirrup. As she gazed over toward Curtis, she was aware that it was the incorrect foot to use. He was trying to hide his laughter from John's watchful eye.

"That's not the proper foot," instructed Uncle John. "You put your left foot in the stirrup and swing your right foot over the horse and put it into the stirrup on the other side."

Uncle John gave Deseray a little push to help her get atop Molly.

Deseray sat on Molly for a moment. She held a rider well and Deseray felt comfortable on her. Since she had taken the joke this far, she decided to take it a little further.

"Do you think you can refresh my memory on how to steer her, Uncle John?"

Curtis laughed so hard that he almost fell off the fence.

"Steer her?" he laughed. "She isn't a car."

Deseray secretly looked at Kachina who was trying hard not to burst out laughing.

"She's bit reigned," began Uncle John, "so when you want her to go left, put pressure on the left side of her mouth and nudged her in the left side. Do the opposite to go to the right."

Deseray sat tightly in the saddle, held the reigns up in the air with both hands and gently kicked Molly with both heels.

Molly's reaction was one of confusion as she backed up slightly and stopped.

Curtis let out a howling laugh that almost sent Molly on

the run. Rocky even startled slightly.

John looked sternly at Curtis.

"This is no laughing matter. You could try to be supportive about this matter. If she cannot ride, she cannot go. If she doesn't go, you may be asked to remain behind as well to keep her company."

At that point, all of Curtis' teasing and laughter turned into real concern.

Deseray decided that she had done enough teasing and was curious as to how she and Molly would work together.

She relaxed the reigns and gave Molly a gentle nudged in the sides as she clicked her lips and teeth to encourage her to move forward.

Molly responded and off they went. There were barrels set up at the end of the corral where Kachina practiced her barrel ridding. Deseray decided to take advantage of them.

She coaxed Molly into a trot and they were off and running. Deseray sat loosely in the saddle and Molly seemed to sense the skill and confidence of her rider. Together they circle the barrels with accuracy and style. No one spoke a word as they watched the horse and rider.

As Deseray rode Molly back to the waiting spectators, she was not sure what the expression on her uncle's face meant.

"You're quite an experienced rider," he commented, "but why all the pretending?"

Deseray sat on Molly, shifting uncomfortably in the saddle.

"It's my fault," added Kachina. "Deseray told me she was a fair rider, but Curtis was teasing her about almost everything, so I thought it would be funny to show him up and be shocked when Deseray could prove that she knows a little bit more then he gave her credit for."

She took a big breath and stopped, looking at John for his reaction.

A gentle voice entered the conversation. It was Elisha.

"You're not going to tell me that you've forgotten what it

was like to be young and play jokes on each other are you?"

John laughed. "I surely hope not."

John turned to look at Deseray who was dismounting Molly.

"I suppose this means you also know how to saddle and take care of your own tack?"

"I'm sorry, Uncle John. I didn't mean to worry you."

Suddenly Uncle John burst into laughter.

"You're not the only one who can play a joke." He said through his laughter.

He looked at Kachina as he opened his billfold and removed a picture.

"You're mother sent this to me a few years ago."

Deseray took the picture from her uncle. She too, began to laugh.

It was a picture of her and Licorice as they stood next to the first-place trophy that they had just won.

Uncle John gave Deseray a hug.

"Since most of the horses are already saddled, you, Curtis and Deseray take that calf out to the range and see if she can adapt. She's old enough now to be on her own."

Elisha smiled. "I'll have lunch ready by the time you get back. After that, you can concentrate on getting your gear ready for the trip." Elisha turned toward the house when she noticed a rider coming up the driveway leading three mules.

John smiled.

"That must be the cook I hired."

As they rider came closer, Deseray smiled with excitement.

"It's Jingles!"

Jingles halted his horse near the group.

He smiled as soon as he noticed Deseray.

"Howdy little lady. Didn't except ta see ya here."

"Do you know each other?" asked John with great curiosity.

"He's the nice man that kept me company on the train."

Deseray turned back to Jingles, "So this is your new job as a cook?"

"Surely is. It's already turnin' out to be a perty good new job."

John walked up to Jingles, extending his hand, welcoming him to their ranch.

The mules that trailed behind the horse were pack mules, each one laden with different types of gear.

The first mule had two leather Panniers with poly plastic inserts. The rectangular shape of each pannier compared to regular saddlebags impressed Deseray. The hard poly plastic boxes made each bag sturdy and roomy. Each pannier had strap closures for easy access.

Jingles opened the pack boxes.

"The first two mules is fer dry goods and shelf staple foods such as powdered eggs and milk." Jingles explained.

The second mule had the same carrying system as the first, except there was a small pack sitting in the center of the panniers.

He slapped his hand on the small pack, "This here is fer the cook tent and my sleeping quarters."

Jingles walked over to the third mule that also had a pair of rectangular panniers but there was no hard ploy plastic insert. The bags bulged with their contents.

"This is fer my pots and pans, lamp oil, lamps and other stuff needed to make a good camp."

Jingles was smiling from ear to ear, very proud of his choices.

"These are real good mules, and they'll serve us well."

John looked pleased with the set-up Jingles' had devised.

"Everything looks well planned out. We can get your horse and mules set up in the stable and go over some trip details. Curtis started to show Jingles where to take his horses and mules. John's voice stopped them.

Uncle John looked at the girls.

By the time you two get back from letting the calf go, it

should be close to lunch." He turned to address Jingles. "You can join us if you would like to."

"Lunch sounds perty good," Jingles said, "Just let me tend to the horse and mules and I'll be glad ta join ya."

Curtis, Jingles and his little caravan headed toward the stables.

Deseray and Kachina returned to the coral and where Kachina saddled her horse.

After her horse was saddled, she said, "I'll get the calf."

A few minutes later Kachina returned leading her horse in one hand and in the other, the calf haltered on the end of a lead rope. Deseray mounted Molly.

"We'll be riding west to find the rest of the herd." She told Deseray.

Holding the end of the lead rope, Kachina swung herself into the saddle and coaxed the calf to follow her. The calf followed easily, and they slowly rode out to the open range.

Within half an hour, they found the herd.

"We'll stop here and take the calf to the edge of the herd by foot. You can just drop the reigns. The horses have been trained not to walk away while the reigns are down."

Deseray dismounted Molly and lay the reins on the ground. Kachina dismounted also, while still holding on to the calf's lead rope.

The two of them quietly walked toward the herd. The calf brayed as though looking for a familiar answer from the vastness of the herd. It had been a long time since she had had contact with other cattle and the sounds and smells of the herd excited her.

Almost as soon as Kachina removed the harness, the calf was off and running, soon disappearing into the herd.

"Did you see where she went?" asked Kachina.

"No, not yet."

The two of them kept looking, hoping to catch of glimpse of her.

Suddenly Deseray pointed.

"There she is."

The calf had managed to find two others calves of similar size and age and seemed to be quite content as she munched the prairie grass with her newfound companions.

Kachina smiled.

"She looks like she'll do pretty well out here."

"Will she ever find her mother again?"

"I'm sure her mother had forgotten her by now. Besides, she is too old to be mothered anymore, so it is not important. Her mother will go into heat and be breed again and it won't matter to her anymore even if it once did."

"It sounds so cruel."

"They live by instincts and that is what makes them survive. Come on, let's get back so we can get some lunch. We have a lot of packing to do."

"I can't wait until we get going." Deseray exclaimed.

When the girls returned to the house, John and Jingles were sitting on the porch, the table covered with papers, laughing as they talked.

Elisha was standing near the door, wiping her hands on her apron. She addressed Jingles.

"I'm about to put lunch on the table, so if you don't mind eating someone else's cooking, you're welcome to join us."

"Sounds like an invite I can't turn down, replied Jingles, "Just let me know where to worsh up."

Curtis stepped off the porch and walked up to Deseray and Kachina.

"I'll give you a hand with the horses."

Once lunch was done, Elisha, Kachina and Deseray cleaned up the dishes while John showed Jingles where he would be sleeping in the bunkhouse.

"Jingles seems like a very nice man," commented Elisha as she handed Deseray a dish to place into the cupboard.

"He was very informative on the train, telling me about the mountains and the names of some of the animals we'd seen. It seems really strange that we were going to the same place and didn't even realize it."

"It's funny how things work out sometimes." Elisha added with a smile.

As the last dish found its place in the cupboard, Deseray and Kachina turned their attention the trip.

"Mom," Kachina said to Elisha. "If you don't need our help anymore, we want to get started with our packing."

"Thank you for your help with lunch dishes. You two go and get your things ready. I'm going to put Louis down for his nap."

Deseray realized that she had not unpacked anything. She had been wearing the same jeans for the past two days. She placed a rather large suitcase onto the bed.

Inside she had put her notebooks, camera, and a tape recorder in which she would use to document the trip and their activities.

"I hope we find some relics to confirm that the Lakota had a tribe in Montana. History places them in South Dakota for the most part. It seems strange that they had their Sun Dance at Little Big Horn if they all lived in the Dakotas." Deseray showed Kachina some of the research she had brought.

"I think they gathered at Little Big Horn that year," Deseray explained, "only because a lot of different tribes were having a meeting to discuss the white man. Little Big Horn was a central location."

"I do remember reading something about that," Katrina said. "Maybe a small band separated from the rest of the tribe. Maybe they decided to stay in eastern Montana. I guess that's what this excavation is all about."

Both girls laughed with enthusiasm as they continued searching for just the right clothes to take along.

After about two hours of sorting pants, shirts, sweatshirts, socks, and underwear, the final selections found their way into saddlebags designed specifically for wearing apparel.

Extra hiking boots and toiletries were also packed.

"Curtis will be proud of you. You managed to get all the

things you would need into two saddle bags!"

Deseray laughed at the thought of playing another joke on Curtis by taking along a trunk full of clothes but thought better of it. She did not want to upset her uncle.

They put their saddlebags on the front porch where they would remain until they were put into the truck.

Deseray packed a small backpack containing her diaries, camera and tape recorder so they could be with her in the truck. She could begin her diary and the beginning of her thesis.

That night after supper, talked turned to last minute needs for the trip. The trip would begin early the next morning.

John looked at Jingles.

"Do you know Jake Spinally, Jingles? He's going to be our trail guide."

"Can't say as I have. I don't know the fella."

"He said he would be here sometime today but hasn't shown up. I have never met him either, but I have been told that Jake Spinally is one of the best guides around. I've only corresponded with him in a letter myself. I guess he'll show up in the morning, I hope."

Everyone was excited about the trip except little Louis. He wasn't too happy that he had to stay behind with his mother. He really wanted to go.

"Daddy," he pleaded with John, "Why can't I go? I'm big enough."

"I know you're big enough," John began, "That's why I am putting you in charge of this whole big ranch."

John reached over and put Louis on his lap.

"You see," he continued, "We can't put just anyone in charge. We need someone who already knows the operations and that can be responsible. I need someone I can trust."

Louis raised his eyebrows with surprise.

"You trust me, Daddy?" He asked.

"You bet I do," John said, "If I can't leave you in charge here, I wouldn't be able to go on the trip. I'd have a terrible time worrying about this place."

Louis put his arms around John's neck and gave him a hug. "I'll do a good job!" he beamed.

"Well," John announced, "It's time we all got some sleep so we can get an early start."

John put his coffee cup into the sink, as he wondered when Jake Spinally would arrive.

"Guess he'll show up in the morning." John told himself as he headed toward his bedroom.

"Remember, everyone, morning is going to come early."

Deseray entered the bedroom she shared with Kachina, just ahead of her. It gave her enough time to secretly reach into the top drawer of the dresser, remove the jewelry case containing the feather and quickly slip it under her blouse.

"I think I'll go for a little walk and look at the stars. I won't be long."

"Don't worry about waking me when you come in, I'm so tired I could sleep thorough anything."

The night air was a bit chilly, so Deseray grabbed a light jacket from the hallway on her way out of the door.

The night sky was as she had expected, filed with many stars. Deseray felt as though she was looking at every star in the universe all at once. The clear sky was so vast; she now understood why they called Montana "Big Sky Country".

The brightness of the full moon illuminated the darkness, casting a soft glow in which Deseray was able to make her way around in the night. Near the house was a groove of pine trees encircling large boulders, now used for decorative purposes as hosts to Elisha's flower garden.

Deseray chuckled as she climbed upon the largest boulder.

" What's with me and boulders?" She laughed.

Once comfortably positioned upon the large boulder, she reached under her blouse and produced the velvet jewelry case. Carefully opening the case, she was pleased to see that the feather was undamaged from the long trip. She ran her fingers gently along its soft length. As her fingers trailed along the feather, her thoughts drifted to those of Reg.

She missed him and hoped he would not give up on her. She wished she had been able to see him again before she had left.

Her thoughts came back to the feather. It was important to keep the feather with her. She knew that it had a power that she would soon discover. Reg had said to be sensitive to the world around her. Each time she held the feather, it was as if it had a message for her. "Now you're being silly", she told herself, "a talking feather?"

A voice from behind her made her jumped so abruptly, she fell off the boulder landing on shaky feet.

"Perty night, isn't it?" It was Jingles.

As luck would have it, the case snapped shut hiding the feather from view.

Jingles quickly helped Deseray to gain her balance.

"Didn't mean ta scare ya'"

"That's ok; I was enjoying the stars so much I was just surprised that someone else was out here. And yes, it is a pretty night."

Deseray sat down on some smaller rocks, not so far off the ground this time. Jingles sat on some of the larger boulders, his feet touching the ground as he sat.

He noticed the case Deseray held in her hand.

"Must be somethin' perty important in that case. You seem to keep it with ya quite a bit."

Deseray spoke slowly. "Yes, I guess it's important."

"Can ya share it with anyone?"

"I'd rather not. It's not that I don't want to," she continued, "but I promised that I would keep it a secret."

"A secret?" said Jingles. "A promise is a promise. If we don't keep our promises, our world wouldn't have any honor or respect. Ya keep yer promise." He concluded and then continued.

"Can't sleep huh?"

"I guess I'm just excited about the trip."

"It seems like everyone is excited about this trip. I've never bin on a dig before. It should prove ta be perty interesting."

Jingles stretched as he stood up.

"Guess I'd better git these 'ol bones ta bed. Ya better do the same."

He turned to leave but stopped.

"By the way," he continued as he stuck his hand under his jacket and pulled something out from under it.

"You might find it easier ta carry yer case in this."

In his hand was a leather pouch with fringes, beadwork and leather ties.

He handed it to Deseray.

"It's a medicine pouch. Indians use it ta carry their special things round in."

"It's beautiful and so soft." Deseray rubbed the soft leather against her cheek.

"I can't take this," she protested. "It's too valuable."

"Now don't ya worry 'bout that little lady. I know ya'll take good care of it and if yer inclined ta, you can give it back after the trip. It's not necessary though."

With that, Jingles limped off toward the bunch house. Deseray wondered about the limp. Maybe someday, she thought, he will tell me about it.

Deseray slipped the case into the leather pouch. It was a perfect fit. She pulled the ties on the pouch closed, engulfing the case and feather within the soft leather.

As she walked back to the house, she felt comfortably sleepy and was looking forward to the next day.

Chapter Five - Trails Away

The clouds whirled and raced across the sky so furiously, Deseray felt as though she were about to be carried away. The valley below was misty with the light rain, yet through the mist, Deseray could still see the small herd of buffalo grazing near the river. The herd seemed apprehensive in the high winds and muffling rain.

As Deseray scanned the shoreline, the ground began to rise slightly. Jagged edges emerged through the grasses as the incline became steeper. Her eyes continued to follow the edge of the rising ravine until her they happened upon a form standing alone in the mist.

Deseray gasped. It was a white buffalo. How fortunate she felt to have seen two white buffalos in one lifetime. She continued to scan the upper edge of the ravine and saw yet another form standing in the mist. The form was that of a man about 100 yards from where she was standing.

He called to her, waving his hand, indicating for her to come toward him. She could not hear his words but began walking toward him anyway. Suddenly she heard what he was saying. He was calling her name.

"Deseray, come this way."

When she came close enough to him, to her utter surprise, she realized it was Reg.

How did he know I was here? She wondered, as she continued walking toward him.

In her haste to reach him, she came dangerously close to the edge of the ravine. The force from the winds caused her to lose her balance for a moment. She regained her footing just in time to prevent herself from tumbling down the steep embankment into the river below.

Before she could reach Reg, he began walking. Instead of toward her, he walked toward the white buffalo. Gazing once again at the white buffalo, she realized it was White One.

She wondered how they had found her and why they had come.

"Wait for me," she yelled to Reg. "Wait for me."

He continued walking toward White One while calling her name.

"Deseray, Deseray."

The voice no longer belonged to Reg, but to Kachina.

Deseray sat up in bed so suddenly; her head almost collided with Kachina, who pulled back just in time to avoid the collision.

"Deseray, are you alright? You were dreaming and thrashing. It seemed as though you were running or something. Are you ok?"

Perspiration was trickling down Deseray's forehead.

"I'm ok. I was having the strangest dream."

"What was it about?"

"I'm not sure. It was very strange. I was trying to catch up to a friend of mine, but he kept walking away from me. He would not wait. He just kept walking. I was trying very hard to catch him, but I couldn't."

Kachina walked down the hall to the bathroom and returned with a glass of water.

"Here, drink this; it might make you feel better."

Deseray slowly drank the water.

"You're right, it did help. What time is it?"

"It's about four in the morning. Do you feel like going back to sleep?"

"No, not really. I think I'll go for a walk. You go back to sleep though."

Kachina laid in bed and pulled the cover over herself, "I will, only if you're ok."

"I'm fine. I've had strange dreams before."

Deseray silently got dressed as Kachina went back to sleep.

A sudden chill came over Deseray as she stepped into the early morning air. She wrapped her sweater tightly about her. Feelings of frustration and confusion chilled her as deeply as the air.

The implied reality of the dream affected her as deeply as though it had really happened. Reg would not wait for her. She felt the frustration in her soul and that too, upset her.

She longed for a cup of coffee and wondering what time Elisha would wake up. It would be rude to dig around in someone else's kitchen.

Almost by magic, the lights came on in the kitchen. Deseray hurried back into the house.

There stood Elisha, scooping coffee grounds into the maker.

Deseray was concerned she had made to much noise as she was leaving the house.

"Did I wake you?' she asked Elisha.

"Oh, heavens no, dear, I get up at four-thirty every day. I have for many years. There are chores to be done early and I have always felt that chores should not be done on an empty stomach."

"I'm glad to hear that. I would feel just awful if I had wakened you."

"You're up pretty early. Do you get up as this hour too?" Elisha asked.

"No, I had a strange dream and couldn't go back to sleep so I thought I would take a walk. It might also be that my time zone is an hour earlier than yours."

Elisha took some cups out of the cupboard.

"Did the walk help?"

"Not much, but a cup of fresh coffee would."

"Well, sit down then and as soon as it's done, I'll pour you a cup."

The air about Elisha was enchanting. She was so calm and

serene; Deseray could not imagine anyone remaining upset or frustrated in her presence.

Elisha and Deseray heard creaks overhead from the floor-boards of the rooms above. It seemed that everyone was going to get an early start that day.

Within minutes, the kitchen was full of cups of coffee and lots of conversation when there was a knock on the door. Upon opening the door, there stood Jingles.

"Good morning, Jingles," exclaimed John. "Are you all set to get started?"

"Sure are." He replied.

"Well, come in for some coffee." John waved Jingles toward the kitchen table.

Jingles carefully wiped his feet at the door before entering.

"Don't mind if I do."

"Did Jake Spinally show up during the night?" John asked Jingles.

"Not that I noticed," Jingles replied as he took a sip of coffee.

A worried expression overcame John's face.

"Maybe I misread that letter. Maybe we were supposed to meet up in Miles City. Elisha where's that letter from Spinally?" His intense frown wrinkled a big furrow across John's forehead. "If he doesn't show up," he said. "I don't know how long it will take me to find a replacement."

Elisha began to warm the fry pan as she took eggs from the refrigerator taking a small detour to the office as the pan warmed. She returned with a letter in her hand. She handed the letter to John.

As Uncle John began to open the letter, he heard the sound of a truck entering the yard. John moved over to the window, looked out, and could see a truck hauling a horse trailer stopped near the front porch.

A look of hopeful relief came to John's face.

"Maybe this is him now."

John and Jingles walked onto the porch just as a tall, slender woman, wearing jeans and a brown cowboy hat stepped out of the truck.

The women stood at the bottom of the steps and looked at John.

"I'm looking for John Case. You happen to be him?" she asked.

"Yes, I'm John Case. How can I help you?"

"Great!" the woman replied. "I'm Jake Spinally, your guide."

John tried very hard not to let his mouth drop open. A woman, he thought, a woman guide. Jingles suppressed a grin as he watched John's face.

"Won't you come in?" John waved his hand motioning toward the front door.

Jake took off her hat as she stepped onto the porch and long brown hair tumbled about her shoulders.

"I suppose you're surprised that I'm a woman, aren't you?"

"A little," replied John. "With a name like Jake, I guess I just assumed you were a man."

"Most people do," she answered. "My given name is Jacqueline, but my dad wanted a boy, so he began to call me Jake and it stuck. It's the only name I use now."

John smiled and led everyone into the kitchen.

Rather than sit at the table, Jake stood near the door and waited.

"I hope it isn't a problem that I'm a woman," she said. "I'm still one of the best guides in Montana that you'll ever find."

John motioned to Jake to sit down.

"I'm reassured to hear that. As far as you being a woman, that's no problem. It just takes some getting used to, that's all."

Elisha offered Jake a cup of coffee.

"Thank you," she said as she smiled gratefully to Elisha. "I'm sorry I'm late, but my horse threw a shoe late last night when I was out riding. My horse takes a specialized shoe, and my regular blacksmith was out of town. I had to hunt up a new blacksmith to make a new shoe. I had a couple extra made for the trip, just in case."

Jake took a sip of coffee before she continued.

"You do have extra shoes for your horses, don't you?" she asked, "I can shoe any horse as long as I have the proper shoes."

"That's no problem," replied John. "All the horses have been freshly shod, and their shoes are packed."

Elisha was setting silverware on the table.

"Now that's got to be the funniest thing I've ever heard." Elisha laughed. "Packing shoes for horses."

The room filled with laughter.

"It's settled then," said John "I'd like you to meet everyone and get a little acquainted before we head out. We can do it over breakfast,"

Jake set her hat on her knee.

"Good idea." Elisha turned to Jingles "Are you going to join us?"

"No, mam." Jingles replied. "I treated the boys in the bunk house ta the best flapjacks and sausage breakfast they've ever had. Enjoyed it myself. If we're bout ready ta go, I'm goin' ta git my mules ready ta load."

With that, he disappeared out the door.

Introductions to Jake were made at breakfast.

Deseray and Kachina were fascinated that their guide was a woman.

After breakfast, John, Jake, and Curtis moved onto the front porch to discuss final details before starting the drive to Powderville. John laid out a detailed map, which had several red circles marking locations between Missoula and Miles City.

"We'll travel on the main highways until we reach Miles City. Then we will head south to Powderville." John explained.

"The red circles are the locations I need to take soil samples for the state. I figured I would combine this expedition with my responsibilities. I figured I could do that on the trip back. That way if you and Jingles want to go on ahead, you will be free to do so. It's the only way I could get the time off to go."

John carefully folded the map.

"I want to take advantage of the travel time to show my niece Deseray, some of Montana's countryside and show her some of the work I do. She's an archaeology student and it will be a good learning experience for her."

"I'm all set," Jake said. "I've got my own truck and trailer. I'm hauling two horses. One horse is for my gear and bedroll and the other horse I ride. How many horses are you bringing?"

John counted on his fingers. "Each of us is taking our own horse. That would make four. I also have two equipment horses and with Jingles' three mules and his horse, that makes a total of ten. I have two trucks and two trailers. Each horse trailer holds four. That gives me two horses without a ride."

Curtis turned to Jake.

"I remembered that you mentioned in your letter you had a four-horse trailer. If you don't mind can my horse, Rocky, ride in your trailer with your horses?"

"No problem. That's why it's a four-horse trailer. I can take another one as well."

John continued. "That's one less problem to worry about. Curtis here will drive one truck and I will drive the other. Both girls drive also, so if we need to change drivers, we will have that option."

Jake smiled at Curtis.

"Sounds like a nice little caravan. What time are you planning on leaving?"

John rose to his feet.

"We'll load the gear first and as soon as the horses are loaded, we can be on our way. Say by ten o'clock?"

Jake rose to her feet also.

"That sounds good to me."

Jake smiled at Elisha.

"Do you mind if I freshen up before we leave?"

Elisha showed Jake where she could wash up and handed her a fresh towel.

"Make yourself at home," she said. "And if you need anything, just let me know."

About nine-thirty, everyone met at the coral. The trucks and trailers were standing ready, waiting for the horses to be loaded.

Curtis led Rocky easily into the Jake's trailer along with her two horses and one of John's packhorses mules. Next into the trailer on John's truck, was Molly, followed by Kachina's horse Maiden. Jingles led his horse in next, followed by John's horse, Blaze. Jingles mules were loaded on the trailer of the third truck along with one of John's packhorses.

"A perfect fit," piped in Curtis.

All the gear was stowed into the trucks and everything was set to go.

"Deseray, you will start out by riding with me," announced John. "Curtis, you and Jingles can ride together and Jake, if you don't mind, can Kachina ride with you?"

Kachina smile as she looked eagerly at Jake.

"No problem. I love to talk."

"Great!" exclaimed Kachina, "I have a lot of questions. If you don't mind?"

Jake smiled.

"I don't mind. Like I said, I love to talk."

Deseray, Kachina and Curtis all gave a big hug to both Elisha and Louis.

Then Elisha and John walked a short way from the house stopping under a grove of trees. They talked for a movement and then kissed each other. John walked toward the trucks, patting Louis on the head as he passed. Elisha took her place next to little Louis who had been sitting on the porch steps.

John briskly rubbed his hands together.

"Well, if everyone is ready, let's get this show on the road!"

John swung himself into the truck, leaving the door open, giving last minute instructions.

"After our first stop, we can switch drivers if anyone wants a change, but we'll start out this way. There will be a quick stop in Missoula. We can use the cell phones to communicate along the way so we're all in the same frame of mind."

The closing of his truck door gave the signal that everyone was ready to leave. The three trucks, pulling a horse trailer each, started down the long driveway, heading south.

Elisha and Louis waved from the porch as the little caravan began its adventure.

John and Deseray took the lead, followed by Curtis and Jingles, while Jake and Kachina pulled up the rear.

Deseray was so excited she continually asked her Uncle John questions.

"Have you decided where we will go yet?"

"Once we get to Miles City, we'll head south toward a small town called Powderville. I have a friend who has a small artifact and stone shop there. He said we could leave the trucks and trailers there. Then we will head out on the horses. We'll go northeast about 20 miles or so and make camp. We'll be in the general area where the hunters found the arrowheads."

Deseray positioned her notebook and tape recorder neatly on the seat beside her.

"Do you think the arrowheads are authentic?"

John checked the rearview mirror to assure himself that the caravan was intact.

"The hunters who found the arrowheads went to my friend's shop. He verified that they were authentic. Then he called me. Word got out about them being Sioux and before I knew it, we had a sponsor and an expedition. Amazing how things work out, isn't it?"

A big smiled formed on Deseray's face.

"I'm glad they did. This is one of the most exciting things I've ever done. It's all working out nicely with my senior thesis. I get to have fun and get my college work done all at the same time."

Within a few hours, the small caravan came upon the north end of Flathead Lake.

"This is the most beautiful lake I've ever seen!" Exclaimed Deseray as the lake came into full view. It's so clean and blue. Those trees on the other side are so pretty with all those white blossoms. What kind are they?"

"Those are cherry trees. We'll have to come back when the cherries are ready for picking. They are delicious and taste the best when they are fresh picked. Most people usually get them days after their picked and they just don't taste quite the same."

Deseray admired the beauty of the trees.

"I bet Jingles could make some mighty fine pies out of them."

They both laughed as they thought of Jingles. He had such an easy air about him, which made him immediately likable.

Checking his rear-view mirror, John announced, "We'll be heading south towards Butte, but stay over in a hotel in Anaconda. The driving is easy since its interstate all the way. Some of the mountains in the pass are high altitude, but you would never know it. While driving on the freeway, it's a breeze. I've already made reservations at the hotel."

As the small caravan neared its destination for the evening, John suddenly took an exist off the highway.

"Before we continue onto our hotel," John told Deseray, "we're going to pretend to be tourists. I've talk to everyone and it's agreed you need to see the Bison Range. You interested?"

Deseray smiled.

"Sure. I've heard about the Bison Range. Thank you, Uncle John, for thinking of me."

Everyone met just outside the entrance to the park.

"If you don't mind," said Jake, "I'd like to pass on going through the park. I'll take care of the horses while you guys go in. That way you can drop one of the trailers and just take a truck through the park. The roads are pretty rough, and the bumping would be hard on the horses."

John agreed.

"If ya don't mind," piped in Jingles, "I think I'll pass as well. Bin here a few times already."

John agreed.

"It's mostly for Deseray's benefit anyhow," he commented.

Curtis and Kachina climbed into the truck and Deseray squeezed in next to them, happy she had the window side. John sat behind the wheel and pulled the truck up to the park entrance.

A ranger greeted them at the entrance.

"Howdy folks, and welcome to the Bison Range. Just a few words of advice before you enter the park. Don't get out of your vehicle. It's a driving tour. All you have to do is keep following the road. There are turnoff areas if you want to linger in one place or another. The elk and the buffalo have a lot of new calves and are very protective of them, so for your own safety, remain in your vehicle."

The ranger handed John a brochure to use on the tour.

The ranger tipped his hat.

"You folks have a nice day."

John took the brochure and handed it to Deseray.

"Thank you," he said. "We will."

After a modest donation for the park, Uncle John steered the truck onto a rough dirt road. The fences were made of wire about eight feet high, consisting of many tight squares, supported by large round wooden posts.

The recent rains had deepened the already existing road ruts and as the truck jerked from side-to-side, causing everyone to toss from side-to-side. John did his best to maneuver from one edge of the road to the other trying to avoid the ruts, but it seemed like a hopeless cause.

Deseray found the whole thing quite humorous as Curtis and Kachina sat with their arms out full length holding onto the dash, trying to avoid clunking into each other's heads.

Everyone became accustomed to the jostling after the first half mile, and then able to concentrate on the scenery and wildlife.

A small herd of bison was drinking from a small lake as

they came to the top of the first hill. The ranger had been telling the truth when he said there had been many calves that spring.

Every cow had at least one calf by her side.

"Awe," were the first words from both Deseray and Kachina while Curtis just grunted.

Deseray thought the scenery was much like that of Wisconsin except for the proportionately greater number of evergreens and pine trees and of course the huge mountain range as a bold backdrop.

The majority of the time, the driving tour consisted of looking at the scenery with an occasional glimpse at a wolf or two, a few antelope and some mule deer.

The ultimate moment came near the end of the tour.

Occupying the vast majority of the horizon was a large herd of elk.

"There must be over a hundred elk in that herd," exclaimed Curtis. Finally, something caught his attention, creating excitement for him, for the first time since the tour began.

The setting sun silhouetted the herd against the crimson sky, creating a radiated backdrop for one continuous accumulation of animals.

Deseray took pictures as she dictated, recording the view she was enjoying. Taping a narrative while she took pictures was a habit she had developed at an early age.

"I'll make copies of these pictures if anyone is interested."

Curtis smiled. "I'll take a couple of those."

When they returned to the parking lot, they found Jingles and Jake laughing and enjoying a cup of coffee.

"So how was the tour? Jingles asked.

"It was awesome," replied Deseray.

John backed the truck up to the horse trailer while Jingles guided it to the hitch. Once secured, John announced they would make it to Anaconda after dark.

The small caravan was on its way.

Long after night fell, the small caravan pulled into the hotel parking lot in Anaconda.

Deseray stretched as she got out of the truck.

She met Kachina at the door. She appeared to be as worn out as the rest of them from the long drive through the mountains.

"Are you ready for some rest?" She asked Deseray.

"It wasn't so bad, just too much sitting. It feels good to walk around."

John signed everyone into the hotel. Deseray, Jake and Kachina shared a room, as did Curtis, John and Jingles. The rooms were side by side.

As John slid the key in the slot for their room, he announced, "There's a restaurant across the street. We will meet in the lobby in an hour and have a late supper. That should give everyone time to freshen up," announced John.

Everyone agreed as they entered their rooms.

Before the hour was up, everyone met in the lobby and then headed for the restaurant, clean and refreshed.

The restaurant had a decor of the old west. Replicas of famous artists such as Frederic Remington and C. M. Russell adorned the walls and shelves. Indian artifacts, wagon wheels and a variety of early western tools were scattered about the restaurant as well.

Huge cut logs served as the table as did the benches. The condiment holders were small sized chicken feeders, which utilized the feeding holes to hold the variety of downsized condiments.

Deseray found the whole theme very entertaining. She also imagined that the menu would probably be one that featured beef and potatoes.

As she gazed that the menu, she discovered she was right.

"I never imagined that beef could be prepared in so many ways!"

"They also have chicken on the menu if you prefer," stated Jake.

Deseray continued looking at the menu.

"No, beef is fine." replied Deseray, " I just have never seen beef made in so many different ways."

A cheery server, in a red dress with a red gingham apron, took their order.

John took out his map and notes and began to go over their plan.

"Once we get to my friend Carl's place, we'll unload the horses and get them settled for the night. I imagine it will be late by the time we get there, but the sooner we get them settled, the quicker we can get some sleep ourselves."

John continued, "Kachina, would you like to drive my truck with Deseray? That will give me a chance to talk with Jake. Carl will be able to give us more details about where the artifacts were found once we get there."

Kachina was excited.

"That will be great! Deseray and I haven't talked for almost a whole day."

"It's settled then," John said as he re-folded the map. "Jake and I will lead."

The server soon returned with sizzling platters of beef and baked potatoes.

Deseray opened the foil surrounding her baked potato.

"I really liked the Bison Range," she said, "I have never seen so many elk in one place before."

Curtis eyes lit up.

"I've lived here all my life and I've never seen so many in the same place either."

Deseray added sour cream to her baked potato.

"It was nice to stop and break up the drive. How long do think it will take us to get to Powderville?"

"Most of the day," John announced. "The scenery along the route is pretty. We'll be in the mountains most of the way, but the closer we get, the more prairie and open plains we'll see."

The meal continued with talk of the day they had spent and the day that was still to come. Once everyone had eaten, it was time to wonder back to the hotel to turn in for the night.

A cot was sitting in the corner of the room when Deseray, Kachina and Jake returned.

An expression of exhaustion overcame Deseray's face.

"I'm too tired to set up a cot tonight. Kachina? Do you mind sharing a bed?"

Kachina smiled, "Sure, I'm too tired to set it up either. Besides, once it's set up, we'll have absolutely no room to walk around."

Jake nodded.

"I agree with you both about being too tired and about the lack of room."

After changing into sleeping clothes, all three of them sat on the beds.

Deseray sat on the bed slowly brushing her hair.

"Jake, how did you ever become a wilderness guide?"

"My dad got me started. He was a guide and when I was old enough, he started taking me along. He didn't have any sons and wanted to share his life's interest with one of his children. I just became interested and he started teaching me a lot about nature. We spent many hours studying maps and learning survival techniques. I really enjoyed it and when he retired, I just took over. I've been doing it ever since."

"It seems like a rough life." Deseray replied.

Jake smiled.

"It can be at times, but I enjoy it so much that it doesn't bother me to get cold or wet anymore. I just dress right and keep my health up. That way I can handle just about anything."

Kachina laid in bed and pulled the blanket up around her neck as she settled in for the night.

"Do you get a lot of business?" She asked Jake.

"Sometimes there is almost more than I can handle. Many people from the cities want a real nature experience and book trips into the mountains. They know very little about survival and safely in the woods, so I really have my hands full sometimes."

Deseray's eyes become wide with wonder.

"Has anyone ever gotten hurt on a trip?"

"No, I've been very lucky that way. I lay out the rules ahead of time and they listen. I hate to cut this short, but we've got a few miles to cover tomorrow so I think we should call it a night."

Deseray pulled the covers over her as she lay on the bed next to Kachina.

"You're right. Good night."

The next morning, Deseray looked around the room and discovered that Jake was gone. Kachina was sound asleep. She got up and dressed quickly, trying not to wake Kachina, but no such luck.

"What time is it?" Kachina asked in a half sleeping voice.

"Six thirty." Deseray softly replied. "Jake is already up and gone somewhere."

As the words left Deseray's mouth, the door opened and there stood Jake.

The smell of coffee filled the room.

Kachina sat up in bed.

"You're a life saver. Fresh coffee!"

Jake set the coffee on the table.

"I was out feeding and watering the horses. I ran into John. He wants to know if anyone is interested in a quick breakfast before we leave."

Deseray took a sip of coffee.

"I think it's a good idea. That way we can have a late lunch and get some miles behind us."

Kachina dressed as she drank her coffee, "Sounds good to me."

Jake picked up the phone and called John's room.

"We're all for breakfast," she said.

She listened for a moment. "Ok, we'll meet in about an hour."

There was a small cafe attached to the motel, which is where everyone met.

After a hastily eaten breakfast, everyone returned to

their rooms to get their belongings.

After a quick check on the horses, the little caravan was on their way.

The caravan made two additional stops, one for their late lunch and the other for an even later diner.

The last stop was in Miles City for dinner. Shortly after the dinner stop, the caravan arrived in Powderville. They drove an additional 10 miles to reach Carl's place.

As soon as the trucks pulled up in front of the house, Carl was standing on the porch waiting to greet his visitors.

John was the first to reach Carl.

"Hi Carl, it's been a long time. It's good to see you."

They embraced hands. Carl smiled.

"It's good to see you too, John."

Carl turned to face the rest of them.

"So, this is your group of eager explorers. I understand a couple of them are yours."

"This young man here is my son, Curtis and this bright little red head is my daughter, Kachina.

"This here," he motioned Deseray to come closer. "This is my niece, Deseray."

Jingles put his hand toward Carl as John made introductions.

"This is our cook, Jingles," and gesturing to Jake, he said, "This is our guide, Jake Spinally."

Carl shook Jake's hand.

"Jake Spinally?" Carl asked.

"Yes sir."

"I've heard of you. You're supposed to be the best."

"That's what I'm told, and I do my best to prove it." Jake smiled.

Carl motioned his arm toward the front door. "Why don't you all come inside?"

"We'd love to," replied John, "but our horses need tending to first. Do you mind showing us where we can put them for the night?"

Carl tapped his forehead with his opened palm. "Hell, I'm sorry. I plum forgot about your horses. The barn is this way."

Carl flipped a switch on the wall next to the front door. The yard immediately flooded with bright light. The brightness was so intense one might wonder if the sun had suddenly risen.

Curtis led Rocky to the stable while Deseray took the lead of Molly. Each rider combed and fed their horse. Jingles cared for his horse and three mules. John asked Curtis to care for the two packhorses. Reluctantly he obliged. Once the horses settled comfortably in the stables, everyone headed back up to the house. Carl opened the door and motioned everyone to enter.

"This is a pretty big, old house," he said, "and there is plenty of room for everyone. Come in and meet the Mrs. and we'll all have some of her huckleberry pie and some fresh coffee."

The inside of the house was a huge as it appeared from the outside. The first room Deseray saw was the grand room, which was off to the right of the front door. The furnishing consisted of antique furniture, including a fainting couch.

Carl led them to the left, which brought them into the main dining room. The table was large enough to sit at least twelve people. A protective cover topped the large antique table, followed with by a coverlet of a fine linen tablecloth. A vase of fresh wildflowers sat in the center of the table. The thick legs of the table and chairs were a carved dark oak, highly polished.

The table had been set with coffee cups and saucers and a large, glass coffee urn filled with steaming hot coffee. The sugar bowl and cream pitcher matched the cobalt blue floral pattern of the coffee urn. Sitting next to the coffee service were two freshly baked huckleberry pies.

"Please sit and have some dessert." Carl's wife said in a soft, inviting voice.

"This is my wife, Donna. Donna, these are our guests I'd been telling you about."

After introductions, everyone sat at the table for dessert.

Donna poured everyone a cup of coffee and proceeded to cut the pies.

"I'm sorry these are not fresh huckleberries, but huckleberries aren't in season until late June. I freeze pints of them for use during the winter and spring months."

"I've never had huckleberry before," mentioned Deseray. After taking her first bite, she exclaimed. "This is delicious. I have never tasted anything so sweet and tart at the same time. Thank you."

After enjoying the pie and coffee, Donna led the women to the rooms that would be theirs for the night and Carl led the men to their rooms. Donna stopped by the first room right at the top of the stairs and motioned to Kachina and Deseray.

"You ladies will share this room. And Jake will have this one." She motioned to the room on the right.

Carl disappeared to the right of the staircase with John, Curtis, and Jingles.

"This is a huge house." Deseray exclaimed, as she entered the large bedroom that she and Kachina would share.

Donna smiled. "A long time ago, it used to be a boarding house. Carl and I raised nine children so it was perfect for us. We started ranching and with the land and the house we had plenty of room for everyone."

"The kids are grown now, but we decided to keep the house. We don't do as much ranching as we used to, and Carl keeps busy with his rock shop."

The room contained two freshly made beds with clean towels lying on each bed.

"There are four bathrooms in this house. One with a shower is just down the hall to your left. Feel free to clean up and turn in when you please. If you need anything, do not be afraid to ask. It is nice having company. Donna squeezed Kachina's hand.

"It's nice to have all of you for a visit." Donna smiled, closing the door as she left.

"Thank you" piped Deseray and Kachina at the same time.

Donna showed Jake her room.

Kachina flopped down on the bed closest to her.

"This is really a nice mattress."

The room was very feminine decorated with horses and wildflowers. Deseray pressed her hand on the other bed.

"Sure feels nice enough. This room must have been their daughters. I couldn't imagine someone like Curtis sleeping in here."

As they settled themselves under the blankets, Deseray noticed how bright the moon was that night.

"The moon has a special glow tonight, don't you think Kachina?"

"I think it looks special because we are tired, and these sheets feel so good. Are you having a good time?"

"The best. I'm really looking forward to tomorrow. I can't wait to start exploring the sites for artifacts. Do you think we'll find anything worthwhile?"

"I sure hope so." Kachina pulled the blanket up to her chin. She yawned passionately. "I'm exhausted," and closed her eyes. "Good night."

"Good night."

Deseray found it difficult to fall asleep. For the first time that day, she thought about Reg and White One and the feather of which she now kept with her at all times in the medicine pouch Jingles had given her. No one had asked about the pouch and she did not offer an explanation.

She carefully placed the pouch next to her on the bed, and sometime amidst her thoughts about Reg, she fell asleep.

Chapter Six - The First Grid Site

Before dawn, the house was alive and active with people. Donna was in the kitchen getting breakfast.

Jake rose from her chair and took the eggs from Donna's hand.

"Let me make the eggs."

Many glances of surprised passed through the people sitting at the table.

It seems everyone had the same thought at the same time.

Jake returned the glances with a smile as she tied her long brown hair into a ponytail and washed her hands.

"I can cook, you know."

Laughter filled the quaint farmhouse kitchen as Jake began cracking eggs into the cast iron pan.

The aroma of bacon rose from another pan as Donna placed one slice at a time onto the hot skillet.

Carl opened the refrigerator, bringing out a large pitcher of orange juice as he proclaimed, "I'll pour the juice. Anyone want to volunteer to make toast?"

Within seconds, Jingles was carving the loaf of homemade bread like a real expert.

Deseray began handing dishes to Kachina who set them on the dining room table. A plate of toasted bread followed this, as did a large platter of fried eggs and a platter of crispy bacon.

Donna filled the coffee carafe as everyone found his or her place around the table.

Rays of sunshine began streaming through the window about the time everyone was placing their dishes into the sink. Once again, everyone took an active role in cleaning up the kitchen.

"My!" Donna exclaimed. "I haven't had so much help with a meal since our last holiday. It sure is refreshing!"

John gave Donna a gentle hug.

"Thank you for the wonderful breakfast. We hate to eat and run, but we want to get started so we can find a good place to make our base camp yet today."

"I understand. It was wonderful having the company."

"We won't be too far away and since we're leaving our trucks here, you can be assured we'll be back."

Deseray remained in the kitchen to help Donna finish the cleaning. Carl led John to a large storage room.

A large refrigerator stood on one wall with wooden crates stacked next to it.

"Here are the supplies from your list you asked me to get. Everything you wanted is either in the fridge or the crates."

"Thank you, Carl. It is convenient to have our supplies so close to the dig."

Carl continued, "I got some dry ice, so you have fresh meat for a few days. After that, you have to go with dry goods and shelf staples."

John smiled.

"I have confidence that Jingles can turn anything into a good meal. Thanks for all your help Carl."

"Happy to do it," Carl replied.

John walked outside where Curtis and Jingles were standing.

"Supplies are in the storage room. I'll let you two get them loaded on the mules."

"Sure thing." Jingles replied as Curtis followed him the supply room.

As the kitchen became tidy, Donna smiled at Deseray. "It's wonderful to have you all here for a visit. Your uncle John and my Carl had been friends for a long time. They went to college together for a while, but Carl dropped out. He never lost his love for rocks though. That is why he decided to open a rock shop."

Donna handed Deseray dishes to place in the cupboards as

she continued, "He gets so excited when he finds nice rocks to polish and turn into jewelry or sculptures."

Deseray placed the last dish on a shelf and closed the cupboard door.

"Uncle John speaks highly of Carl. I think he wishes Carl could come with."

Donna smiled.

"Carl would have loved to go with, but this is our busy time with the shop, but you will be close by so if we have a slow day, he can peak in on you."

Deseray gave Donna an affectionate hug.

"I had better join the others before they leave without me."

She disappeared out the door.

Within the hour, everyone gathered near the stables. The horses were stamping and whinnying as the riders entered the stables. They were anxious to begin the trip as well. One by one, the horses were led out of the building into the coral. Curtis had Rocky saddle first, so he helped John load one of his packhorses. Deseray interrupted him.

"Curtis?" asked Deseray as she struggled with the cinch on Molly's saddle.

"Is there some reason why I can't tighten this cinch?"

Curtis laughed.

"Someone forgot to tell you. Molly blows out her belly when a saddle hits her back."

Curtis gave Molly a little smack on her flank. She jumped slightly and at that precise moment, Curtis pulled the cinch tight.

"You'll have to remember that, when you saddle her again."

"Thank you." Deseray smiled.

Jingles led out the three mules bearing the panniers and packs he and Curtis had filled earlier. Deseray watched as Jingles mounted his horse, noticing that his bad leg was not much use for supporting his weight. Again, she wondered how he had hurt his leg.

Swinging up upon Molly, Deseray immediately felt comfortable. Kachina rode up alongside of her.

"I'll ride next to you if you don't mind. I'm so excited I can hardly wait to get going."

Looking at the early morning sky, Deseray smiled, "It's hard to believe we're finally on our way."

Jake swung herself up upon her horse with the expertise that had preceded her. The motion of herself and her horse became one as she took the lead of the horse-mounted caravan.

As the mounted riders waited patiently, John stood next to his two packhorses with a checklist in hand. He was audible as he went over his checklist, picturing in his mind where he had put each item on the horses.

"Shake screen frames, screen and rope; check, trowels, shovels and transit; check. Soft soled boots; check." He suddenly looked at each of the riders.

"You guys did remember to bring soft soled shoes or boots, didn't you?"

Everyone nodded with compliance.

"Good. Now we're ready to go.'

John walked over to Carl and shook his hand.

"Thank you for the hospitality and all your help in getting this expedition off to a good start."

Carl tightly clasped John's hand.

"You're welcome John. I only wish I was going with."

"If you find some free time, just stop out for the day if you can. We can always use a sharp eye and steady hands."

Carl smiled. "I'll do that."

Deseray knew that Uncle John took the expedition more seriously than anyone else and was excited for him. The men grunted their farewells as Deseray and Kachina waved to Donna who stood on the front porch watching her guests leave. Her warming smile could make the sun blush. She waved as they headed northeast toward the rising sun and whatever mysteries they would find. High spirits and even higher expectations sent the eager explorations on their way.

John brought his horse up alongside of Jake's.

"You're the expert, so lead the way!"

Jake smiled. The enthusiasm of the small group was contagious as she found herself looking forward to the trip as much as the rest of them.

"It's only about twenty miles to the site I've chosen for the base camp. Since the arrowheads were discovered in an area between the Powder River and O'Fallon Creek, I figured this would be the best place. It's near water and there is good grazing for the horses."

A slight wind cooled the riders and horses as they made their way through gently rolling hills and sparsely tree covered terrain. Within five miles however, trees began to sprout out of the earth conforming to the rolling hills and shallow gorges, which governed their ability to take root and grow.

Deseray felt comfortable sitting upon Molly as the day moved on.

"This is peaceful country. I guess I imagined it being more mountainous than it is."

Kachina pulled up closer to Deseray.

"This area is very diverse," she explained, "Occasionally there will be some high peaks. Of course, nothing as dramatic as the Rockies near our house. We'll see foothills and small canyons and rivers winding throughout this area. The vast prairie country is further north, but there's still prairie around here too."

Deseray patted Molly's neck.

"Uncle John seems quite at home out here isn't he?"

Kachina readjusted herself in her saddle. "He spends most of his life outdoors taking mineral samples and digging in the strangest spots. I'm never sure what he's looking for, but he keeps looking."

The two figures riding in front of Deseray and Kachina suddenly disappeared from site. Upon reaching the spot where

John and Jake had disappeared, Deseray and Kachina saw a steep ravine and thick trees on the other side.

They followed, as did Jingles and Curtis. Branches poked Deseray in the face and she wondered why Jake had not found an easier way to get through the trees. She realized what Uncle John had meant when he had told her that it could get rough at times.

Upon emerging from the trees, Deseray not only saw John and Jake, but one of the most beautiful rivers she had ever seen. The emerald green waters rushed quickly by, filling the air with the sound only running water could make.

Jake was already giving instructions on the best way to set up the base camp. The horses edged toward the river for a drink of the cool water. Curtis began sinking stakes into the ground to tether the horses once they had finished drinking.

John and Jingles began removing packs from the mules and packhorses, placing the large bundles onto the ground. Within one of the bundles were the tents they would be living in for the duration of the expedition. John located a larger tent bag and held it up for Jingles to see.

"Here is the two-compartment tent, Jingles. I'll help you set it up. You and I can bunk in one side and the second side we'll use for storage."

As John and Jingles set up the larger tent, the remaining members of the expedition began the task of setting up their own. John and Jingles had their tent set up with record speed. John grinned from ear to ear.

"Looks pretty good, don't you think?" he proclaimed.

Jingles laughed. "Sure does. I'll git the dry goods and such in ta the 'kitchen' area."

John left Jingles to his chores as he looked at the progress the rest of them were making.

"I'll check to see if anyone needs my help with their tents."

John walked to where Curtis was setting up his tent.

"I was going to offer you some help, but it looks like

you've got things under control."

"These tents go up pretty fast, don't they?" Curtis said with a big smile, feeling quiet proud.

Jake didn't need John's help either, as her tent was up, and she was carrying her belongings inside. He was impressed with her efficiency. It was then that John noticed she was carrying a sidearm pistol.

"I hadn't noticed your pistol before" John commented.

"It was in a saddle bag. I have a rifle too. You never know what type of critter may want us for lunch. I use it mostly to scare them, but I have had to kill a bear or two at times."

Deseray and Kachina seemed to be struggling, but John decided it would be a good experience for them to try it on their own. He decided not to offer them any help, for the moment.

John began to sort out the remaining equipment while Jingles was busy putting the cooking supplies and dry goods away.

Soon, everyone was standing around watching as Deseray and Kachina tried to put up their tent.

They had small poles poking out in complete disorder, from both inside and outside of the tent. Curtis began howling with laughter.

"Come on! These tents are so easy. Just pull the poles apart, let them pop into each other and slide it through the carriers on the tent. Then poof, drop it on the ground. Done! What could be easier?"

Curtis started toward the two girls, but John held out his hand to block Curtis' progress.

"Let them do it themselves," laughing he said. "It's a lot more fun!"

Deseray and Kachina continued to laugh as the springy cords that held the individual poles, kept pulling the poles past the holes where they were supposed to stop. Their antics proved to be very entertaining to the onlookers. Eventually they were able to get the poles together end to end. The process of threading the poles through the tent carriers was much easier for them and soon they had the tent together and standing.

"See, we could do it." Deseray chirped proudly.

"Yah!" added Kachina.

They tents were located near the trees which would serve as a wind block but facing north to prevent the summer sun from scorching the inhabitants.

Within a short time, the camp was set. The sun was beginning to lower in the western sky prompting Curtis to gather wood to build a fire. The luck of being near trees provided them with kindling to start the fire and dead trees and logs to keep it going. Propane lanterns were available, but everyone was looking forward to sitting around the campfire.

Jingles put up a cooking rack over the pile of kindling and the wood Curtis had placed in the burning pit he had dug. "Guess I'd better git some grub going. I'm sure everone is hungry by now."

Soon the fire was roaring in the pit and a stew was cooking in a pot. In another pot Jingles was making some biscuits to go along with the stew.

"Hope everone is real hungry. This is the best stew ever."

Adorned with light jackets or sweatshirts, the hungry explorers gathered around the fire as Jingles pass the tin plates filled with stew and biscuits.

Deseray retrieved tin cups from the storage tent and walked over to the fire and the pot of brewing coffee.

"Let me pour everyone some coffee," she offered.

A circle of logs formed around the fire served as chairs. John balanced his plate on his lap, set his coffee cup on the ground near his share of the log and whistled.

"This is a real fine camp. One of the best I've ever seen. Some of the best company too." He winked.

Jake sat on the log next to John.

"We're about six miles west of the Medicine Rocks State Park. From the information you have gathered, the arrows were found about a half-mile northeast of where we are located. I have a map with markings indicating the location where arrowheads were found. I figured we could go over that area in detail in the morning."

John took a sip of his coffee.

"Once we locate the spot where the arrow heads were found, we can decide where to set up the excavation grids. The hunters showed Carl the exact spot the arrow heads were found and marked it with a flag."

Jake nodded with approval.

"That will make it much easier to find," she replied.

Deseray sat down on the other side of Uncle John.

"What kind of things should we be looking for?"

"If there was a village near here, there should be items such as fleshing tools, more arrow heads and any other objects made of stone. The tepee fires would have left discoloration in the ground from fire pits. There may even be depressions in the ground where there may have been a cache pit used for food storage."

"This excavation will be a good learning tool for you. Remember to keep a journal for yourself, but for the team, you need to log anything and everything you see or find. When we combine the logs of the rest of the team, we will be able to form a complete picture of what may have been here in the past."

Excitement almost overwhelmed Deseray. "So how do we get started?"

"The first thing we do is to decide where to begin the dig. Once we decide on that, we create a grid. You know what a grid is, don't you?"

Deseray swatted her uncle on the shoulder.

"Don't be silly, sure I do. We mark six-foot-by-six-foot squares on the ground by using stretched string tied to corner posts for each square. Right?"

John pretended to be amazed. "That's right! Now my sister can be rest assured that the money spent for your college education has been well worth it."

Deseray laughed. She then realized how much she missed her mom. It had only been a week since she had left, but the thought of fifteen hundred miles away from each other made her feel a bit lonely for her family. She was happy that part of her family was with her as she smiled at her uncle.

"I'll make you and my mom and my professor all very proud of me."

John hugged Deseray. "I know you will."

Jingles began collecting the dishes while lasts cups of coffee were finished. John stood up and handed his dish to Jingles.

"That's was very fine stew. Thank you, Jingles. Since we want to start at first light, I suggest you get some sleep. It is a big day tomorrow with many things to do. I, for one, am turning in."

Deseray and Kachina began helping Jingles with the dishes and quickly had the camp cleaned for the night.

The girls walked over to their tent. Kachina opened the flap. She looked at Deseray.

"Have you ever slept in a tent before?" She asked.

"Sure, my dad is big on camping."

Curtis's voice echoed from across the camp.

"Have you ever slept in a tent where there are lots of really wild animals before?"

Kachina stood by the door flap.

"Shut up Curtis and go to sleep."

"Don't get eaten by a bear." He added and was quiet.

"Are there really bears?" Deseray asked with a concerned look.

"Probably, but Jingles has all the food carefully closed and there isn't anything to attract them to us. Don't listen to Curtis. If a bear does come through, he'll just smell us and go away."

Nevertheless, Deseray snuggled deeply into her sleeping bag.

"Goodnight Deseray. Tomorrow will be great fun!"

"I know it will. Goodnight."

As Deseray lay in her sleeping bag, she could hear the wind rustling the branches of the trees. Occasionally the side of the tent gently moved in and out. She was relieved that Jake had picked a site protected from the wind. She liked Jake, but she seemed quiet. She was skilled at her trade but rarely offered any information about her personal life except how she got the name Jake and her guide business.

The combination of the soothing sound of the nearby river and the gentle movement of the tent soothed Deseray into sleep.

The sound of pots and pans clanking together woke Deseray from her sound sleep.

She was dripping wet, even though she had flung off her sleeping bag earlier in the night. Her dreams had been full of visions that left her confused.

Kachina looked at Deseray.

"Are you alright? You're covered with sweat. You'd better changed into dry clothes."

"I've been having those strange dreams again. I don't know why they are so intense. I used to have wonderful dreams. Whenever I woke from them, I felt refreshed with a sense of freedom. The dreams I've had lately have been confusing. I am going somewhere but I don't know where I am going. I recognize some of the people, but they are going somewhere too and won't wait for me."

"It's just dreams. You need to relax. Get excited now. We are finally going to start exploring and setting up our dig. This is real. Your dreams are just that, dreams."

Kachina gave Deseray a reassuring hug.

Deseray smiled as she began changing her clothes.

"You're right. I guess I take my dreams to seriously sometimes."

Kachina sniffed the air.

"I smell breakfast. Jingles must be up and cooking. Let's go eat."

Deseray finished buttoning her shirt. The dry clothes felt comforting.

"I'll be right behind you."

The smell of Jingle's cooking did not seem to have an effect on John and Jake. Instead of divining into the great food, they were busy discussing directions and final plans. Curtis was caring for the horses. Fresh air mingled with the smell of bacon, as Jingles placed more bacon into the pan. Deseray caught up with Kachina as she headed for the chow line.

"That smells good!" said Deseray as she took a plate from the stack.

"There's some pancakes under this lid," Jingles said as he lifted the cover from a pot.

"There's syrup in that ther little pot on the fire and some eggs in the other one."

Deseray filled her plate.

"You know, I'm going to gain ten pounds if you keep feeding us like this."

John laughed.

"Once we get started digging, I promise you, you won't get a chance to put on ten pounds."

A slight breeze rustled the nearby trees. Deseray took a deep breath as she sat on her section of the log.

John smiled at her.

"Are you having fun?"

Deseray swallowed the pancake she had been chewing.

"Yes, I am having great fun. I can't wait to start digging."

John stood up to get a plate of food. As he placed pancakes and syrup on his plate, he smiled at Deseray.

"Jake and I have worked up a rough lay out for the digging grid. We will work in teams of two per each grid and lay out four grids for each team. Each team will work only one grid at a time. If someone should discover anything, then we can concentrate on the surrounding grids. Get done eating and we'll get started."

Curtis washed his hands in the nearby stream and took a plate.

"How far from here are we going?" he asked.

Jake finished eating quickly and placed her dirty plate in

RITA K KASINSKAS

the wash bucket. She reached into her pocket, took out a map, and held it out for Curtis to see.

Jake showed him the lines and circles her and John had made on the map.

"We'll set up the grid about a mile from here. This circle here," she pointed at a red circle in the center of the grid, "It's where the arrowheads were discovered."

John finished eating and handed his plate to Jingles.

"Just put yer dishes over by my worsh bucket and I'll git them done."

Kachina swallowed her last bite.

"Uncle John?" She questioned, "You made it clear that we all had soft soled shoes or boots. Why is that?"

John smiled. "It's very simple. Once we scrape the topsoil off, the ground underneath will be much softer, soft soles prevent deep imprints that could damage the site."

"I see." Kachina put her plate into the wash bucket.

John smiled at Deseray as she placed her dishes in the wash bucket.

"I am so excited!" she proclaimed.

"Slow down a little," he laughed, "The site isn't going anywhere."

"I'm just so anxious to be a part of this. I didn't think I would be part of an excavation until after I graduated."

John smiled as he enjoyed the enthusiasm his niece showed.

"Well then, get your things together and we'll be on our way."

Cutis finished his breakfast and walked over to Rocky. Rocky muzzled close to his master's face. Curtis pet him affectionately.

"Good boy. Now we can get some exercise."

Removing his saddle from a nearby rack, he placed it upon Rocky's back. Rocky was anxious to be on his way as well. Curtis felt anxious as well as he tightened the cinch.

"Come on," Curtis exclaimed, "Let's quit dawdling and get

moving."

It did not take much coaxing to get Deseray and Kachina on their feet.

As she began to saddle Molly, Deseray remembered what Curtis had told her about Molly's little trick. With a light smack of her hand, Molly let the air out of her belly and Deseray quickly tightened the cinch.

She smiled at Curtis.

"See, I remembered."

Curtis swung himself up onto Rocky's back.

"Good for you. I guess we can teach you a thing or two after all." He smiled.

Kachina piped in.

"Curtis, Be nice."

"I am being nice. I gave her a compliment, didn't I?"

"If that's what you call it."

Kachina swung herself atop Maiden. Deseray dropped her reins to the ground and began walking toward the tent.

Kachina watched as Deseray had disappeared behind the flap.

"Are you coming? What are you looking for?"

Deseray appeared a few moments later.

"I wanted to bring my camera and journal. I want to document the whole process from the beginning."

Jingles began washing the bucket of dishes but paused long enough to offer instructions for the anxious explorer.

"I'll have supper ready fer ya about dusk, even if ya don't find anything. Jake's pack has yer lunch."

John laughed. "That's very kind of you, Jingles. But I don't hold out much hope of making any earth-shattering discoveries today. It's more of a preparation time than anything else. But a hot meal will taste good, just the same."

John turned to the rest of the group. "Are we ready?"

He didn't need to ask as he looked at the mounted riders and the anticipation of the horses. "Let's go then."

Jake took the lead, taking the group northeast of their

campsite.

A variety of grasses grew among the shrubs and small tress. New grasses were short waves of green with occasional tan scrubs accenting the terrain. Brown sagebrush bushes, whose life cycle had ended, clung into the earth with their expired roots, not wanting to give up their last hopes of life. Inevitably, strong gusts of wind won the battle and the bushes reluctantly let go and began their journeys to nowhere across the Montana plains.

When they arrived at the right location, Jake pulled her horse to a stop and dismounted.

"This is the spot." She announced. She dropped the reins to the ground, as did everyone else as they dismounted.

Deseray found it interesting that all the horses were well trained not to wonder far from their riders. Everyone began to unsaddle their horse.

"Uncle John, why don't we tie the horses, so they don't get away?"

John placed his saddle on a nearby stump as he replied.

"Montana is full of predators and a horse would make a good meal. If we tie the horse, they become sitting ducks with no chance to survive. They'll stick together and return on command."

Deseray put her saddle next to Uncle Johns and placed her saddle pad on top."

"I'm glad to hear that, I wouldn't want to walk back to base camp."

The equipment John had brought was carefully unloaded from the two packhorses and laid out on the ground.

"Be careful with that one," John warned Curtis as he carried a bundle over to the group.

"That one had the transit in it."

John took the transit from Curtis and looking at the map, set it up near the proposed grid site.

Kachina watched John as he carefully leveled it.

"What is that for?"

Securing the transit on level ground, John answered.

"We'll use it to take certain measurements. If we discover artifacts, we can measure the exact depth of the discovery. This is important because it can help us to establish a time-period. If artifacts are found at different levels, we can determine the time based on our measurements between the levels."

John made some marks on a piece of paper, obviously doing mental math as he wrote.

"First, we'll use it to establish the individual squares of the grid."

Deseray smiled as she loving watched her Uncle go to work. He gave left and right directions as the corner stakes were placed strategically into the ground per his instructions.

Individual squares were marked off with taut strings stretching from the four corner stakes of each square, creating a carefully established grid.

"We'll work in teams. One team member will remove the soil and place it into the shaker screen. The other member will operate the screen, carefully looking for anything that may be pertinent. Does everyone understand?"

Three heads bobbled up and down.

The agreement was unanimous.

Two sets of shaker screens were set up for the teams. Bins placed under each shaker screen would be emptied as it they were filled.

"Curtis, you team up with Kachina," John instructed. "You've done this before, and you can give her some advice. I will work with Deseray. Jake, would you like to join us?"

Jake had propped herself against a nearby boulder a few yards away opening her backpack.

"No thank you. I'd like to make sketches of you while you're working, if you don't mind." She took out a sketchbook and pencils. Deseray looked at Jake.

"You're an artist?"

"Somewhat. I spend so much time outdoors; I've gotten into drawing and painting what I see."

"That's wonderful."

John walked over to Jake looking over her shoulder.

"Mind if I take a look?"

Jake opened her sketchbook and angled it toward John so he could get a better look at its contents.

"No, go ahead."

Jake carefully turned the pages. Sketches of birds, trees and people filled the pages.

"These are very good," John complimented. "Maybe we can use some of the ones you draw of us for our documentation?"

Jake was pleased at having been asked to be a part of something so important.

"That would be fine with me."

After taking one last look at the sketches, John returned to the grid area. He laid out a map of the grid.

"I've put each team's name in each square," John instructed, "These will be each team's responsibility to dig. Be sure to document your activities and hopefully we will hit pay dirt!"

"By the way, be sure to drink plenty of water! This is hard work, and I don't want anyone passing out on me!"

With a trowel in hand, Deseray began removing the top surface of her first square. Her hands were shaking from the sheer excitement. She carefully placed it into the shaker screen and Uncle John worked it with back-and-forth motions.

"Be sure to dig the walls straight up and down. This helps us to evaluate both the vertical and horizontal relationships and any artifacts we discover. Do you understand?"

"Yes, I do, Uncle John. I'll be very careful. Thanks for letting me dig first."

"You're welcome. It's a good learning experience."

The work was harder and slower than Deseray had imagined. Noon arrived and still no discoveries. Everyone was feeling a bit tired. John emptied his soil bin.

"Let's take a break for lunch. Jingles packed us some sandwiches and a thermos of coffee and one with milk. There's more water in one of the packs."

After lunch, the teams traded positions and the digging continued.

Jake wondered over to get a closer look. She didn't say anything but began drawing in her book.

The afternoon ebbed away, still with no discoveries.

As the sun started setting in the eastern sky, John announced that they would stop for the day.

"I think we've done enough for today. Let's head back to the campsite."

There was very little conversation during the return to camp.

From the expressions on their faces, Jingles assumed there had not been any luck.

He smiled brightly with a big smile.

"Ther's always tomorrow, but tonight, ther are brownies!"

Deseray looked surprised.

"How can we have brownies without an oven?"

"I just baked them in a big kettle."

Deseray stared at the big black kettle. "Can you do that?"

"Yep, and I did."

After washing up in the river, everyone ate silently.

John broke the silence.

"Sometimes its weeks before any discoveries are made. You have to remember that we may be on a wild goose chase. The experience will be good for all of us and has its own rewards. Besides, we've only just begun."

"How long will before you give up on a site?" asked Deseray.

"We'll play it by ear. We've only have so many funds to continue the dig, and it we don't have positive results, we will have to abandon the project."

John looked around at the long faces.

"I would say we have enough to spend at least a month at

it. Chin up, you guys, there's always tomorrow."

Deseray and Kachina went to bed early. Deseray rubbed lotion on her dry, sore hands.

"Even with gloves on, that digging is pretty hard on the hands, isn't it?"

Kachina rubbed her knees. "I don't know about you, but I think you guys are all crazy. Why you want to dig in the ground all day and get tired and sore is beyond me. Curtis wants to look for dinosaur bones while you and John want to find things buried in the ground. Pretty crazy interests if you asked me."

Deseray smiled, "Why did you come along?"

"I didn't want to be left behind. I love the outdoors and camping is great fun. Besides, I thought I would try to take an interest in what Curtis and John enjoy so we can have things to talk about."

"What do you want to do that interest you?"

"I'm not sure. I think I want to be a taxidermist."

"You mean you want to clean the insides out of dead animals and mount them? And you say we're crazy!"

Their laugher broke the silence of the camp.

"I can't paint like Jake and I'm lousy with a camera, but I really love nature. Taxidermy is an art form in itself."

"So why haven't you pursued it?"

Kachina continued putting lotion on her knees. "I don't have the money to study right now and I wouldn't feel right asking John to help out."

"Why not?" Deseray wondered.

"Because he's not my real dad. Curtis knew what he wanted a long time ago and has been saving over the years. I don't feel right asking my mom to take money away from the ranch. I figured I would just get married. I didn't think I would want a career. Now that I want one, I'm not financially prepared."

"I think you should talk to Uncle John. He is so supportive of education of any kind. You should talk to him."

"I guess I will when the time is right." Kachina snuggled

into her sleeping bag. "Now it's time to get some sleep."

Deseray turned off the lantern leaving them submersed into a silent darkness. Deseray put the feather under her pillow. She was hoping the closeness of the feather would influence her dreams to be positive ones, instead the disturbing dreams she had been having.

The next morning Deseray woke feeling refreshed and peaceful. She had not dreamed.

The digging continued for two weeks. During that time, nothing of significance was found. At the end of the two weeks, John gathered everyone together to discuss their next step.

"We aren't having any luck with the grid located where it is. It's up to you guys if you want to abandon this project or move to another location."

"Uncle John?" asked Deseray, "Do you feel we have found the subsoil? We have gone down about eighteen inches. From what I remember, each inch of soil is about 100 years. That means we have gone down about 800 plus years. Right?"

"Yes, Deseray, you are right."

"I would really like to move to a new location," said Deseray."

The agreement was unanimous. John was pleased to see that the enthusiasm they had when they started with was still there.

"So how do you want to decide where to move next?" Jake interrupted.

"In my opinion, if I were to have a village of people, I would want them to be near water. Everyone needs water for daily living."

John nodded. "That's a good point. Do you have any suggestions?"

Jake took out the area map.

"The arrow heads were found here," she pointed to the mark on the map, "which could have been from a small hunting party. If that is the case, the village could be nearby, only closer to the O'Fallon River, such as near our campsite. That's one of the reasons I choose our campsite in the first place. The trees protect it and there is game nearby. Of course, I understand that three hundred years ago the vegetation would have been different, but we can speculate, can't we?"

"Those are good points," John agreed. "How do you guys feel about it?"

Curtis took the map from Jake.

"I think Jake is right. We should scout the areas along the river and use our sense of logic to decide where we would have made a village if it had been our decision."

"Does everyone agree with Curtis?" John asked.

There was total agreement.

"OK, then, we will clean up our dig site and put it back as close to the way we found it."

The next days were hard work and plenty of sweat but the first excavation site was returned to normal as much as possible.

John and Jake took out their map once again.

"We decided to explore the east side of the O'Fallon about four miles north of here. There is more rocky terrain and dense vegetation. I hope that three hundred years ago the area was similar. Jake and I feel this would be a good place to start. We'll break camp here and move it north."

Once camp was broke, they began their journey north along the river and a new dig site.

Chapter Seven - So We Will Not Miss Each Other

Deseray kept looking at the sky as they journeyed north to the new site. The clouds were becoming gray and dense.

The approaching storm seemed to have no effect on the horses, but Deseray found herself becoming apprehensive. She never liked storms, especially as violent as they could get in Wisconsin.

She leaned over toward Kachina.

"Do you guys get tornadoes here?"

"I've never seen one. I think is has something to do with the mountain ranges."

John rode back to join them.

"Looks like we might be in for a good-sized storm and it's going to come on quite fast. There is a small canyon about a mile up from here. Jake thinks we'd be best holding up there. It will offer us protection. It has trees along the upper walls of the canyon, which will protect us from the wind. We won't be able to do much about the rain except wear our ponchos."

The small group of travelers hurried their pace. As they rode along the air had grown colder. Deseray reached into her saddlebag to get her jacket. As she was putting it on, her hand bumped into the medicine pouch, she had attached to her belt. The thought of it brought her comfort.

Howling winds began to surround them, causing the horses to respond with restless mannerism. The sky grew darker and blocked out the sun.

John rode beside Deseray.

"The storms out here aren't as fierce as the one in the Midwest. The rain comes down hard, but we don't get the high of winds like the ones you're used to. It will just make us cold and wet and miserable for a while."

"How comforting," thought Deseray.

"I guess I just get nervous in storms. I'm used to tornadoes."

"We'll sit it out for a while and then we can find a good place to make camp. Maybe we'll even consider camping here for the night. We'll just put up a couple of tents and share them."

Jake had gone ahead to scout out the canyon and soon returned.

"The canyon is just ahead and as luck would have it, there's a large overhang big enough to for us to fit under. It will be perfect to strike a quick camp," she explained.

She looked at the dark sky.

"The storm looks like it might last a while."

Deseray thought the canyon was beautiful. It was like a room with three large walls consisting of red and brown colors marbling throughout the layers of rock. Large tamarack and lodge pole pine lined the top edges of the walls. This gave Deseray a feeling of security.

Jake began to unsaddle her horse.

"The horses need to be unsaddled and the gear put under a tarp to keep it dry."

John dismounted and began to unsaddle his horse.

"I think we should pitch a couple of tents as well. It looks like the storm is going to last longer than we thought."

Jingles searched through one of his bundles looking for a small portable propane burner.

"I'll git some coffee goin."

John put his saddle on the top of a large rock pile.

"We'll put all the gear on these rocks and cover it with a tarp. Since we will be close to the horses, I think it would be a good idea to tether them. The storm is spooking them. I don't want them to run."

Jake unsaddled her horses and tethered them. As Deseray

and Kachina cared for their horses, Jake and Curtis put up a tent in record time. Deseray, Kachina and John worked on another one.

Luck was on their side and the tents were up, the gear safety tucked under the tarps and fresh coffee brewing and still no rain.

In a way, Deseray found the whole thing exciting. There they were, out in the open spaces with nature letting them know who was boss, subject to her demands and reacting to her.

The sky remained dark, but within the walls of the canyon, the winds were not noticeable. The clouds were taking their time releasing the heavy burden of water they contained.

Jingles unpacked the cups and after filling each one, he handed them to the eager and chilly recipients.

"I made some hot cocoa too, if anyone is interested."

Deseray decided on the hot coffee, which began to warm her with the first sip. The warmth also made her aware that she needed to go to the bathroom. She set her cup of coffee down.

"Can I go for a walk? I won't go far."

John assumed she needed to go to the bathroom so gave his approval.

"Make it very short. I don't want you out in the rain when it decides to break lose."

"I won't go far. Deseray started walking along an animal path that led up the side of a hill. Thick trees and bushes flanked either side of the small path.

"Be careful of the wind," Uncle John warned her, "I wouldn't want the wind to come along and swoop you away. I wouldn't know how to explain that to my sister."

The path was easy to follow but rose up steeper than Deseray had first thought. She held onto tree limbs and branches as she lifted herself up the path. She slipped a few times and low growing scrubs caught her in the face. As she emerged through the thick trees, she came to a small clearing and stopped.

She found herself overlooking a large water filled canyon. Groves of trees lined the river as it traveled along, drinking the refreshing water as it passed by.

Deseray used caution as she stood near the edge. The wind was gusting, causing her to sway closer to the edge than she wanted to be.

Relief crept over her as she stood all alone overlooking the valley below. It was the first time she had been alone since she arrived in Montana.

After relieving herself, she sat on the ground and took the medicine pouch from her belt. She carefully removed the jewelry case from the pouch and gently picked up the feather.

As she held the feather, the wind caught it slightly, causing the feather to glide gently up and down. Deseray wondered how it must have felt to be the eagle the feather had come from and soared through the sky in dominant flight.

Still allowing the feather to glide up and down, Deseray rose to her feet and whirled around in a circle. She held the feather in the air as though it belonged to her, preparing to take flight over the mountains.

As she whirled around, she could not stop herself. She whirled faster and faster. Her head began to feel dizzy and light. The alluring clouds were engulfing her with their magic. Everything became misty and white, as the feather seemed to be pulling her faster and faster in the circle.

As the white clouds thickened, Deseray thought she could see White One running at the head of a large herd of buffalo. They ran faster and faster in a great circle, causing the white mist to greatly thicken.

"Don't leave me behind, White One," Deseray pleaded. "Take me with you!"

The swirling mist of clouds lifted Deseray into the air and placed her up on White One's back. His massive muscles flexed and moved under her body. She wrapped her arms tightly around White one's shoulders and held on.

Deseray's heart thumped and her head began to spin. Her head soon became as cloudy as the air around her. She was becoming sleepy as the whole world just slipped away.

A strange calm overcame Deseray as her head cleared. The ensuring storm had disappeared. The wind was a gentle breeze, and the sky was bright and sunny. As she looked up, she saw White One disappearing into the tall grass.

She quickly looked around for the feather. At that moment, her concern for the feather disappeared and was replaced with a new concern.

She could hear herself say. "What is going on?"

She no longer wore the jeans and jacket she had been wearing. She was clad in a light brown buckskin dress with fridges and colorful quillwork. Colorful quillwork moccasins covered her feet. In frustration, she raised her hands to her head. Her long hair which had hung in a ponytail, trailed down either side of her head in thick twisted braids. The end of each braid adorned a small feather. The only familiar thing about her clothes was the medicine pouch she had gotten from Jingles.

"I think I'm going crazy!" she yelled.

The tall grass she was sitting moved gently in response to the wind. The feather, she thought, where is the feather? She looked frantically in the grass but could not find it. It was gone.

As she placed her hand on the ground to help herself up, it bumped against the medicine pouch she had gotten from Jingles. She quickly opened it. The jewelry case was gone but the feather nestled inside. She took it out of the pouch and examined it. It was the same feather, except now it had a decorative ornament attached to the quill end of it. The ornament was a red circle covered with different colored quills wrapped around it. It reminded her of a medicine wheel. The ornament's presence added to her growing confusion.

She put the feather back in the pouch and looked around.

"I have to figure out where I am and how I got here.

The grass was tall and thick. The air about her was surprising fresh and clean. There were no familiar odors in the air. It was the smell or the lack of it that was so refreshing.

Deseray became aware of a distant sound and stood up to get a better look. The sound was that of someone yelling. No, not yelling, more like a whooping sound. Before she could identify the sound, she felt a pressure on her wrist and heard "Run!"

The stranger pulled Deseray into a full run before she even knew her feet were moving. A young male American Indian had a tight hold of her wrist, forcing her to keep pace with him as he ran through the tall grasses, only looking behind them occasionally.

"Let go of me! What are you doing?"

Deseray tried desperately to free her wrist from his grip but was unsuccessful.

With great strength, the young brave suddenly flung Deseray onto the ground. Before she could catch her breath, another American Indian dressed differently than the first one, came leaping through the air, aiming his body at the one who had taken Deseray captive.

A bone chilling sound filled the air, as the body of the attaching warrior lay motionless on the ground. Blood oozed onto the ground beneath the dead warrior's head as he lay against the earth. Deseray put her hand over her mouth to keep from throwing up as she continued to watch the blood soak into the earth. She quickly gazed at her capture, as he remained poised, with tomahawk in hand, as though he awaited another attack.

The attack came moments later. The attacker was dressed like the one lying on the ground. The second attaching warrior came through the grasses swinging his own tomahawk at the defending brave. This warrior too, met with the same fate as the other first attacker as he crumpled to the ground, motionless.

"We must go before the rest come," said the young brave.

"The rest who?" Deseray demanded. "Leave me alone."

"You must come with me or die!"

He grabbed Deseray's wrist with his strong grip and pulled her into a full run. Even as Deseray began to tire, the young brave would not slow his pace. She wondered why he seemed so harsh by not asking her if she was tired as she strained to keep up at this pace.

As difficult as it was for her to continue running, she sensed it was important that she did not slow them down. She was able to find the strength and stamina to continue running.

They came to a clearing where the grasses had become shorter. The young brave slowed his pace and soon stopped.

"We will rest here." He said as he sat down.

"Who are you? Don't' you understand English?"

"I do not know what English is."

To her surprise, she understood his words. It suddenly occurred to Deseray that she was no longer speaking English. Her confusion continued to increase as the scenario about her began to unfold.

She had an overwhelming desire to run away from her capture, but her fear of the unknown lurking in the tall grass prevented her running away.

They sat in silence for a while, both of them regaining their strength.

The bone breastplate the young brave wore had shifted from the front of his chest slightly to the side. Under the breastplate, he wore a leather thong necklace. The design of the necklace looked strangely similar to the pattern she had used for the necklace she had given to Reg.

She wanted to reach out and touch it, but she did not dare.

The young brave spoke.

"I see your journey was a safe one." He laughed gently. "You could have picked a safer place to arrive. But the Spirits must have chosen that place, as it was the Spirits who guided you here."

Once again, she understood his words.

"Do you know English?"

"I do not know what English is."

Again, she had understood his words. She realized to that he also had understood her words. Deseray's mind whirled with confusion.

"I'm dreaming," she said, not realizing she had spoken

aloud.

"You are not dreaming," he responded. "The Sprits have guided you here using the powers of the gift feather you carry with you."

"The feather!" exclaimed Deseray. "How do you know about the feather?"

The young brave laughed and said nothing more about the feather.

"We will rest here. It is still a long journey to the village. You close your eyes and rest. Our enemies may come this far, and we may have to leave quickly."

He sat quietly, looking in the direction where they had just come.

Deseray found him strangely attractive. She imagined he must be handsome as well. His handsomeness was hard to determine due to the paint that covered his face. There was a familiarity about him, thought Deseray. Her fear began to fade as a small degree of comfort replaced it.

Her tired body welcomed the coolness of the grass as she laid her face against it. She did not close her eyes though. Looking upon the young brave sitting next to her made her wonder how he knew so much about her.

As he straightened his breastplate, she could no longer see the necklace he wore underneath it. She suddenly felt tired and drifted off to sleep. Someone pushing on her shoulder awakened her.

"We must go now."

She expected to open her eyes and see her Uncle John, but instead saw the young brave who had saved her from attack.

"I'm not dreaming, am I?"

"You are not dreaming. We must go."

He rose quietly to his feet and began to walk.

Deseray followed. They walked for a long time with no words spoken. She wasn't sure if it was safe to talk as they walked, so she remained silent.

Her legs began to ache from the constant walking but

feared to mention it to the young brave walking next to her. He must have known her thoughts and stopped walking.

"We will rest here," he said and sat down.

It felt odd for Deseray to "just sit down" where she had just been walking.

He opened a leather pouch removing some dried meat and handed it to her.

"Eat."

She took the meat. It was shriveled and dry. She took a bite. She wasn't sure if it tasted good, or it tasted good because she was hungry.

Next, he handed her a leather pouch that held water.

"Drink, only a little."

They both ate some meat and Deseray drank a little water. The young brave drank no water.

"Don't you want some water?" she asked of him.

"Later, I will drink."

"Tell me, where am I and why am I so confused?"

"You are in the land of the Dakota. We are on our way to my village near the river. You will be a guest among my people. The Spirits have brought you here from your own time. The spirit of the one you call White One has requested the Spirits honor you by giving you the desire of your heart."

She was surprised that he knew about White One and about her desire.

"How do you know these things?"

"The Spirits have chosen me to be your protector and teacher while you are among our people."

He laughed a friendly laugh.

"You do not remember me, do you?" he asked.

Deseray was confused. He reached under his breastplate and held the necklace for Deseray to see. To her surprise, it was the necklace she had made and given to Reg.

"Reg? Are you Reg?"

He laughed.

"That is not my name among my people. I am called Tall

Trees."

"How can this be?"

"Remember when I told you there are many powers at work that we do not understand? The Spirits have many powers and many messengers. These messengers are not always two-leggeds, but can be four-leggeds, like the white buffalo, you named White One. The Spirits heard his plea for your desire to be with my people in the time that has passed. Now you are here to fulfill it."

"I'm not sure if I believe it or not, but it feels so real it must be."

"We must go."

Just as the sun was setting, they arrived at village of Tall Trees' people.

Tipis nestled along a beautiful river dotted the magnificent skyline.

The authenticity of the scene that lay before her, mesmerized Deseray.

Smoke ebbed his way skyward, circling around the crossed poles that supported the many buffalo hides that formed the structures. Children ran at play with dogs chasing close at their heels.

Stretched hides suspended from poles, dried in the heat of the sun. Women were busy around cooking fires preparing the evening meal.

Deseray's heart raced within her chest as she realized that her wish to have had a glimpse of the heart and soul of early American Indians stood before her for the taking.

She was living it.

Before they entered the village, Tall Trees made a deep whistling sound, to which a similar sound came as a response.

"When we enter the village, everyone will be curious about you. They will touch your clothes and your hair. Do not be afraid."

"You look like one of the people of the Southern Cheyenne, who are our friends, so no one will harm you. The customs of the Cheyenne are different from my people, so if it is noticed that you do not understand our ways, there will be no suspicion of you."

Deseray took a deep breath. She was nervous and excited. The village seemed so big with a lot more people than she had imagined.

"I will not say if it is and I will not say it is not, but many will think I have brought you to our village to take you as a wife."

His words surprised Deseray.

"We will let them believe this for now. It will save trying to explain you. Many will become suspicious if I tell them you were guided here by the Spirits."

Deseray tried desperately to keep her eyes fixed to the ground.

"What if I do or say something wrong or offensive. Will they hurt you for it?"

"I am a great warrior and respected among my people. They will not harm you or me. I will take care of it."

"You will stay at the lodge of my sister. She has a great understanding of the powers of the Spirits. She will welcome you as a friend and a special guest. Listen to her. She is wise and will teach you the many things you have longed for."

"Speak no more until you are in my sister's lodge. She will prepare you to meet my people when you are ready."

As they entered the village, Deseray found that Tall Trees had spoken the truth.

Children and women came up to her, pulled on her clothes, and touched her skin and hair. She was aware of the lightness of her own skin as she watched the dark hands reach toward her. Deseray feared that someone would guess that she was not American Indian and do her terrible harm. Since she had not seen any evidence of the white man's influence within the village, she assumed they had never seen a white person. If this were true, what else could she be but a American Indian from a different tribe?

This thought comforted her as she walked by the many women, children and men.

She wanted to look around at the tipis, the children and all the people, but Tall Trees had told her to keep her eyes to the ground and not to look around. Wondering eyes often belong to those of an enemy who had come to spy on their village. It was hard for her not to satisfy her curiosity, but she respected Tall Trees and trusted his words. She looked only at the faces of the people who came close as they touched her.

Deseray was relieved as woman come close to her and put her arm around her as she spoke. "I am Woman Who Sings. I am the sister of Tall Trees. You will come to my lodge and rest yourself."

Deseray allowed Woman Who Sings to lead her away from the curious crowd to the quiet and safety of her tipi.

When they got inside, Woman Who Sings motioned Deseray to sit.

One area of the tipi seemed to be reserved for sleeping. Two low platforms sitting a small space apart held tanned buffalo hides. Near the platforms were two square boxes. They appeared to be some type of hide carefully formed to create almost perfect boxes. Each box was beautifully painted with a variety of colorful designs.

In the center of the circle was a small fire. A type of chair with no legs was sitting near the fire. Next to the fire stood a tripod of sticks from which a fleshy looking bag containing some type of food hung.

"You are the one the Spirits have guided to our people." She wasn't asking Deseray, she seemed to be telling her.

"I do not understand how or why you are here, but my brother, who is very wise for his age, understands. He has asked me to teach you the ways of our people. I will do this, for my brother has asked me to."

The woman did not seem unfriendly, only suspicious. Deseray could not blame her. She did not quite understand it all herself.

"It is late. My husband is on a scouting party looking for the buffalo. I will give you food and then we will sleep. When the morning comes, after you have rested, we will talk more."

Woman Who Sings walked over to the large fleshy looking pouch suspended from four sticks poked into the ground. From the pouch, she scooped out what appeared to be stew and placed it into a bowl made from a buffalos' horn. She handed the stew to Deseray with a spoon also made from some type of bone and motioned her to eat.

The stew was hot and tasty. Deseray was curious about the meat in the stew but decided not to ask. She was afraid if she knew what it was, she wouldn't be able to eat it.

A soft cry and movement came from across the tipi. Woman Who Sings walked over to the sound and picked up a naked baby. Deseray could see it was a girl baby.

"This is my daughter."

Woman Who Sings sat herself comfortably against a sitting board and began nursing her baby.

Deseray finished the stew and placed it next to the cooking pouch from where it had come.

As Woman Who Sings continued to nurse her baby, she motioned Deseray to a pile of buffalo hides sitting against the edge of the tipi.

"You will sleep there."

Like the rest of the sleeping areas within the tipi, the hides lay on a low platform about three inches high.

Deseray felt uncomfortable as she pulled the heavy hide over her body. Not knowing what else to do, she kept her clothes on.

The softness of the inside of the hide surprised her and she adored the silkiness of the fur on the outside.

She could feel the tension of the day slowly slipping away as she tried to sleep. It was difficult for her to comprehend all that had happened. Maybe, she thought, it is only a dream and when I wake, I will be home.

That night Deseray had no dreams, but her sleep was

peaceful and relaxing.

Early the next morning as Deseray awoke, the heaviness of the buffalo hides confirmed that her journey to the past was indeed reality. Woman Who Sings was sound asleep as was her daughter who was snuggled close to her mother's warm body.

Deseray felt a degree of discomfort being among strangers and realized she needed to go to the bathroom. She wondered where they went when they had to go. She quietly slipped out from under the hide and carefully made her way to the entrance of the tipi. Gently lifting the flap, she stepped outside. What do I do now, she wondered?

A quiet voice brought the answer to her question.

"There is area over there for you to use."

It was Tall Trees. He sat soundlessly next to the tipi.

Deseray smiled without a word and headed for the direction of which he was pointing.

Once Deseray was out of sight, she carefully examined the clothes she was wearing. Her tunic was made of highly tanned deer or elk. She lifted her tunic to examine her underwear. She discovered that her underwear was a breechcloth much like the ones the men wore.

A leather belt tied to her waist with rectangular cloth pulled up through both the front and back of the belt. She was surprised at how comfortable it was to wear.

When she returned, Tall Trees was speaking to his sister.

She smiled at Deseray and seemed more welcoming to her then she had been the night before.

"Tall Trees wants to go for a walk with you," she said. "Do not take long. There is much to be done this day."

Tall Trees walked toward the river as Deseray followed.

"I'm afraid of all of this," she told Tall Trees. "It's all so different and I don't know what to do or how to treat people."

"Don't worry." His smile was reassuring. "You will learn quickly. My sister believes the Spirits brought you from the village of the Cheyenne to become my wife. She understands that you are not familiar with our ways and has agreed to teach you the ways of our women."

"Listen to her and do as she tells you. The women work hard. Among my people, you are not a girl as you are in your own time. Here you are a woman."

"I told my sister that you were separated from your own people and were unable to find them again. This is true since your own people are in a different time and you cannot find them in my time. My people will accept you if they do not wonder if your own people cast you out and if you ran away. People will not ask you questions, but they will ask my sister. This will give her something to tell them that will satisfy their curiosity."

Tall Trees sat on the sand near the river's edge. Deseray sat next to him.

"Why does your sister think I am here to become your wife?"

"Many times, when a captive or a woman from another tribe comes to be with a tribe other than her own, the warrior who brought her intends to marry her. You are not a captive, but a guest. It is your right to choose the husband you wish to have."

"But I have not thought about a husband. Aren't I going back to my own time after I have learned?"

"If you cannot find your way back to your own time, you must find a husband to care for you while you are here among my people. It is our way. Even if you are here only for a short while, the time may come to choose. Unless a woman is a shaman or has something wrong with her, she has been long married with babies by the time she is your age."

"Our lives are very simple. The women prepare our food for use and storage, sew our clothes and homes, and raise our children. The men become good hunters and fighters to protect the village. It is very simple."

"I can see the simplicity, but I can also see the hardness of your lives."

Tall Trees stood and smiled down upon Deseray.

"You will fit in here. It is in your spirit to be here."

Deseray stood next to Tall Trees. She felt a great affection for him. She thought to herself, as she looked upon him, if she had to choose a husband, why not Tall Trees. She wondered if he would want her. After all, it was not his choice to be responsible for her. It was thrust upon him. Maybe he would rather have someone else as his wife. She decided not to think about such things; after all, surely the Spirits would return her to her own that time before that came.

Her concerned turned to that of her family.

"What of my family. What will they think when I am gone?"

He gently touched her cheek. It made Deseray's heart pound faster.

"I do not know what to tell you. The Spirits did not tell me of your family or how it would be when you are gone."

He gently cupped her face in both hands.

"Be comforted. I will be your family while you are among my people as will my sister and her family."

Deseray's heart was still heavy as she thought of the pain her absence would cause for her family. Tall Trees removed his hands from Deseray's face. She wanted to reach up and hold them there but did not. His touch gave her comfort. Tall Trees turned to face the river, and then returned his gaze to Deseray.

"Today the women are helping another woman to sew her new tipi. You will help with this. It is a social gathering for women. They talk, laugh, and share ways to do things. You will learn to understand how our women do many things by listening. They will not talk to you. It is not because they do not like you, it is not good manners to ask questions of a guest."

Deseray was relieved to know that she would not have to answer questions. She was not sure of what she should or should not say. She knew she could not tell anyone that she was from a time that had not yet come.

"How did I get here?" She asked Tall Trees.

"The Spirits guided you here."

"But how? Was it the feather?"

She removed the feather from her pouch and showed it to Tall Trees.

"I do not understand the spirit world. I had visions of your coming. This is the way the Spirits spoke to me and told me the things I should know. I learn and do the best for my people."

"What do you mean visions?" Deseray asked.

"Visions are thoughts and imagines that come to you sometimes when you are asleep and sometimes when you are not. They are like dreams."

"Can anyone have a vision?"

"If it is the will of the Spirits, yes."

"Before I came here, I had many dreams I did not understand. They seemed very real. I was riding White One with a herd of brown buffalo. In my dreams, there was a warrior. I guess that must have been you."

Tall Trees nodded.

"The spirits gave you the vision to prepare you for your journey. Now that you are here, you no longer need the vision."

Deseray showed Tall Trees the circular ornament now attached to the feather.

"This wasn't here in my time. What does it mean?"

Tall Trees held the ornament in the palm of his hand pointing to the colors, explaining each one to Deseray.

"The circle is the sacred hoop of my people. We do all things in circles. Nothing ever ends. It continues always, like the circle. If one of us enters the afterlife, his life does not end, it continues in the lives of those who are left behind. The light is always followed by the darkness, which is always followed by the light. It never ends."

"The colors are the four winds or four directions. We always begin with the direction of the rising sun, the new day.

He pointed to the east.

"The color for the new day is red. The red is also for the red-tailed hawk, the messenger.

The bottom of the circle is yellow. It is for the warm winds this direction brings to us. It is also for the buffalo. These winds bring the warmth of the season that dries our meat to give us food during the cold times."

Continuing around the circle Tall Trees pointed to the west.

"This direction brings the darkness and ends the day. It is black. This direction is for the thunder being or the thunder-bird that brings the thunder, lightning and the rains that give us life.

The direction of the motherland is white. It is also for the eagle. He is the symbol of leadership and is the closest to the Great Spirit of all creatures. We believe that the wings of the eagle have touched the face of the Great Spirit. The winds from this direction bring the cold which teaches us endurance that we may become strong."

Deseray was silent as she thought about what he had just said. It wasn't so much what he had said, but how he had said it. His voice was reverent and serene. The beliefs he shared with her touched her soul in a way that nothing in her life ever had before.

She took the feather from Tall Trees and carefully placed in back in her pouch.

"I have so much to learn," she said.

"You will not learn it all. Learning begins from birth and continues through life. There will never be enough time to learn all there is to know. I will teach you the ways of my people and my sister will teach you the ways of the woman. Return to her now and I will talk with you before the sun sets."

Tall Trees walked along the river and left Deseray alone.

Upon returning to Woman Who Sings' tipi, a fire was burning near the buffalo paunch-cooking kettle. Woman Who Sings was adding dried buffalo, roots and dried berries to the water in the paunch. As Deseray watched Woman Who Sings use forked antlers, she scooped up several hot stones from the fire and dropped them into the paunch, making the water roll and bubble from the heat, thus cooking the contents inside.

Deseray was amazed at the creativeness of this cooking method.

Deseray watched carefully, taking in every detail as Woman Who Sings opened the flap of one of the two decorated pouches. Inside she could see a variety of bowls, eating utensils and cooking tools. The pouch appeared to be made of un-tanned hide stretched into the shape the of an envelope or elongated pouch. Deseray suddenly realized the pouches were parfleches.

Parfleches were used to store household goods and, much like a suitcase from her time, used to transport these items.

Not wanting to appear naive, Deseray admired the beauty of the artwork, even though she really wanted to ask how to make them. Deseray assumed all women would have known how by her age, so she decided she'd ask Tall Trees about it.

As the meal finished, Women Who Sings picked up a cradleboard. While holding it steady, she began lining the inside of the cradleboard with a fluffy materiel. Deseray smiled. She recognized the fluffy materiel. It was fluff from matured cattails. She then recalled that the cradleboards were lined with cattail fluff and served the same purpose a modern-day diaper. She then opened a small basket and patted a powdery substance on the baby's butt. She could see the confusion in Deseray's eyes.

"Powdered buffalo dung. It keeps the sores from forming on her bottom side."

Deseray smiled and nodded, letting Woman Who Sings know she understood. To prevent diaper rash, thought Deseray.

Once she finished putting on the powder, Woman Who Sings placed her daughter into a cradleboard and strapped it on her back.

The cradleboard had tines sticking up on either side of the top edge, which straddled the baby's head. From her studies, Deseray knew the purpose of the tines were to protect the baby's head if the papoose where to fall from a height, such as from a horse, then the tines would stick into the ground protecting the baby's head from injury.

Again, Deseray was impressed with its creative design.

"The men of the scouting party have seen a small herd of buffalo one sun from here. There are only a few men in the village today. The rest are looking for the larger herd."

"When the buffalo are found," she explained, "There will be many things to be done. Tall Trees has asked me to tell you he has left to join them. When he is successful, he will kill many buffalo to make a fine lodge of your own." She ended with a smile.

A lodge of my own! Again, Deseray realized that all believed that she was to be married to Tall Trees. Deseray had not imagined herself married. She had too many things she wanted to accomplish with her life before she would consider it. However, in this time, all other women her age of the village were married and already had several children. Not yet, thought Deseray, I am not ready.

"You have come here on a good day. Today Walks Slowly will host a tipi sewing for her new lodge. She is a new bride and she and her husband are ready to leave her parent's home. Horse Woman will be the lodge maker today. Her joy and happiness will keep Walks Slowly's home from being smoky. If she is in a bad mood and directs us how to make the new tipi, the tipi will always be smoky. This will not happen. Horse Woman has been invited to be the lodge maker for many happy homes. Come, it is time."

Many women had gathered by the time they arrived. No one asked who Deseray was. They already knew, for the news had traveled to each lodge before the sun had set the night before.

"Dry Sands," directed Woman Who Sings, "You will work here." She pointed to a pile of buffalo hides, scraped clean of their hair and flesh. Several of them lay on the ground already sewn together.

"Listen to Horse Woman for guidance."

Deseray realized that she had called her Dry Sands. She

laughed to herself. That must be what Tall Trees had told them to call her. It felt strange to her to hear her new name.

As the women gathered, Deseray noticed small square leather pouches attached to each woman's belt. From these pouches, they removed the tools they would need to complete their task. Deseray watched as the women carefully arrange the 15 hides, under careful scrutiny of Horse Woman, to form the outer covering of the tipi. One woman was moving along the edges of the hides with a bone awl, skillfully making holes along the edges to pass the tendon threads through.

Deseray opened the small leather bundle that a woman gave her. Upon opening it, she saw the small balls of moist sinew tendons to use to sew the hides together. She had no idea what to do next.

As she helplessly stared at the small balls in front of her, a young girl leaned close to her and whispered.

"I am Otter Tail. We will work together."

Deseray smiled.

Otter Tail took the bundle from Deseray and removed one small ball of sinew, carefully wrapping the rest to keep them moist.

To Deseray's horror, Otter Tail put the small ball of sinew into her mouth.

A few moments later, she pulled one end of the ball out of her mouth and threaded it through a bone-sewing needle. Then she began running the needle through the holes along the side of the hide, carefully pulling the edges together to form a strong connecting seam.

Otter Tail could see the horror on Deseray's face.

Otter tail removed ball from her mouth.

"I know some of your people live in lodges of grass and twigs so this may be new to you. I will teach you how my people do it."

She spoke softly so others would not overhear her. She wanted to save face for Deseray's lack of knowledge.

"The sinew will become hard and brittle if it is not kept

wet as it was when it was removed from the buffalo. It is best to use it at that time but is not always possible. She handed the small bundle to Deseray indicating to her to take one of the balls and placed it in her mouth.

Deseray felt as though she would gage as she picked up one of the balls. Reluctantly she placed it into her mouth. She forced herself not to throw up as she felt the stringiness and bitter taste fill her mouth.

Otter Tail smiled as she handed Deseray a sewing needle made from a bone splinter.

She spoke no more to Deseray, but worked close by her, giving her non-verbal instructions as the progressed.

The hostess, Walks Slowly, encouraged many breaks so she could feed her guests. The moment the small ball in their mouths was gone; the women would put food in their mouths, ate for a few moments before putting in another ball of sinew.

Where two women worked closely together, Deseray noticed their heads touching as the talked and laughed. She could not imagine how they managed conversation with the horrible little balls in their mouths.

Everyone seemed to be having a good time. The babies, placed in cradleboards, were propped up against small trees, stumps and bushes, near where the women worked. The babies were quite content to sleep in the refreshing breeze and warm sun.

Deseray's fingers began to become stiff and sore as she worked the needle through the holes. No one else seemed to be having the same problem so she decided to endure the discomfort. She did not want to embarrass Tall Trees by appearing to be weak and lazy.

A couple of the women disappeared and returned shortly, dragging long poles behind them. The leaves, branches and bark had been stripped from each pole. These poles would become support for the outer covering they had been sewing together.

Once raised, the long poles formed an upside-down cone shape. Additional poles added gave strength to the structure.

Attached to the few poles were lengths of rope. As Deseray examined the rope, she realized it had been made from buffalo hair carefully weaved together. How clever, she thought.

The women raised one pole with a rope attached to it, up into the air. Another woman took the other end of the rope that dangled down from the pole and began walking round the tipi poles, securing them together at the top.

Another woman attached the other end of the rope to the new tipi cape. Another woman put wooden pegs down from the top to about halfway down the buffalo hide. The wooden pegs are called lodge pins used to close the open side of the cape. While raising the last poles the cape went in the air with the poles. When the poles were properly place, the women pulled on the ends of the rope until the tipi cover went to the top.

As the new covering draped over the cone shape poles, more wooden pegs were used to close the open side of the new cape. The pins continued from the top to near the bottom. The very bottom section left unpinned serves as the door.

The efficiency with which the women worked together amazed Deseray, as did the quickness by which they completed the tipi. Their skill was exceptionally proficient.

Where the lodge poles stuck out of the top, the covering had not been joined either, leaving two flaps near the top.

A pole attached to each of the flaps allowed a woman to either open or close them as her needs suited her. The openings allowed smoke to escape when open or to prevent rain from entering when closed. Around the base of the tipi, bone pegs were place in the ground to secure the bottom of the tipi. When the tipi was complete, Walks Slowly began to move her possessions from her parents' home to her own.

Retrieving her baby from a nearby stump Woman Who Sings started walking toward her own home.

"Walks Slowly's husband will be proud to sleep in such a fine home," Woman Who Sings said. "It is time to go home now."

Otter Tail smiled at Deseray as she slipped away across the village.

The rest of the women gathered their tools and babies and parted to their own homes.

Deseray was looking forward to getting some rest, but when they returned, Woman Who Sings handed Deseray a couple of buffalo bladder bags.

"Take these to the river and fill them."

Deseray was tired and wanted to rest. Her fear of embarrassing Tall Trees by not being strong and obedient, gave her the strength to go to the river to fill the bags.

The rest of her day consisted of many chores that Woman Who Sings instructed her to do. For a while, she was scrapping the hair and flesh from an elk hide.

Deseray knew the next step was to soften the hide with buffalo brains and fat to use for clothing. Deseray hoped she wouldn't be the one to soften the hide. The idea of touching buffalo brains made her stomach queasy. She still had the nasty taste of sinew in her mouth.

As night neared, Woman Who Sings placed her hand on Deseray's shoulder.

"You are a good worker. Go to the river and freshen yourself. You are done this day."

Deseray was excited to find some time to call her own. She walked to the river and found a large boulder to sit on. She was tired and her muscles ached. She couldn't remember having worked so hard for so long in her entire life.

The moon had already risen, and the stars were twinkling brightly.

She wondered where under the night sky Tall Trees was sitting at that same moment.

She missed his gentle voice and reassuring smile. He had told her he would see her again before the sun set. That was before she knew he would leave with the rest of the men out scouting for the buffalo. Deseray knew if they did not find the buffalo, he would not return. He had not returned.

Deseray looked toward the river once more before returning to the village hoping to see Tall Trees coming toward her.

She saw a familiar figure outlined in the moonlight. Could it be? Yes, it can.

She leaped from the rock and ran up to the figure. It was White One!

She pet White One's burly head and whispered, "I was hoping I'd see you. It seems you're the one responsible for my being here."

White One gently nudged Deseray. He was clean and strong. His hair was softer and fuller than it had been in her time. She noticed an unusual sparkle in his eyes.

"I know why you're so happy," she said softly, "Because you are free. In this time and place, you are free. That's how it should be."

White One slowly backed away from Deseray.

"Where are you going?"

Just then, she heard someone calling her name and realized this was why White One needed to leave.

It was Woman Who Sings.

She walked up to Deseray while looking in the direction from which White One had disappeared from view.

"I must be dreaming," she said, "for I thought I had just seen a great white buffalo."

Deseray stood and said nothing.

"It is late," she told Deseray. "The presence of the white buffalo is a good sign. They will find the buffalo tomorrow. It will be a busy day. We must rest."

She turned and walked toward the village with no more words. Deseray followed.

Chapter Eight - A Way of Life

As the sun rose upon the sleeping village, people began to stir. Dogs trotted about looking for any forgotten scraps. An occasional baby's cry disturbed the morning peacefulness.

As she looked at the village, Deseray noticed that all the tipis had a slight slope to them. They were not perfectly round or straight up as she had always imagined they would be. All the doors faced the same direction. Throughout the center of the village of tipis were of clusters of common fire pits. In the center of the entire village was a much larger fire pit surrounded by a large circular space.

Deseray thought about what has happened to her. She kept asking herself, "Is this real?" If it were a dream, it was intense.

"Dry Sands?"

Deseray turned in the direction of the voice. It was Women Who Sings.

"Today we will gather camas roots."

Deseray watched as Woman Who Sings placed harnesses on two dogs. Her hands were strong but weathered as she attached a travois made of heavy branches to each harness. She easily stretched a piece of tanned leather over each tri pod frame and secured them into place.

The dogs waited patiently. This was their job and if they wanted to eat, they obeyed. Without a word, she went into the tipi and returned shortly with a cradleboard on her back. She also carried pieces of elk horn in her hand.

"Come, the roots are this way."

Deseray followed and did not ask questions. She wondered if she was already supposed to be familiar with camas

THE WHITE BUFFALO'S FEATHER

root gathering. She was nervous.

The fifteen-minute walk ended by a large field of wilted wildflowers. Some of the plants were almost three feet tall, even in their wilted state. Woman Who Sings propped the cradleboard up against a tree with several other babies. They all slept peacefully inside.

"Since camas does not grow as far south as your people, "Woman Who Sings began, "you may not have knowledge of gathering. I will teach you."

Deseray was relieved.

"Follow," she said. A few moments later, they stood at the edge of three pits. Each pit was quite large and a few feet deep. Five inches rocks and occasionally large flat stones lined the bottom of each pit. Women were already placing wood to start a fire in each pit.

"Other women have already cleaned the roasting pits of which we use each year."

The men had already gathered the wood and were leaving the area.

"We cannot begin roasting until the men are gone."

Deseray wondered why the men had to leave.

Woman Who Sings sensed her confusion.

"If men are near the roasting pits, the camas will not roast properly."

She handed Deseray one of the antler bones she carried. Woman Who Sings then turned to the fields of flowers and began digging at the base of a plant. The leaves were very thin and very long. Some leaves were as long as three feet. The wilted flowers had been a variety of light lavender, white and even dark purple.

As they women gathered the roots, the dogs slept, patiently waiting for the gathering to begin.

Slowly Woman Who Sings continued digging around the base of a plant.

She pointed to the plant next to hers and motioned Deseray to dig.

The ground was firm, and the antler proved to be inefficient for such a task, but served its purposed. It did however manage to loosen the dirt as she pried it into the ground.

The field was quickly filling with women and young girls who had joined them in the gathering. The importance of this root, to the food supply became apparent to Deseray. She wondered what it tasted like and knew she would soon find out soon.

Deseray's hands and fingers began to ach as she continued to dig the plants. The day was hot and the sweat trickled down the middle of her now aching back. She noticed that the women tending the fire had begun to gather alder branches and wet grass from the nearby creek. She realized that it was slough grass, which grew annually near wet areas.

As the travois was filled, Deseray led the dog over to the pit area where she unloaded the roots they had dug near the pit. She repeated this throughout the day. The pile became much larger as the day progressed.

Sometime after the sun was at its highest point in the sky, the women stopped working to tend to their babies and eat some lunch.

Their lunch was, as always, very simple. Today they ate pemmican and drank water.

As Woman Who Sings nursed her baby, she spoke to Deseray.

"You are a good worker. We will continue to gather until near sunset. Then we will fill one of the roasting pits with what we have gathered today."

After lunch the digging continued.

"The roots will stay in the pit for three suns. We will wait three more suns for the roots to cool. Then we will gather them from the pits. Some we will eat soon and some we will dry for our cache."

As Woman Who Sings had said, the digging stopped just before sunset. The woman gathered near the roasting pit and began adding the alder branches and the wet grasses to the pit. Piles of bulbs went on top of the grasses. On top of the bulbs, the woman put bark and dirt. Deseray had noticed the piles of dirt next to the pits, but thought they were only there from digging the pit.

Soon another fire gently burned on top of the dirt that now covered the roots.

The sun had long set by the time the top fires were burning. Women began gathering their tools and babies and returned to the village. The bright, full moon guided them as they walked through the night. Deseray laughed to herself, "A harvest moon in June."

Deseray was soon sound asleep when she heard her name.

"Dry Sands?" It was Woman Who Sings.

"We will eat breakfast and then return to the harvest."

Deseray wanted to moan and protest, but she darn not, as she did not want to embarrass Tall Trees.

She rose from her sleep, ate her simple breakfast, and followed behind Woman Who Sings to repeat the day before.

"We will have one more pit to fill and be done with the gathering." Woman Who Sings explained to Deseray.

As the day ended, Deseray missed Tall Trees. She wondered where he had gone. The last time she had seen him was days ago when he left to join the hunters.

After another backbreaking day, Deseray was eager to sleep and rest her aching body. She could not recall when all of her body hurt so much.

The next morning Woman Who Sings noticed how tired Deseray had become. Woman Who Sings also noticed Deseray's weariness.

"I can see you are not used to such work. I would like to do some visiting today. I will leave my daughter here with you if you would like to rest in the tipi for a while."

Deseray hid her true thoughts. She cherished the idea of resting during the day, even for a short while.

"I would very much enjoy watching your daughter while you visit."

"I will return by the middle of the day meal and will feed

the baby when I return," she said as she picked up a bundle. She walked across the village and disappeared from sight.

The baby was still nestled in her pile of fur, sleeping soundly. Deseray sat next to her and pulled the hide Tall Trees had given her close to her. She smelled the hide. The scent of Tall Trees lingered on the fur and brought joy to her as she filled her nostrils with his scent. Pulling the hide over her, she snuggled next to the baby and slept.

Deseray woke with a start. She thought she heard screaming. She looked at the baby next to her who also began to stir. The screaming was outside.

Deseray jumped quickly to her feet, lifting the flap, looked outside. People were running everywhere screaming and yelling. Most of the commotion came from the opposite end of the village. The village was under attached!

To her horror, Deseray recognized the intruding warriors. They were the same kind of warriors Tall Trees had killed the first day she had arrived from the future.

The intruders were shooting arrows at anyone who moved. The few remaining warriors in the village were attempting to hold the enemy at the far end of the village, allowing the women and children to run into hiding. The women of the village were grabbing children and running to hide in the thick vegetation and bushes along the river.

The enemy, thought Deseray, as feared filled her very soul. She suddenly realized she had no idea what to do. She turned and looked across the tipi. The baby was awake and fussing now. I've got to save the baby, she thought.

She remembered what she had overheard the women saying one day, as they explained to the young children that they were to find a place to hide in the brush if the enemy ever came to their village. "Do not cry out from your hiding places" they were told, "no matter what happens, even if you are afraid or see someone killed."

She knew she needed to get the baby and find a place to hide in the bushes. She ran over to the baby and was about to lift her into her arms when she heard someone stop suddenly outside the tipi. The enemy! She took a large robe and threw it over the baby. Then she frantically looked around the tipi for some type of weapon.

Before she could locate one, the flap burst open and there stood an enemy warrior with paint all over his face. She felt such intense fear that she felt as though she would throw up. Her attention returned to the situation at hand.

She had to save the baby. Deseray moved slowly around the outer edge of the tipi, away from the baby, making her way toward the flap. The warrior snarled and laughed as he watched the fear in Deseray's eyes. As she moved, she continued looking around for some type of weapon. Her eye caught the edge of Woman Who Sings' tomahawk slightly hidden by some small pieces of tanned hide. It was closer to the enemy than Deseray and she knew she would never be able to reach it before the warrior would overtake her.

Just then, the baby cried out. The enemy snarled again and seemed thrilled by the idea of killing a baby too. He turned his head in the direction of the sound. He kept an eye on Deseray as he edged toward the pile of hides that concealed the baby.

It's now or never thought Deseray. She deliberately moved toward the hidden tomahawk. The enemy didn't seem threatened by her movement and turned fully toward the baby and pulled the hides off to reveal her lying there.

Before Deseray realized what she was doing, she grabbed the tomahawk, raised it in the air and brought it down as hard as she could onto the top of the enemy's skull. There was a loud crunch as the enemy fell onto the edge of the hides. Blood oozed from his skull and flowed freely onto the hides, turning them dark red.

She ran over to the baby and snatched her into her arms. She pulled a hide from under the pile where the dead enemy lay, crawled to the farthest edge of the tipi and pulled the hide over her and the baby so only Deseray's head and one hand showed.

With the bloodstained tomahawk clenched tightly in her

exposed hand, she sat and waited for the next enemy to come.

She wasn't aware of the time as it passed. She no longer heard any sounds outside. She blocked them out.

The walls of the tipi began to darken as the sun set.

Soon the flap of the tipi once again flung open.

"Deseray!"

Deseray sat rocking back and forth, clutching the baby and staring at the body of the dead enemy.

Tall Trees put his arms around Deseray and the baby and led them outside. Things weren't much better. Dead bodies lay on the ground, women were sobbing, and small children cried with confusion.

"Deseray, it is Tall Trees." He forced the tomahawk out of her clenched hand and let it fall to the ground.

"You are all right now."

Deseray looked into Tall Trees' concerned eyes. She didn't notice the blood the oozed from the wound on the side of his face.

She opened the hide wrapped around her and showed Tall Trees the baby.

"She is safe," she said and handed the baby to him.

Woman Who Sings came running up to them relived to see that they were safe, especially her baby. The babe was crying and Woman Who Sings took her from Tall Trees.

As she hugged her baby, she looked at Deseray.

"Thank you for keeping my baby safe."

Tall Trees motioned his sister to look in the tipi. She gasped as she saw the body of the dead enemy surrounded by a pool of blood.

She walked over to Deseray, putting her arms around her with the baby between them and said softly, "I will always be grateful."

Tall Trees lead Deseray away from the village toward the peacefulness of the river. The village mourned with sorrow and the peacefulness that thrived there days before now echoed with pain and sorrow.

Tall Trees handed Deseray a bladder bag filled with water. "Drink."

At first, she didn't want to drink, but with coaxing from Tall Trees, she took a small drink.

She suddenly noticed the cut on the side of his face.

She gently touched the side of his head. "You are hurt."

She poured some of the water into her hand and rinsed the wound.

Tall Trees took her hands and pulled them away from his wound. She realized that it was not proper for her to fuss over his battled wound. It was a symbol of great bravery, so she left it alone.

He looked lovingly into her eyes.

"You were very brave today."

"But I killed someone."

"You killed our enemy. You saved the life of my sister's baby. I too, am grateful. I am grateful to the Spirits that you are also alive."

"I've never killed anyone before, not even an enemy."

Deseray put her face into Tall Trees chest and sobbed.

He put his arms around her and let her cry.

Deseray cuddled in Tall Tree's arms as they sat under the trees near the river. He let her sleep undisturbed until morning.

"Are you better this morning?" he asked as she awoke.

"Yes. But I am still disturbed because I killed someone."

"It is our way. Most warriors fight to show courage. We do not fight for territory or land. The land is mother earth and belongs to all the people. Many times, when we fight, we take coup. This is when we touch or strike our enemy without killing them. This is a sign of great courage."

"I have heard of counting coup. So, if fighting is to show courage, why did the warriors that came yesterday kill people?"

"Those are called the Crow. They are not a warring people. We trade with them. With every tribe, some members go on their own and give a bad name to their people. I do not understand their ways."

"Neither do I." commented Deseray.

"You have gained your first pony this day," Reg told her.

"Why is that?" she asked.

"It is the pony of the enemy you killed. By rights the pony is yours."

Deseray was thrilled to have her own horse, but sad as she recalled how she had earned it.

The next few days were very difficult, not only for Deseray, but for the entire village. The air was filled with morning and many funerals were being held. Men, women, and children died in the raid. Deseray had been right when she thought the enemy had been the Crow.

Tall Trees seemed especially concerned about the recent attach.

Deseray and Women Who Sings kept busy processing the meat that had not been stolen, scraping hides, and slicing meat for drying.

"We were fortunate that my husband and my brother were not killed," Woman Who Sings said to Deseray. She looked over to where her daughter laid in the sun and then at Deseray.

"My daughter too," She squeezed Deseray's hand. "You were very brave. Songs will be sung of your bravery. I wish to honor you and name my daughter after you. I shall caller Little Dry Sands."

Deseray didn't want to think about the dead enemy but was delighted that Woman Who Sings wanted to name her daughter after her.

"I am honored. Thank you."

Then her expression became serious.

"Why is Tall Trees so far away these past few days? Does he feel pain of losing someone special?"

"He once again feels the pain of losing our parents. It is not proper to speak of the dead, but you did not know them so I will speak of them only once. If we speak their name, we will be calling them back from their journey to the afterlife. They will become lost. Never again would I speak of them."

"When he was a small boy, our village was raided. When the enemy came, I took him and hid in the brush as I was taught to do."

"We could see the fighting from where we hid. My mother was running to hide with my younger sister when the enemy came upon her. Tall Trees wanted to cry out to her, but I covered his mouth, as we were taught not to cry from a hiding place, so we did not endanger all who hid. The enemy killed both my mother and my sister as we hid there and could do nothing."

Woman Who Sings seemed to be reliving that day in her mind as she spoke.

"I think he was angry with me because I would not let him leave our hiding place to save our mother and sister, but he was so young and not yet skilled in hand-to-hand combat with the enemy. I feared he too, would be killed."

"After the fighting was over, we learned that our father had been killed and the enemy took his body. Tall Trees then became the head of our family, and someday be a chief as our father had been. He was still so young. Our relatives raised us until I was of the age to marry. When Cries In The Wilderness and I were joined, Tall Tress was adopted by him and he was raised as his own."

Deseray's heart ached for both Woman Who Sings and Tall Trees.

She gently touched Woman Who Sings' arm.

"How sad to lose most of your family in one day," she said.

Woman Who Sings continued.

"Tall Tress concentrated on his fighting skills. He tried harder than anyone I have ever seen and achieved many great things at a very early age. They sing many songs of his greatness. The recent fighting within our camp brought back the memories. The never-ending circle of life."

Woman Who Sings said no more about the dead.

Deseray was quiet for a while.

"If Tall Trees lives with you, where had he been staying since I came here?"

"He had been staying with friends. He believed it to be respectful to you if he did not sleep in the same tipi until you make your decision to marry. I would be honored to have such a brave woman as you for my new sister."

Married, there was that thought again. Deseray realized why they married so young. The risk of early death existed for everyone, almost every day in this time. Deseray could not think of marriage to Tall Trees because deep inside she knew she must return to her own time and her own family.

"How is it that Tall Trees is not yet married?

"The young girl, Otter Tail, has found favor in his eyes, but he has waited to marry her. When I spoke to him about it, he said the Spirits had a task for him and when the time was right, he would know when to marry. I think the Spirits were waiting for you to arrive so Tall Trees would take you as his first wife."

"His first wife!" exclaimed Deseray, realizing her voice had given away her complete shock.

"Why would he want more than one wife?"

"Do you mean the men of your people do not take more than one wife?"

Much to Deseray's relief, she did not wait for an answer.

"Among my people, a chief has many duties and must entertain to keep his importance in the tribe. He must also have many children. This creates much work for one woman. Many times, the first wife is grateful when her husband takes another wife, as she will then have someone to help with all the work and help with the children. Often the second wife is the sister of his first wife."

Deseray realized that it was true, the woman worked hard each day and the idea of sharing the work seemed welcomed. As she thought about how hard the women worked, she was quickly reminded of this fact when Woman Who Sings interrupted her thoughts.

"We must return to the roasting pits."

160

Group by group, the woman and dogs returned to the roasting pits. The warriors kept a more watchful eye on the village since the recent attach.

After much work of removing all the dirt and burned grasses, they cooked roots were ready to be divided among the women. As the pits lay emptied of the roots, the women returned to camp with their shares.

Woman Who Sings gave careful instructions to Deseray on drying the roasted camas roots to be prepared for storage.

"The roots will dry for seven suns. Once they are dried, we will crush some into a powder to make flour and the rest we will save for soups."

Women Who Sings smiled, "Today, we will eat them freshly roasted."

She instructed Deseray to take a bite of one of the roots. It tasted much like a sweet potato. She liked it.

A few weeks went by and the women went to gather local berries that were ready for harvest. Once again, the dog and travois were used to carry the gathered berries.

When they returned to the village, Woman Who Sings instructed Deseray how to dry the berries for future use. Deseray realized that food preservation was the daily pastime for the women during the warm months while the men spent their month hunting deer, elk, and rabbits. The hides from these animals provided their clothing and different bags for carrying either scared or personal items.

The meat from the summer hunts was eaten as quickly as they were hunted. They provided their summer food combined with the many roots, berries and nuts; the woman gathered.

The greatest hunt and much of their winter food, blanket and tipi covers came from the buffalo hunts. The summer hunt provided food throughout the summer months and be used to turn into pemmican and dried for winter use. The fall hunt would provide more food, clothing, and coverings for warmth during the winter months.

Deseray was excited to see the hunt and learn from

Women Who Sings the ways they butchered the buffalo, tanned the hides, and dried the meet. She could hardly wait!

Chapter Nine - The Hunt

Tall Trees sat motionless on the edge of the ravine as he looked up at the star filled sky. As he stood guard, keeping an eye on the horses and a watch for an enemy, Deseray filled his thoughts.

He was impatient to find the buffalo, not only to secure the much-needed meat and hides for the upcoming winter, but also to return to camp to see Deseray.

While deep in thought of her, he imagined that the ground began to rumble. Focusing only on the vibrations, he realized that indeed the ground was rumbling. He lowered himself to the ground and place one ear near to the earth. He could almost feel the earth's movement as he listened.

The magnitude of the earth's vibrations could come from only one thing, a large herd of buffalo on the move.

He rose from the ground, cupping his hand next to his mouth sounded a high-pitched shrill. Another of similar degree answered it. Tall Trees could not leave his guard. His call singled to the others of his desire to speak.

Within minutes, several other hunters surrounded him.

"The ground rumbles with the power of many buffalo. After the sun rises, it will be time for the hunt."

As the elected hunting chief, it was Tall Trees' duty to organize the hunt. No hunter or pony could proceed with the hunt without his say so. It was his duty to enforce the rules of the hunt.

The sun would rise in a few hours providing the hunters time to prepare themselves and their ponies.

"Send a runner to the village and tell them of the coming hunt."

The runner left for the village immediately. Even before the hunt would begin, the woman from the village would be on their way.

It would take the village the rest of the night and half of the next day to reach the hunters.

Early morning came as Tall Trees braided his pony's tail and tied it up with a brightly colored piece of dyed leather. Opening a leather pouch, he removed small bundles of colored cream. He covered his palm with a bright red cream and placed in firmly upon the chest of his horse. Before the paint dried, he pressed his hand just behind the first mark, leaving a second hand imprint on his horse. This symbolized that he had fought in hand-to-hand combat with an enemy.

Upon his horse's forehead he made several slash marks one below the other to symbolize he had counted coup upon his enemies.

It was good medicine to display one's accomplishments upon his horse during the hunt.

Tall Trees gently tapped his pony upon the side of his neck.

"You are a good hunter my friend. Both of our lives depend upon your skill this day. I have trained you well and you have learned well. Now is the time to show what you have learned."

Tall Trees tied a piece of leather upon his pony's back and tied a feather to the leather guide tied around his muzzle.

"Once again, my friend, we will go on the hunt together. We will be victorious and kill many buffalo for our people and have many hides for a new tipi."

He thought of Deseray.

Tall Trees spoke to his pony as a form of honor for his sure-footedness and his loyalty. Once they were in the middle of the rushing herd of horned buffalo, Tall Trees' life would depend upon the skills his hunting pony had learned and upon his own balance and skills as a hunter.

Tall Trees painted a few lines upon his cheeks and tied his

hair back away from his face.

After each hunter completed his preparations for the hunt, they mounted their ponies, riding in the direction the promising herd. The scout sent to locate the herd soon returned. The band of hunters followed the scout who led them to the grazing herd.

As they approached the herd, they dismounted and crept closely to the ground until they came to the top of a ridge that kept them out of sight of the heard.

The wind was coming from the direction of the rising sun. To prevent the herd from catching the scent of the hunters, they approached from the opposite side of the revealing wind.

The hunters returned to their ponies, circle to the south and rode in as close as possible before the herd could notice them coming.

A cow with a calf near the edge of the herd bellowed a warning and broke into a run.

Tall Trees kicked his pony. The hunters knew that the hunt had begun. He raced into the now running herd. He no longer held the reins of his pony, as he needed his hands free to take an arrow from his quiver, place it in his bow and aim. He locked his knees tight to his pony's sides and relied upon his pony's abilities to prevent them from being gored by the buffalo horns.

It was Tall Trees' riding skills that prevented him from falling off as his pony veered from side to side, avoiding either a running buffalo or an attaching one.

Releasing his first arrow, it pierced the neck of a big bull. He tumbled to the ground, his chest colliding against the earth with great force. His legs twitched for a moment and then he lay motionless. Tall Trees did not wait to watch the buffalo surrender his life. He continued the hunt. He carried only enough arrows in his quiver to mark the number that would satisfy his needs, no more. He had to make each one count.

The hunters wearied as they continued the hunt. The herd was large and there were plenty to kill. More than they would need. When the hunt yielded enough to satisfy the needs of the village, Tall Trees announced the end of the hunt. It would be a great dishonor to the buffalo to continue the hunt if it meant the waste of buffalo lives.

The tired hunters and ponies were now unable to continue the hunt.

Miles and miles of the rolling prairies were dotted with the carcasses of the dead buffalo.

Tall Trees dismounted his pony. Each of his arrows had resulted in a killed buffalo and as he looked into his quiver, it was empty. His hunt had been successful.

"The Spirits favored us this day. It was a good hunt. Now we must seek our dead and wounded. The women will be here soon."

Several hunters remounted their ponies to complete the grim task of gathering up the wounded and dead because of the dangerous hunt.

Tall Trees had noticed a young hunter, White Tail fell from his pony during the hunt after a large bull had gorged his pony. He had not noticed if White Tail had escaped severe injury.

He did not have to wonder long, as hunters carried White Tail's injured body into the small camp. He was severely injured, but not dead. The medicine man, Spirit Walker, examined him.

"His injuries are great, but he will live. Bring him to the shade and I will tend his wounds."

The warriors placed White Tail in the sparse shade of a few scrawny trees and left him to the care of the medicine man.

Two hunters lost their lives during the hunt and three injured. White Tail's injuries were the most severe. The families of the dead hunters would now become the concern of the whole village. No one in the village would starve or be naked due to the loss of the family hunter. It was the way of their village. Tall Trees was the hunter for three families who no longer had a warrior to hunt for them. Today there would be two more families in need of a hunter.

It troubled Tall Trees to have to tell the families of the loss of their loved one, but as the Hunting Chief, it was his duty to do so.

Soon after the hunt was completed, the woman appeared on the horizon.

The hunters timed the start of the hunt to allow time for the woman to arrive as soon as the hunt ended. Once the rider reached the village to bring the message that hunt would begin, the village was spurred into activity.

Deseray wasn't sure what to expect from the news but was up and moving with everyone else. Some of the women began to remove all their personal belongings from their tipis and piled them outside.

Woman Who Sings said nothing to Deseray, but Deseray seemed to understand what her task was, simply by copying her actions. It seems that the tipi of Woman Who Sings was one of the tipis for use during the hunt. The size and type of poles used for tipis was hard to find, so tipi poles were used to make the temporary travois needed to return the meat to the village.

Woman Who Sings had five horses and Deseray had one.

After removing the lodge poles, the huge covering fell to the ground. Woman Who Sings and Deseray tugged the huge hide flat onto the ground, folding it several times.

The largest tipi poles formed a travois. Deseray harnessed the travois to her horse. Several women pulled the huge hide onto the poles, lashing it into place along the pole's edges.

As the group effort of preparing the horses for the journey continued, it was surprising how quickly the task was completed. Of course, the dogs would also pull smaller travois.

On top of the dog travois, Woman Who Sings placed some change of clothes, a water supply and her tools she would need to cut and skin the buffalo.

She turned to Deseray.

"The hunt was close so the whole village does not have to move. The older women will remain here to care for the children and elderly. Please take my daughter to the home of my cousin, Young Doe, who will care for her while we are gone."

Upon Deseray's return, she found a line of horses already on the move toward the hunting grounds. Woman Who Sings had sensed for some time that Deseray lacked the stamina of the rest of the women her age.

"You may ride the horse if you choose."

Deseray noticed that no other women rode any of the horses.

"No, I am fine. I will enjoy the walk."

Woman Who Sings smiled at Deseray with a great sense of pride.

Half the night passed as the women continued the journey. The brightness of the moon guided their way. They did not stop, even for food. They drank water as they walked. Still, they did not ride the horses.

"The horses must be strong to carry the hides and meat back to the village." Women Who Sings explained to her.

Her feet ached and she felt her energy draining. As the sun emerged from the horizon, a lone rider met the caravan of women.

"You are close. The hunt will soon begin," he said, and he rode away in the direction of the upcoming hunt.

Women Who Sings handed Deseray a change of clothes.

"These will be more comfortable to work in. Change and then we will go and get the meat when the hunt is done."

Other women were changing their clothes as they prepared themselves for the butchering of the buffalo. They simply slipped off their "good" clothes and put on the old ones.

It took some forcing on her part, but Deseray managed to overcome her great shyness and slipped off the dress she was wearing and put on the butchering one.

The clothes were clean but darkened and stained with blood.

Women Who Sings laid down in the grass.

"The hunt has not yet begun," she said, "We will rest until

the hunt is over."

As they women sleep, it reminded Deseray of a "power nap" people would take in her time.

Great rumbling from the ground that seemed to pulsate through her entire body disturbed her sleep. Almost as soon as she opened her eyes, a rider appeared.

"The hunt has begun," he announced and rode away.

The women quickly gathered their needs and walked toward the direction of the hunt.

Upon cresting a small ridge and the vast prairie that lay before them was covered with dead buffalo.

Woman Who Sings shaded her eyes against the sun.

"The men have not returned from the end of the hunt. They are looking for the injured and dead. When they return, the men will help with the cutting up of the buffalo."

She offered no more to Deseray but walked from buffalo to buffalo searching for the arrows of her husband and those of Tall Trees.

"The hunt looks to be a good one," she said, " let us hope our men were among the lucky ones to have a good hunt."

Women Who Sings handed Deseray a flattened stone with an extremely sharp edge. It looked similar to the stones she had used to scrape hides, but with a much narrower edge and definitely much sharper.

Woman Who Sings stopped by a large bull.

"Tall Trees", she said as she bent down near the animal.

Since Tall Trees was the hunting leader, it seemed likely that he would kill the first one.

Deseray noticed a large hole cut into the buffalo.

"Why is there such a large hole in the buffalo?" Deseray asked.

"It is our customs for the hunter to eat the liver of his first kill. It is strong medicine."

Deseray swallowed hard as she imagined Tall Trees tearing out the liver and eating it raw while it was still warm.

She had a lot to learn so she watched Woman Who Sings

with committed attention.

With great skill and expertise, she began to cut the buffalo down the center from the neck to the groin. Entrails, liquid, and blood spilled out on to the ground. She quickly found the intestines and began pushing the organs inside.

Deseray felt sick as she watched. She did not dare cover her mouth as the nausea crept up from her stomach. She had never seen an animal skinned before. The smell of warm blood made her want to gage as Women Who Sings reached her hand inside of the buffalo as though she were looking for something particular. Soon she pulled out the buffalo stomach. She forced one end of it open, catching blood before it landed on the ground. She watched as the other women caught blood in the stomach pouches as well.

When the stomach was full, Women Who Sings tied the ends to prevent to blood from escaping. The women worked throughout the day and well into the night until the majority of buffalos had been cut opened and the blood run out of them. It was important to do this so the animals would not bloat and ruin the meat.

Covered with dried blood, Deseray's stomach was still unsettled. Deseray stuffed liver, organs, hearts, and other internal parts into the intestines for safekeeping.

Deseray could feel her hair matting as the blood dried to her head and body. The smell was overpowering, and she realized how difficult it was to get used to the smell.

Her arms and hands began to ache, but she continued to follow Women Who Sings, going from animal to animal looking for a familiar arrow. Deseray tucked the filled intestines inside layers of meat, as were the tongue and the brains. Also placed within the folds of meat was the decapitated heads containing the hump portion of the shoulders needed for a variety of future use.

The women worked well into the night, using torches to see. Once all the buffalo were opened, they stopped. The cold night air kept the meat cool enough to allow the women to eat and rest before they continued work. It was important to save as much meat as possible.

As Deseray sat with her food, she had no desire to eat. She was covered in dried blood and her nausea had not improved. She never imagined butchering the buffalo would be so physically demanding. She slept without eating.

As soon as the slightest amount of light appeared in the morning, the woman continued their work.

"Now we must remove the hides and cut up the meat." Woman Who Sings explained to Deseray.

"All parts of the buffalo has a purpose," she continued, "the tendons remained within the sections of meat to keep them moist. If they became dried, they would be brittle and useless. When we return to the village," Women Who Sings instructed Deseray, "The tendons will be stripped from the legs and stored in moist pouches until used."

Deseray continued to fight her nausea as she carefully followed Women Who Sings instructions as she began to carve at the layer of fat and skin that secured the hide to the animals. Slowly she carved, peeled, carved, and peeled until the hide began to separate from the body. This continued until the hide separated from one-half of the animal.

Women Who Sings then began to cut large portions of the meat away from the huge body and piled it up upon the ground.

As though as magic, when it was time to turn the huge buffalo, Tall Trees and Cries In The Wilderness suddenly appeared. He said nothing to Deseray, only smiled as the butchering continued. Deseray was relieved to see that he had survived the hunt.

The strength of the men to turn the huge animals during skinning increased the speed the women were able to work. The lit torches allowed them to work long into the night. Once again, the cool night air helped to keep the meat from spoiling as quickly.

As the sun rose and they could carry no more, a new procession led the way back to village.

The ponies and dogs pulled their heavy loads as the exhausted women walked along side.

By late evening, they arrived at the village. Everyone soon became involved in the distribution and preparation for the drying and storage of the meat.

Deseray was exhausted. She wondered how everyone kept going, even without sleep. It did not seem to affect anyone but her.

That night would be a night for celebration and stories to tell.

As Deseray helped Women Who Sings unload the last of the meat from the travois, the erection of the tipi began. Once Women Who Sings' tipi stood tall against the sky, Deseray was amazed at how quickly the dwelling had returned to its original place.

Women Who Sings returned her possessions to the inside.

"I am going to my cousins to get my daughter. Please make sure the meat is well covered for the night."

As Deseray finished pulling the heavy, fleshy hides over the piles of meat, she felt a hand on her shoulder.

It was Tall Trees.

"Come with me."

Deseray felt sticky with blood. Some of it had refused to dry. The dried blood flaked off her skin as she moved. Her clothes were completely covered.

The stench from her body combined with the stink of all the blood was overwhelming. She desperately wanted so badly to take a nice, hot bath, in a real tub.

"The moon is full," He said, "and the water in the river is warm. You can bath there."

"I was worried for you today. Someone had said hunters had been injured or killed. I prayed you were not one of them."

Tall Trees smiled at her.

"Never."

When they reached the river, Tall Trees sat under a small grove of trees and Deseray continued to the river's edge.

"I will wait here."

Deseray felt shy about bathing in the river, as she was certain someone would see her. Yet it wasn't such a big deal to anyone else. After all, they had spent their entire lives bathing in the river. The desire to get the blood washed off helped her to overcome the reluctance.

Deseray left her bloody clothes on as she entered the water. The dry caked blood made it almost impossible to remove them without washing off the dried blood first. Tall tress was right.

The water was warm. After removing her clothes, she set them on the riverbank and slowly walked back into the water. She was still amazed at the warmth of the water. Usually rivers fed by the mountains were cold, but this river was warm. She lowered herself into the water and finally dunked under. It felt good to wash off the stickiness and foul smell as the water relaxed her sore aching body.

The thought of putting the washed but blood-stained clothes back on made Deseray cringe. As she went to get her clothes that she had placed on the riverbank, she discovered that the bloody clothes were gone, and her original clean clothes had taken their place.

Tall Trees was nowhere in sight.

Deseray got dressed and began to walk toward the village. Before she knew it, Tall Trees was walking next to her.

"Let us not return to the village yet."

He took her hand and guided her back toward the river.

Hanging on the trees were her slaughtering clothes, washed the best they could be and hanging out to dry.

She smiled at the thought that Tall Trees had done women's work just for her. She never mentioned it to him though. Some things were best left unsaid.

As they stood looking at the moon, Deseray noticed how closely Tall Trees was standing next to her. She could hear him as he breathed.

"Did you learn much today?"

"I learned that I don't like the smell of blood and that the women work very long and hard each day."

"I spoke to my sister. She tells me you worked as hard as any of the other women. She tells me that you endured much today and made her proud. You have made me proud as well."

Facing her for a moment, he kissed her on her forehead.

Deseray's heart quickened at his closeness. His display of affection for her caused her body to tingle. She could feel her face become flushed and hoped that in the moonlight, Tall Trees would not notice.

"There will be much celebration this night. It was a good hunt. The family of the dead will mourn and will be remembered as we celebrate not only the hunt, but the lives that were given for the good of all."

"Do many hunters die during the hunt?"

"Each time is different. The size of the herd and the skill of the hunters decide if anyone dies or becomes injured. Someone always becomes injured, but not always does someone die."

"How can you celebrate if someone has died?"

"Our village will not go hungry this winter. The celebration is to show thanks to the buffalo that gave their lives for my people. A hunter and their family know that hunters do not return from the hunt. It is our way of life and we accept it. The hunter is prepared to die before he leaves."

As they reached the village, the celebration had begun. A huge fire burned in the center of the circle of people. In a smaller circle around the fire, dancers where circling to the sound of the beating drums. Dancers dressed in colorful clothes chanted along with the drummers, whopping and screaming their joy.

The circle of dancers moved clockwise to the beat of the drums. It was a pow-wow in celebration of the successful hunt. Male dancers wore porky roaches on their heads that bobbled back and forth, as they danced. Circular bustles made of eagle feathers adorned their lower backs as they spun and dived, each one performing their own personal dance.

Some of the women dancers jingled as they moved, causing the shells that adorned their dresses to hit each pother making a festive sound. Other dresses were adorned with carefully planned patterns created from dyed porcupine quills sewn into patterns to display each one's personal expression.

Ankle bracelets decorated with bits of bone and shells added to the festive sound as the young girls danced with enthusiastic vibrancy, swirling with their arms in the air circling and half circling as the beat of the drums filled their souls.

As the drummers played, they sang songs to honor the buffalo and songs to honor the brave hunters. They sang songs to honor Mother Earth for her generosity to them.

The smell of roasting meat filled the air as everyone gorged themselves on the fresh buffalo meat. Dogs lay contently gnawing on the bones that had been tossed there way.

Hunters told many stories of their bravery of that day. They told stories of how each had conquered and slain the beasts. As they told their stories of the great creatures, Deseray could sense the reverent respect each felt for the spirit of the buffalo they had slain.

Deseray sat quietly at a distance as she watched all the activity around her. Part of her wanted to dance too, while another part of her just wanted to sit and watch and learn. As she watched the families share their joy, she began to miss her own family. Tears fell down her cheeks as she thought of them. They must wonder what has happened to me, she thought. Suddenly she wished she could go home right now.

She wondered if she would ever be able to go home.

The past two days had been long and tiring ones for her, so she laid her head down for a moment to rest. The ground felt cool and refreshing and she was soon asleep.

When she woke the next morning, the only thing left of the evening's celebration was the great fire, which smoldered in the center of the village.

A buffalo hide covered her, protecting her from the chill of the morning air. As she looked around, she saw a couple of dogs fighting over a bone while another dog sat quietly, chewing on his prize, a piece of meat.

Tall Trees lay next to her, who had been quietly watching her as she slept.

"Did you sleep well?"

"Yes, surprisingly, I did. Why didn't you wake me so I could sleep in the tipi?"

"I thought about it, but last night was the first night Women Who Sings has seen her husband, Cries In The Wilderness for some time. I knew they would want to spend some time together and I was not sure how comfortable you would be sleeping near them as they visited."

Deseray blushed.

"I was always near," he smiled. "I am your protector, remember?"

Deseray removed the buffalo hide and handed it to Tall Trees.

"This is yours?"

"You may keep it, as a gift."

"Thank you." Deseray replied as she hugged the hide close to her.

Her affection for Tall Trees grew with each passing day. She enjoyed looking at his face and his closeness made her feel safe and comforted in such a wild world.

His presence also helped to ease the pain she felt as she thought of her family. She missed them but felt powerless about her return to her own time, wondering if that time would ever come.

Her heart ached as she thought of her return to her own time. She knew she was falling in love with Tall Trees and she felt a great closeness to Women Who Sings and her daughter. At the same time, she missed her own family. She knew she could not have both worlds and knew the Spirits would make that choice for her.

Tall Trees sat closely near Deseray as he spoke. She enjoyed his closeness.

"There will be much to do this day. The hides will need to

be scraped and the meat must be dried for winter storage."

"It seems to me," Deseray replied, "That everyone works very hard all the time. When do you enjoy life?"

"We enjoy life every day," he said. "Being able to place my hand upon the earth or being able to see the eagle in flight is enjoyment. If we have enough meat for winter and a warm fire and the cold and snow of winter is kind to us, we find many times of joy. During the months of snow, we repair our weapons, make our tools and carve new pipes. Our women and girls have time to do their quillwork, sew new clothes and play with the children. The men hunt for any fresh meat we can find and hopefully have furs of other animals for pouches and linings for our winter clothing."

"My sister will teach you how to scrape the hides and tan them for clothes. She believes my hides from the recent hunt will make a good tipi for this winter."

As Deseray and Tall Trees talked, the village began to wake and was soon bustling with activity.

"Do males ever live alone?"

"Not usually. Even the medicine man has a wife. Why do you ask?"

"Because you said your sister believes that your hides would make a good tipi for this winter."

Before Tall Trees could answer, Women Who Sings was approaching them. Tall Trees and Deseray rose to their feet.

Women Who Sings looked at Deseray.

"You sleep well?" She had a glow in her eyes as she asked.

"Very well."

"This is good, as we have much to do this day."

Like every day, Deseray thought to herself.

Woman Who Sings motioned in the direction of her tipi. "Breakfast is ready in the tipi. After you have eaten, we will begin."

Deseray smiled at Tall Trees as he disappeared across the village. She put the hide he had given to her in the tipi and ate the food she found waiting for her.

Women Who Sings' daughter had spent the night visiting with her grandmother, and she was now on her way to pick her up. Deseray had no idea where Cries In The Wilderness was. She had no idea what he even looked like, as she had not yet met him.

By the time she finished, Woman Who Sings entered the tipi with her daughter of whom she bundled into some furs to allow her to sleep. She motioned Deseray to follow her.

She was carrying the clothes they had worn while processing the buffalo on the prairie.

"I will teach you how to clean your clothes after a hunt. We must go to the river."

Once they arrived at the river, Deseray expected her to put the clothes in the water. Instead, she laid them on the ground and began digging a hole near the river's edge.

She smiled at Deseray as she continued her digging.

"I am digging for white clay. It is the best for cleaning tanned hides."

Upon discovering the sought-after material, Woman Who Sings began rubbing the moist wet clay into the fabric of the hide clothing.

Deseray followed her lead and proceeded to rub the clay into her own clothes.

Woman Who Sings gathered the clay-soaked clothes into her arms and headed back to camp. As they walked, she continued the instructions for Deseray.

"After the white clay is dried, you will need to brush all of it from the clothes. The wet clay will have absorbed the blood and dirt as it dries. You then brush it away as you remove the dried clay."

Deseray was impressed.

After laying the mud-laden clothing out to dry, Woman Who Sings led Deseray to a large pile of buffalo hides they had left near the tipi. Already, the flies were swarming around the hides, dinning on the flesh that still clung to them.

"Stake these hides in this area and stake them with the

hair side down. Make it as tight as you can to prevent the hide from shrinking. I will instruct you how to scrape them properly,"

"You will need water as you work. These hides are fresh, but you can see they already begin to dry. If the hide becomes to dry, put water on it as you work. "

Deseray was still trying to get used to the smell of raw buffalo flesh and hair laden hides. She didn't think she ever would. As she dragged the heavy hides across the grass and began to stretch them out, she tried not to think about the smell.

Women Who Sings gave her a flat edged bone. The bone had been sharpened by rubbing it against a rough surface, such as a rock, to form it into smooth edge. She used the sharpened edge to scrape flesh and hair from the hides.

Deseray secured the hides in place with sharpened wooden pegs and kneeled on one hide and with Women Who Sings careful instructions, began scraping the clinging flesh from the hide. The flies buzzed all about her as she worked. She found them extremely annoying but refused to let anyone know of her bother.

As she held the fleshing tool in her hand, she was amazed at its design efficiently. She had seen such tools in archives, but they were naturally very old and worn. It was fascinating for her to think, that maybe someday, this tool could be unearthed, maybe even by her, in search of the past.

Dogs stood around her, waiting as she scraped and removed the flash, leaving little piles the dogs scampered for and consumed. The dogs seemed to get the most enjoyment from the hunt. It was the only time they ate so well.

As Deseray scraped the hides, Woman Who Sings began slicing the meat into strips. She carefully placed the slices of meat onto drying racks.

"We will make some of the meat into pemmican which will get us through the winter," explained Woman Who Sings.

Chapter Ten - A Forever Promise

Preparation for the many preservation techniques took place in the days that followed the hunt. Deseray watched as Women Who Sings carefully cut the thick hump and shoulder area of the buffalo hide she was working on. She held out the thick hide for Deseray to examine.

"Tall Trees will take this to the medicine man to have him make a new war shield for him. A war shield made by the Shaman has powerful medicine. Tall Trees is a great warrior and a great provider. You will do well to take him as your husband."

Deseray still found the idea of being married very frightening. She had been with the people for over two months and had adjusted to many of their ways. She still thought of herself from her own time, a time when she had no plans of marriage. In this time, she realized that it was expected that at her age to be married. Still, she was finding it difficult to accept the idea of sharing a husband with another wife. She found many things in this life-style hard to understand. They worked and lived together with respect and honor and took care of each other. No one went hungry or was left in need.

"Does Otter Tail favor Tall Trees?"

"She does, very much, ever since they were young children. She is much younger than my brother, but as she becomes a woman, her interest in him grows."

"Does she resent me for being favored by Tall Trees?"

"She does not. She has told me she thinks that your household as Tall Trees' first wife and she as the second wife would be a strong family."

The thought of her marriage to Tall Trees filled Deseray

with a special joy. Yet the joy was overshadowed by the fact that she was not from this time and wondered if or when she would return to her own time.

Woman Who Sings seemed to sense Deseray's thoughts about her marriage to Tall Trees.

"The hides from a summer hunt make the best lodge covers. They are the easiest to clean since the fur is much thinner. There are enough hides here to make a new lodge for you and Tall Trees."

Deseray looked at all the work that lay in front of them but had a sudden need to speak with Tall Trees. Women Who Sings seemed to sense her need.

"He is on watch for the enemy. You can find him near the horses."

"But all this work?" Deseray exclaimed.

"I will continue to work until your return," she said. "Go now."

Deseray laid her tool on the hide she had been working on. She wiped her hands on the grass to rid herself of the blood that clung to them. It wasn't perfect, but again, it was the way things were done.

As she made her way across the village, in the distance, she could see new scaffolding that would hold the dead. Her heart ached for the relatives who had lost loved ones. As they placed the bodies upon the scaffolds, personal possessions were laid with them. Things like favorite bows and arrows for the men, beautiful beadwork for the women and favorite toys for the children. Each also received a pouch of tobacco to honor the Spirits along their journeys to the other world.

Tall Trees was sitting upon a huge pile of boulders. Deseray climbed carefully to prevent falling as she made her way to his side.

A smile crossed Tall Trees' face as he watched her approach him.

"It must be important that you would climb on the rocks to speak to me."

Deseray sat close to him.

"It is important. I have many questions that I cannot find the answers."

"I do not know if I have the answers either."

Deseray enjoyed looking at Tall Trees. His presence made her feel safe and content.

Deseray wasn't sure how to open the conversation about her possible marriage to Tall Trees, so she just blurted it out.

"Woman Who Sings speaks of your marriage to me. I don't know if I can return to my own time."

"I do not know if you can return to your own time or not. The Spirits have not told me this."

He was quiet for a moment.

"If you can not return to your own time, you must take a husband. If you do not favor me, you may favor another."

Deseray laughed.

"Of course, I favor you."

Tall Trees bent close to Deseray and whispered softly.

"I favor you."

His lips softly touched hers. Her heart pounded quickly as she yearned for another kiss. Tall Trees felt the same desire and pressed his lips against hers more completely and passionately then the first time.

Tall Trees spoke softly in her ear.

"We will live our lives as though there is no tomorrow. When tomorrow comes, we will deal with it, only then. I love you. I do not want to see you return. I am not concerned if you someday return to your own time. We must live our lives in the present as though you may live the rest of your life in this time. If the day comes when you must return, we will face that day when we must. Not now."

Tall Trees held her close to his body. The smell of him transcended her into a world where only the two of them mattered. She so loved him that the thought of leaving him made her heart ache.

"Before I came here, I dreamed of you." Deseray said softly.

"I did not know it was you at the time. I know now. Why I am here, I can't answer, but I am here. You are right. I need to live in the present as the present is all I have."

Tall Trees faced Deseray. The love in his eyes penetrated her soul. She knew he was a good man. She felt that if her mother knew him, she would share her joy.

"I miss my family. My heart feels saddened when I think of them. I know they have not been born yet, neither have I for that matter. When I think of being married, I miss them even more because I want to share my joy with them."

Tall Trees gently placed his arm around her shoulder.

"I am sad for you that you miss your family. You have been here a short time. We can wait a time longer before you decide to marry. Among my people, the proper way to ask you to be my wife is to ask your father or brother and then present them with fine furs or fine ponies. You have no family here, so I have no one to ask but you."

Tall Trees paused, "When I think the time is right, I shall ask you to marry me. Not until then. I will approach Cries In the Wilderness, as you live with them and they are as your family."

Deseray did not speak again. She simply smiled lovingly at Tall Trees.

"The spirits will tell me and then I will tell you." Tall Trees kissed Deseray on the forehead and left her with her thoughts.

The days turned into weeks and the weeks became months, and Deseray remained in the past with the people she learned to love.

While working the hides on a warm day, of which Deseray believed to be September, Deseray smiled. The hides from the summer hunt were cleaned and ready to become a tipi.

Woman Who Sings taught her well.

She carefully inspected Deseray's work.

"You have learned well. My brother had better ask for you to be his wife. I have heard there are a few young men ready to ask. He may lose you if he is slow. Since you live with me and my husband, it would be proper for them to ask One Who Cries In The Wilderness. I will mention it to my brother."

Woman Who Sings' smile was mischievous.

Deseray smiled. It seemed that the Spirits were not sending her home. She knew she had to have a life in this time. She too, hoped Tall Trees would soon ask.

Women Who Sings planned her encounter with Tall Trees a few days later.

"Have the Spirits told you that it is time to take Dry Sands as your wife? Many are waiting in line."

Tall Trees looked at his sister.

"You speak boldly for a woman."

"No, I speak boldly as a sister." She simply smiled and returned to the village.

The next morning as Woman Who Sings and Deseray worked on the hides near the tipi, they noticed laughing and sound of cheer coming from the end of the village. Cries In The wilderness emerged from the tipi and stood near Woman Who sings. Soon they saw Tall Trees leading two beautiful horses through the village.

He stopped in front of Deseray.

Tall trees handed the reins to Cries In The Wilderness

"This is for payment at the loss of Deseray's work for you."

He took the reins, which was the customary way of accepting Tall Trees proposal to marry Deseray. The village sounded with joyful cheers.

Tall Trees whispered into Deseray's ear, "Will you be my wife?"

She replied softly.

"Yes, I will be your wife."

Woman Who Sings smiled.

"I have no need of you right now," she told Deseray. "You two should speak of your upcoming marriage."

She led the horses away.

Tall Trees and Deseray walked to the river.

Tall Trees held her close.

"I have longed to be one with you since I first saw you in your own time. When the Spirits brought you to my time, my desire for you has grown each day. I find it hard to wait until we are joined as husband and wife to feel your body next to mine."

Deseray was surprised that she and Tall Trees were actually taking about making love as they sat on the rocks watching the ponies graze.

She could feel the quickening of his heart and the labor of his breathing.

His desire for her was obvious to her, but she wanted their first time together to be the most special moment she would experience in her life.

Deseray blushed. "As much as I long for you, I would like to wait until we are married."

"I find it hard to wait until we are joined as husband and wife. I speak of this, so you do not fear our wedding night."

Deseray was touched at his concern as to whether she had not been with another man.

"Would it displease you if I told you I have been with another?"

Tall Trees squeezed her tightly.

"Not at all, I know your ways are different from our ways," he paused, "I have been with another woman. It will make our joining more pleasant as I will not worry about hurting you, as happens with some woman. Then they learn to hate the joining."

"What do we do now?" Deseray asked. "Is there a ceremony?"

"We must announce our desire to the village that we will be joined. The medicine man will say marriage prayers over us as he binds our wrist to each other. As the blanket is wrapped around us, we will become one. After this, we simply go away on our own. When we return, we will return as husband and wife."

"That's all there is? How long do we stay away?"

"We stay away for as long as we decide. We use this time

to discover each other's thoughts and desires. It is also the time we use to discover each other's bodies to learn what brings each of us pleasures."

Deseray blushed.

"Where do we sleep while we are away?"

"I have a small tipi I used for long journeys. It is not suitable for a lodge, but suitable for our needs."

Anticipation of her marriage to Tall Trees surged throughout Deseray.

"All but one hide is ready for a tipi. But I want to marry before the lodge making."

Tall Trees grabbed Deseray into his arms and kissed her firmly on the mouth.

"I do not want to wait. Go now and tell Women Who Sings that the hides from my summer hunt will be used to make our new lodge after we are married."

As she cheerfully made her way back to the village, she wondered if she had done the right thing. She had no idea if she would ever return to her own time and longed to be a part of the life she now lived. She did not want to continue to be a burden to Woman Who Sings and her family. She longed for a family of her own. She decided that marrying Tall Trees was the right thing to do.

The glow of joy radiated from Deseray's eyes as she approached Woman Who Sings who had continued working on the hides.

She greeted Deseray with a warming smile.

Woman Who Sings embraced Deseray.

"I will be honored to have you for my sister. There is much work to do to finish these hides for your lodge party. Will you marry soon?"

"Tall Trees wishes it. As do I. We want to marry first. Upon our return we will make our new lodge and move in."

Deseray placed her hand on Women Who Sings' arm.

"I am concerned that I will not make Tall Trees proud. I still have much to learn about your people and your ways. I can not explain to you why I do not know these things, but it is important that I learn."

"Since you came to be with my people, you have learned more than you know. I have watched your skills improve with each passing day. I think you are from the Spirit world that has come here to be as one of us so you will know us better. It is my honor to be your teacher. I will teach in a way that no other will notice you do not have certain knowledge of things. You have killed an enemy; among my people this is powerful medicine. No one will question your skills. They already sing songs to honor you. They sing songs to honor my brother. The songs they will sing once you are joined will be the most powerful."

"You must choose who will be the lodge maker. Horse Woman has always been successful and has supervised many happy lodges."

"I choose you, Woman Who Sings, to by my lodge maker."

Woman Who Sings blushed.

"It will be my first. I am honored."

"You will have to instruct me as to how I prepare for the party and what to feed my guests."

A soft sigh escaped from Deseray. "There is so much I need to learn. You are a great teacher, and I am honored to have you to become my sister."

Deseray felt a tinge of pain as she used the word sister. She has always imagined that her sister would stand up for her at her wedding. As she thought about her marriage to Tall Trees, she knew it would not happen. She never imagined that she would marry someone who had lived almost three hundred years before she was born. Her heart ached with sadness that she could not share this important part of her life with her family.

"You will be a beautiful bride for my brother." Woman Who Sings told Deseray as she fumbled with a bundle she had retrieved from a pile of furs.

"I have a gift for you. It is your wedding dress."

Deseray had not thought about a wedding dress. She assumed that a special dress for a marriage was not part of the ceremony.

Woman Who Sings carefully pulled back the furs revealing a dress of a bright red color.

"This was my wedding dress. My mother made it for me. It is made from a deer hide that she carefully tanned so it is soft to the touch. She died it red since red in a wedding dress symbolizes good luck and prosperity. I thought that one day my daughter would wear in for her marriage."

She handed the dress to Deseray.

"I would like you to wear it as well since I seem to be the only family you now have."

Deseray could feel the tears well up in her eyes. She carefully took the dress and gave Woman Who Sings a warm hug.

"Dry Sands, come and try on your wedding dress."

As Woman Who Sings laced the shoulders of the dress closed, she smiled with great pride, not only at the beauty of the dress, but also at the beauty of the person who wore it. The dress fit Deseray snuggly and had fringes that extended nearly to the ground.

Woman Who Sings stood back from Deseray with a huge smile on her face.

"You make a beautiful bride. The dress fits you well. The dress looks good on you."

"Thank you for the use of the dress." Deseray ran her slender fingers along the dress. "I love him very much and I will make him a good wife. Is tomorrow too soon to marry?"

Woman Who Sings smiled. "When you are in love, it is never too soon to marry."

"I'm a little nervous." Deseray admitted as she stepped out of the dress. She had finally gotten used to the practice of not wearing any under clothes, which were worn only in the winter months. She felt no embarrassment, as she stood naked in front of Woman Who Sings.

She quickly dressed into her everyday clothes. With a new sense of pride and purpose, Deseray picked up her fleshing tool and began to earnestly scrape the remaining flesh away from the last hide needed for their new tipi.

She had become quite skilled at it by now and dreamed of the day she and Tall Trees would sleep in their new tipi as husband and wife. Deseray worked until the sun began to set. Without noticing, Tall Trees had been standing near the tipi watching her as she worked. As she stood from her work, she felt his arms entwined about her waist.

He gently kissed her ear and whispered, "Let's sneak away this very moment. I can hardly wait."

Deseray turned and faced him full on, her nose bumping his as she turned.

"What about the public announcement of our intentions?"

"I will announce it this day when we return to the village." he chuckled.

Deseray swatted him gently on the shoulder with her hand.

"Your sister is pleased we will marry."

"So am I. I will make it public this night. Will you be ready to leave tomorrow?"

"What about our own home when we return?"

"We will stay with my sister until our tipi is ready. Is this good for you?"

"Is that the way it is done?"

"Since my sister is the only family you have and she is my family, yes, this is the way it is done."

Deseray looked deeply into the eyes of the man she had fallen in love with.

"Then that is the way it will be. I will prepare for our journey."

Tall Tress left Deseray by herself. She walked to the river so she could clean the scraps of flesh and the smell from her clothes and body. When she finished bathing, she sat on the shore, looking at the stars that had just begun to peek through the darkness of the night sky.

Her thoughts were full of doubt and anticipation. Was

she making a mistake marring Tall Trees? Did she really have a choice? He was right when he hand told her that she had to choose a husband if she were to remain with his people. She did not know if she could return to her own time and knew she had to make a life for herself here in this time. As the moon showed its' golden color, she found peace knowing she could not have chosen a better man to be her husband, in any time.

Shining and happy eyes met Deseray as she returned to the village. Woman Who Sings walked gently hugged her and smiled. Deseray realized that Tall Tress must have made the public announcement of their marriage.

"Tall Trees has been beaming throughout the village ever since he announced your marriage. He is proud."

Deseray rose early the next morning filled with questions for Woman Who Sings, who was already preparing food for the feast that would be a part of the marriage ceremony.

She smiled at Deseray.

"My cousins are helping to prepare the food for the day of celebration. It is our way to feed people all day as the drums play and the young woman dance. It is to honor your marriage."

The information she had just provided Deseray answered her questions. She felt relieved.

"This is a very important day in your life. You will be united with my brother in a way you have never been before. He is a good man and I know he will be gentle. Trust him when he approaches you and remember he loves you."

Deseray decided not to tell Woman Who Sings that she had been with a man before. It was enough that Tall Trees knew and was not bothered.

"I know that Tall Trees will treat me with respect and love on our first night," Deseray assured her.

Woman Who Sings opened a large leather pouch.

"Here is some pemmican, dried meat, and dried berries. Tall Trees is a good hunter. If you stay longer than your food supply," she smiled at Deseray, "he can hunt more food and you can gather some roots."

Deseray laughed to herself as Woman Who Sings placed the provisions into the rough leather pouch.

She had always imagined that for her honeymoon she would have been packing a silky negligee, perfume and a charge card. She was living a life that she never thought possible, but a life she wished for since she was young. It was now her reality and she was learning to accept the many changes better than she had imagined she would.

Woman Who Sings handed the closed pouch to Deseray.

"After the ceremony you would go to your own lodge, but going away together is also a custom, if you do not yet have a tipi. I know Tall Trees has decided this because you new lodge in not yet ready. You will have a good life with my brother."

Deseray hugged Woman Who Sings.

"I know I will."

By the middle of the day many people had already gather in the center of the village. Deseray was dressed in the wedding dress and felt like a bride. She was anxious to see Tall Trees.

When he appeared, bright red material adorned his clothing, and a passionate and proud smile adorned his face.

The feasting, drum music, and dancing of the young woman continued into evening. Reverently the medicine man appeared carrying a strip of red leather. Four of Tall Tree's best friends followed, carrying a blanket.

Tall Tress took Deseray by the hand and stood in front of the medicine man.

She felt nervous but Tall Trees seemed remarkably calm.

The medicine began to chant his prayers for the couple, as he tied their wrist together. He continued his prayers, as the four friends wrapped the blanket around the couple.

As the medicine man finished his prayers, he released the tie from their wrists. A loud cheer rose from all the people.

As the blanket fell to the ground, Deseray looked into Tall Tress' eyes. She felt a wondrous transition, as she truly became his wife.

As everyone continued the celebration, Tall Trees took

his leave of Deseray. As he did, he gently kissed her forehead and said, "I will return soon."

Deseray went to the tipi to get her belongings. As she stepped outside, she could see Tall Trees approaching, leading three ponies. One of the ponies was dragging a small travois with a large bundle. Deseray suspected that the bundle was the small tipi they would occupy on their trip.

She also recognized one of the ponies being lead as Tall Tress' favorite horse, the other one she had never seen before. As he neared her, Tall Trees handed her the lead.

"This will be your pony, as a wedding gift from me." You have killed an enemy and have earned the right to own ponies. He is yours."

Deseray was pleased to own another horse that was hers. Women usually did not own horses. They owned the lodges they lived in and all the possessions inside. Men owned horses, weapons, and pipes.

Before mounting her horse, she secured the leather pouch of food to the travois. She felt a degree of importance as she sat upon her own horse.

As they left the village, Deseray was aware they were traveling northeast. Tree covered ridges surrounded shallow ravens as they traveled. Intermingled amongst the tree coverage were areas of prairie grass and ground hogs scurrying from hole to hole as the strangers approached.

"Be careful and do not let your pony stepped into a groundhog hole. It will cripple your horse."

Deseray laughed to herself as she remembered that her uncle John had told her the same thing as they had approached the first dig sight.

Excitement and anticipation filled Deseray as she rode alongside of Tall Trees. He looked forward as they traveled, as though he were looking for some particular location or landmark. Peace and freedom surrounded them as they traveled. The horses' unshod hooves gently striking the ground sounded with gentle taps upon the earth, quietly blending in with their

THE WHITE BUFFALO'S FEATHER

surroundings.

Deseray continued to understand the enjoyment of life Tall Trees had tried to explain to her. Serenity with one's self and with mother earth brought a degree of enjoyment that she had only experienced when she had chosen to. In this time and with this lifestyle, it was a way of life, as long as people allowed themselves to be aware of the beauty and tranquility that surrounded them every day.

Continuing northeast, a feeling of familiarity slowly began to dominate Deseray's senses. Within a few more minutes of travel, Deseray saw the source of her feelings of familiarity. She pulled her horse to a full stop and stared. Tall Trees stopped as well and smiled at her.

"I know you are from the Spirits as I can see you already know this sacred place."

"Yes, I do."

Her heart swelled with homesickness and comfort at the same time.

"In my time we call this place Medicine Rock."

She walked over to the large sandstone formations and placed her hands upon a large boulder. Tall Trees was quickly standing next to her.

"Yes, this is a place of strong medicine. Since my people are so far from our scared Black Hills, we use this place for many of our ceremonies and vision quests."

The very essence of the formations drew Deseray into a state of euphoria, knowing finally that the land in this past time was what she knew as Montana. Knowing this provided the answer to her deeply felt hope, that, a Lakota tribe had lived as far west as Montana. The answer was reveille by the very spot she presently stood.

"Tell me," she said to Tall Trees, "How did your village come to live so far from the Black Hills?"

"My grandfathers' grandfather lived in a village near the Black Hills. He had a brother that was born before him. They were very close in age and grew in skills and cunning at much the same pace. Unknown to each other, they had both fallen in love with the same maiden. When she was presented at the Maiden Festival, the festival in which it is made public that a young girl had become a woman and was ready for marriage. Each brother then made it known that they desired the same maiden."

"The maiden favored the younger brother, my grandfather's grandfather, even before it was made public. She chose him. This hurt and angered the older brother. It also hurt my grandfather to think that a woman could come between them."

"My grandfather's grandfather went to his brother and told him that he loved both the maiden and his brother. To spare his brother the pain of seeing him married to the woman his brother also loved, he told his brother they would leave the village and start a new village out of his vision."

In his anger, the older brother agreed and let his only blood brother leave his life forever."

Tears filled Deseray's eyes as she listened to the story. Her heart ached for her own brother, whom she feared too, would never see again.

Tall Trees took Deseray into his arms.

"I'm sorry this story has saddened you so."

"I'm just thinking of my own brother. Please finish the story."

"My grandfather's grandfather and his new bride were joined by many of her family and some friends. They numbered about 30 people. From this small band of Lakota members, a new village began. They journeyed for one moon until the came to the river where we make our summer camp. It has been that way ever since."

A sigh of wonder escaped from Deseray as Tall Trees finished the story.

"Have the two villages ever gotten together again?"

Only once, since my grandfather's grandfather's time have the two villages joined for celebrations. He decided that enough time had passed, and the wounds of the heart should be healed. Our people join the many in the Black Hills to celebrate the Sun Dance."

Tall Trees touched Deseray's arm, releasing her from the mesmerized frame of mind.

"Tell me your thoughts."

"I was just thinking about my uncle and the expedition. I was wondering if they gave up looking for signs that your tribe did indeed live in this area. History does not record that your tribe even existed."

"I can not answer why signs of my people had not been found. Is this important to you?"

"Now that I have lived here, with you and with your people, it is more important than ever. I wish there were some way I could let my uncle so he could know we have been here."

Tall Trees touched Deseray face.

"I do not know how I can help you. We must find a place to set our camp before the darkness comes."

Tall Trees walked over to the horses, cupping his hands together, offered Deseray help upon her horse.

As she was about to swing herself upon her horse, Tall Trees caught her in his arms and kissed her passionately.

"I love you."

Catching her breath, she smiled.

"I love you too. But you said yourself; we need to make camp before dark."

With powerful arms, he set her upon her horse and laughed.

"Yes, you are right. But just wait until dark!"

Laughing, he mounted his horse, taking up stride next to hers.

"There is a favorite place I know of north of here. A small river forms into a small lake. It is warm enough to bath. It is not used as hunting grounds, so we will be undisturbed."

They rode on in silence the rest of the way. Deseray's was still concerned as to whether she was doing the right thing. She was uncertain about her return to her own time. A sigh of decisive relief expelled from her lips. It was done. She was married to Tall Trees. She felt no regret. She decided to be happy with this new life. She hoped that her family's grief at her loss would heal quickly. For all intent and purpose, in her own time, she was dead. A shiver of realization overcame her.

It had been months since her disappearance, and she was certain that they had stopped looking for her by now. Her heart felt sad at the agony they had gone through, but she was powerless to control the future she had left behind.

Surprisingly abundant trees border the slow-moving stream that lay in front of them. Tall Trees turned his horse south coming upon a clear, emerald hued lake. The absence of wind allowed the stillness of the water's surface to be so undisturbed, it reflected everything around it, as though it were a large mirror.

Dismounting his horse, Tall Trees tethered it to a nearby tree. He then proceeded to unload the travois. Together, they were able to erect the small tipi quickly. Deseray moved the buffalo hides and other belongings inside.

Tall Trees started a small fire for Deseray to use to cook their evening meal. While she was preparing the meal, Tall Trees walked to the river. He removed all of his clothing and bathed fully. Deseray had discovered that this was his evening spiritual ritual to the Great Spirit.

She had discovered that each person had his or her own personal and private way to speak with the Great Spirit. For each, it was a solitary act, never to be shared.

Water still clinging to his hair caused it to hang straight about his shoulders. He wore only his breechcloth, of which caused Deseray to find him exceptionally attractive.

With a smile upon his face, Tall Trees helped himself to the food she had prepared.

"I look forward to our joining tonight. Is the time right for you? You are not afraid?"

Deseray blushed slightly.

"I am not afraid. I am a little nervous, but not afraid."

Deseray eat very little. She placed her food on the stones next to the fire and rose to her feet.

"I think I will bath in the river." Shyly she added.

"Would you like to join me?"

His eyes glistened as he rose to his feet.

"I would."

Together they walked toward the river. The brightness of the moon illuminated the river with a romantic glow. Deseray was convinced that the Spirits had created such an evening just for them. As they neared the river's edge, Tall Trees stopped Deseray by pulling her into his arms.

"I love you." He whispered softly. "I desire you."

Deseray tipped her face toward him and kissed him as she had done in her dreams, softly and longingly.

"I desire you too."

Tall Trees slowly untied the leather ties that secured her dress, allowing the ties to fall away and her dress to slide to the ground. Deseray placed both of her hands on either side of his breechcloth, releasing the ties, causing the breechcloth to take its place on the ground next to her dress.

He kissed her firmly on the mouth as he gathered her into his muscular arms. He carried her into the river, stopping only when both of their bodies were submerged. Their lips remained together as they surfaced, cool water adding to the passion of the prolonged kiss.

His long, wet hair trailed across her skin, the wet tingling adding to her growing desire for him.

Slowly he carried her from the water. With her legs still wrapped about his waist, Tall Trees laid down upon the cool grass. Tall Trees stroked her hair.

"I have waited a long time for this moment. Are you ready to be joined with me and be my wife?"

Deseray's heart pounded rapidly within her chest her desire increased within her body.

"I have dreamed of this. I am ready to join with you and be your wife and you to be my husband,"

Under the bright stars that filled the shy, they became husband and wife.

Tall Trees brushed Deseray's hair from her face.

"You have given me pleasures I never imagined were possible."

"You have also given such pleasures."

He gently kissed her.

Deseray snuggled herself next to Tall Trees, as they regained their strength under the blackened sky now accented with bright dots of light that filled the night sky.

The evening had grown cold as Deseray shivered.

"You are cold. We will go inside and get you warmed."

He helped Deseray to her feet. As they returned to their small camp, they retrieved their

clothing along the way. Tall Trees lifted the flap to the small tipi and allowed Deseray to enter first.

Without getting dressed, they slip under the pile of buffalo hides lying inside the tipi.

The buffalo robe felt comforting against Deseray's skin, defending her against what she assumed to be an August night, which felt exceptionally cold.

The look in Tall Trees' eyes revealed his joy and pleasure in his choice of a wife.

"We can only stay a few suns. Winter is coming and the fall hunt is needed soon. I hope this does not disappoint you."

"It does not. The hides for our new tipi are nearly ready and we will soon be in our own home.

Tall Trees placed his arm around Deseray, and he was soon asleep.

As her new husband lay next to her, she took a moment to ponder the events of her wedding. The simplicity of their marriage commitment was not at all how she had imagined, but not at all disappointing. Little by little, she was discovering the true simplicity of the heart of the American Indian. She felt warm, content, and complete all at once.

She was the wife of Tall Trees and truly now a member of

their tribe.

Early the next morning Deseray awakened to the smell of food cooking.

As she emerged from the tipi, she saw Tall Trees preparing their morning food.

"You should have wakened me. It is my job as your wife to prepare the food."

Tall Trees pulled her close and whispered.

"There is no one to see a man prepare food for his wife. Once we are back at the village, it will not be possible."

Deseray felt privileged by his simple display of love.

As they sat and ate their meal, Tall Trees had a secretive look upon his face.

"What are you thinking?" She asked.

"It is important that your family find items from my people?"

"Yes, if they are still looking."

There is a place near what you call Medicine Rock, which has a small cavern below it. We can put some of our possessions like some arrows and a sheath in this cavern. If we are fortunate, they will find it in their time. Then they will know."

After packing up the horses, Deseray and Tall Trees found their way to Medicine Rock. Just as he had said, there was a small cave beneath the rock formation. In this cave, they placed arrows, a sheath, and some ornamental items.

Deseray sighed, "I hope they will find these items."

Secretly she wished she had paper and a pencil so she could write a note to her uncle to let him know she was fine. The idea seemed inconceivable. Who would believe that she was living in a time hundreds of years before her own birth?

Tall Trees seemed pleased at what they had done.

"Does this make you happy?'

She gently kissed him and replied, "Yes."

Chapter Eleven - Winter Camp

After their return to the village as husband and wife, Deseray continued preparing the hides for her and Tall Trees new tipi.

Under the watchful eyes and careful guidance of Woman Who Sings, the hides would soon be ready.

"You have already removed the hair and all flesh from both sides." Woman Who Sings commented to Deseray, "You have fifteen hides for nice size lodge. It will be a good tipi. After the fall hunt, we will use those hides for bedding. The fur on the hides from the fall hunt is thicker than the summer ones. We will use them as bed coverings and linings for the lower walls and floor of your new lodge to protect you from the snow and cold winds. "

As the days past, Deseray knew winter was coming. She noticed the number of birds migrating south increased each day and the hot days had become cold and the nights even colder.

Finally, the hides were ready for the new lodge that she and Tall Trees would soon share as husband and wife. Since Tall Trees had moved into his sister's lodge after their marriage, Deseray was reluctant to join with him. She was not as open-minded when it came to their practices of joining.

Tall Trees and Cries In The Wilderness had been gone for several days with the hunting party looking for the herd of buffalo that would supplement the people for the long winter months. The meat from the summer hunt was dried or turned into pemmican. Yet, it was not enough. The winter hunt would also provide new clothing and soles for winter shoes, as the fall hide is the thickest and best suited for these needs.

As each day passed, Deseray created more things that she

and Tall Trees would use in their new home.

Deseray was excited when the day arrived when she would make her own parfleches. She made an amazing discovery about these storage bags. Each type of pouch or rawhide bag got its name from its use and named according to their purpose. A household pouch is called wizipan.

Deseray was using the hide from Tall Trees' recent deer kill. After butchering and preserving the meat, Deseray removed all the excess flesh and hair from the hide.

Woman Who Sings gave her distinct directions.

"Cut two pieces this long." The size she indicated was slightly larger than three feet by four feet.

"Once the hide is dry, it will be much smaller," she told Deseray.

Using her fleshing stone, Deseray carefully cut two pieces from the deer hide.

"First we will heat the stones we will need."

They built a large fire and placed many stones into it.

"They will be hot enough once we have the pits dug."

Woman Who Sings handed Deseray a tool for digging.

"We will dig a small pit for each piece."

After digging the two pits, Woman Who Sings continued the lesson.

Using deer antlers as carrying tools, Deseray placed hot rocks into each pit.

""Now stretch the pieces over the pits, but do not stake one side. You will lift that side to add water to the pit. Once they begin to dry, you will have to re-stretch them during the day, so they do not become so small or fall into the pit and burn."

"You must tend the rocks throughout the day and add small amounts of water to the rocks so the fire does not become so hot that it will burn the hide."

Deseray carefully staked the hides over the pits. Deseray knew that this was the same process used to harden the hides for war shields.

By the end of the day, the two pieces were ready to shape into pouches.

"Carefully fold one piece to the other end but leave this much," she indicated about a foot, "for the end of the pouch opening."

Deseray realized it would be the flap on one end of the elongated pouch.

Deseray appreciated the skill of Woman Who Sings as she helped Deseray fashion the deer hide to form the rectangular pouches. The pouches were made in twos. Deseray didn't ask why it was done this way. The bags were lightweight but durable.

Carefully Deseray sewed the pouches with sinew and the pouches were soon the correct size and shape for her needs. She would store her household items in them once she was in her own lodge.

When Deseray thought she had finished, Woman Who sings instructed her to place two holes near the flap end of each pouch.

"When we journey," she said, "you will strap the two of them together and place them on your horse."

Deseray suddenly realized why they were made in twos. They were like saddlebags.

Using already made paint colors she had received from Woman Who Sings, she decorated each bag, to reflect her personal life."

Woman Who Sings stood near Deseray, admiring the paintings adorned upon the pouches.

"These are very interesting designs," she said, "You honor the white buffalo with your paintings. I am a little confused by your repeat the use of an eagle feather."

Deseray smiled as she looked at the pouches.

"The feather is symbolic of my journey here to your people."

Deseray had learned that the paintings on tipis, shields and personal items told the stories of the owner's life, adventures, and accomplishments.

"Tomorrow will be your lodge making. Get some rest for morning will come early. I think it would be a good idea to ask someone to help you to serve your guests. Otter Tail has let me know she would be honored if you were to ask her."

Deseray smiled, "Otter Tail had spoken to you about my marriage to Tall Trees? How does she feel about it?"

"She is happy for both of you. She knows there is still time for Tall Trees to choose her before it is her time to marry. She knows that Tall Trees' importance in the tribe will grow quickly and he will soon need a second wife. She is happy to wait for him to choose her."

Deseray set the two pouches inside the tipi.

"I will go and speak to her now."

As Deseray walked through the village to find Otter Tail, she was amazed at how accepting many of their customs were.

When she arrived at the lodge of Otter Tail's family, she was playing with her baby brother. She rose quickly when she saw Deseray.

"Otter Tail, I would be honored if you would accept my request to help serve my guests at my lodge making."

Otter Tail hugged Deseray with true affection.

"I would be honored to serve your guests. Thank you for asking me!"

It was the first time Deseray had spoken to Otter Tail since the lodge making of Walks Slowly and her new husband.

"I know you will be a wonderful wife for Tall Trees." Otter Tail said.

Deseray smiled.

"I hope I will make him proud. I still have much to learn. After our lodge is up, I would be honored if you visited me. I could learn many things from you."

"I will be happy to teach what I know. Thank you." Otter Tail smiled.

Deseray also smiled.

Deseray liked Otter Tail and decided that if Tall Trees

were to someday chose her as his second wife; she would like to get to know her better. Having her serve at the lodge making would give her the chance to do that.

Morning did come early. Before Deseray realized what was happening, Woman Who Sings began gathering together bundles of food into her arms. She smiled.

"I have prepared much food to feed our guests for the lodge making."

Deseray began to load the prepared hides onto a travois to move them to the site they had chosen to raise their tipi. It was within 50 feet of Woman Who Sings' lodge and she would be Deseray's nearest neighbor.

Everyone soon gathered at the lodge site, eager and ready to help. As they hides formed the tipi cone shape on the ground, the sewing soon began. Visiting and eating made the sewing go quickly. Deseray paid close attention to the stitches and techniques the variety of women used. She did have a little experience with sewing the hides together at the tipi making of Walks Slowly's lodge, but she had been so nervous, she barely remembered what she had even done.

Since it would be her sole responsibility to raise and lower her new tipi and make all necessary repairs, she used this time to learn as much as she could, so she would be well prepared when the time came.

Her thoughts centered on her anticipation and pride of a home for her and Tall Trees. Living with Women Who Sings and her husband was enjoyable, but Deseray was still uncomfortable making love in a room with other people. She would enjoy making love to her husband for the first time in her own lodge.

During her own tipi raising party, Deseray realized how much she had learned since she came to be with the people. She cherished her new friends and now her new family. Women Who Sings proved to be a great lodge maker. As the sun began to set, Deseray stood proudly in front of her own lodge. It was done! She felt great pride. She thanked all of her guests who managed to consume the remainder of the food that had been prepared.

The setting sun silhouetted the crossed branches of the peak of her new home against the red western sky. Deseray felt both joy and sorrow as she realized that this, a tipi, three-hundred years before she was born, was the home of herself and her new husband. Her heart ached to have her mother hold her one more time. A tear of sorrow trickled down her cheek as she thought of her family. She so longed to have been able to share all her newfound joy with them.

Before she could dwell any longer in her self-absorbed pity, she noticed the women slowly drifting away. Their smiles were silly and anticipating. The giggling followed them as they disappeared to their own homes.

Deseray chuckled to herself wondering what was so funny.

As she turned around, her nose smacked right into the broad chest of her husband. He too had a peculiar smile upon his face. He grabbed Deseray into his arm and twirled her around in a full circle, setting her down in front of the lodge flap.

"You have made me proud! This is a fine lodge. I am the envy of all the men of our village. I not only have a fine new lodge, but the most beautiful women in the entire village!"

"Your fine and empty lodge. I have not had time to move our things into it."

"What things do we need? A warn buffalo hide is all we will need this night!"

Deseray laughed as she tapped his arm.

"And what shall I make your food with."

"All the nourishment I need this night is the warmth of your body lying close to mine!"

Tall Trees returned to where he had first been standing and picked up a large buffalo hide, he had placed there. He opened the lodge flap and threw the hide inside.

On a whim, he then lifted Deseray into his arms and carried her inside.

Laying her gently on the hide, he began to kiss her face,

cheeks and finally her lips.

Deseray's body quickly responded as she placed kisses all over Tall Trees' face and cheeks and rested longingly upon his lips.

"I love you" Deseray whispered.

"I love you too, with all my heart."

In their empty tipi, lying on a buffalo robe, they joined together.

Tall Trees stroked Deseray's hair.

"You are the most beautiful wife any man has ever had! You have made me proud this day. I am the envy of all who see you. You have learned well, and you do belong here among my people, and with me."

The next morning when Deseray awoke, Tall Tress was not lying beside her. Deseray dressed, realizing that the air was unusually chilly. Her warm clothes were still in Woman Who Sings' lodge, so she entered the morning air, her arms wrapped around herself for warmth.

When she stepped outside of the flap, a physically warm sensation greeted her as a buffalo robe surrounded her shoulders, followed by a loving kiss.

Tall Trees looked as pleased as a kitten with a bowl of fresh milk.

"My sister is awake. You can move your things into our lodge if you would like."

"I would like too very much. I am excited to have a home of our very own."

The honking of geese overhead drew both of their eyes upward. They watched the flock of geese as it re-grouped into a V formation.

Tall Trees pointed.

"Do you see," he began, "that the flock is confused for a moment. The leader became tired and as the new leader moves to take his place, the rest become uncertain of the direction they must go. A leader is important to all community creatures. There is more than one leader, so they share their wisdom and do the right thing for all concerned."

Deseray put her arm around Tall Trees waist.

"Some day your duties as a leader will become great. When this happens, you will take on a second wife?"

"Today, one wife is all I can handle."

Deseray smiled. Inside of her, she felt sadness. Somehow, she knew, that one day she would return to her own time. She mourned at the thought of separation from Tall Trees. She also mourned at the loss he too would feel with her parting. It was important to her that Tall Trees knew she greatly approved of Otter Tail to be his wife.

"Your sister told me that as a leader becomes more and more important; his duties become great as well. She told me that as a leader, you must entertain and have many children. She also explained that it was unfair to place all this responsibility on one wife, so chiefs take more than one wife. I understand this. I just wanted you to know that I really like Otter Tail."

"It is good that the first wife likes the second wife. Then they can become friends and have no fighting in the lodge."

Tall Trees had thoughts of his own. He wondered if Deseray was thinking of the day she would return to her own time. He did not want to think about it. The thought brought him close to anger.

"I do not want to speak of this anymore. You go to my sister's and get your belongings. I have other things to do right now."

Even though his voice was gentle, Deseray know he felt anger. Was she going too far speaking of whom he should choose for a wife? Was he angry because they shared the same thoughts of her departure?

Deseray smiled as he turned to leave. Their eyes met with deep passion.

"I will always love you," she said, "no matter where I am. You will always be a part of me, forever."

Tall Trees embraced her firmly.

"I will always love you. You also, will always be a part of me."

He released her and strode heavily away. Deseray know his heart was sad.

As she walked to Women Who Sings' lodge, she secretly hoped that she would not have to return to her own time. She missed her family; of who she was certain had stopped looking for her a long time ago. Nevertheless, if the choice were hers to make, she would sacrifice her family to remain forever with Tall Trees. She wondered if the choice was hers to make.

Preparations for the move to the winter camp were underway. Deseray packed all the dried meat, roots and berries gathered during the warm months of summer along with all her personal items.

The dried buffalo meat weighed less than fresh, at least 1/3 less. With the addition of the pemican she had prepared, Deseray hoped they had enough food to last most of the winter. Tall Trees had told her that they would have to hunt some buffalo in the winter months, or their will not be enough food to last through the winter.

The carefree days of men's bare chests and women's sleeveless tunics were gone. Yolks of heavy tanned hide had replaced the summertime leisure of little or no clothes. Naked children reluctantly cover their bronzed little bodies with dresses, shirts, and breech clothes in effect to ward off the chilling northern winds that marked the coming of the months of many snows.

Since Deseray and Tall Trees owned several horses, they had the luxury of placing their tipi on a travois as well as their belongings. They also had the luxury of being able to ride during the weeks it would take for the move to the winter camp.

As Deseray loaded one of the travois with her pouches and hides, she became curious as to why they moved their camp for the winter.

Almost as though he could read her thoughts, Tall Trees walked up to her to check on her progress.

"Why do we move the village for the winter?" she asked.

"Once the snows come and the winds blow, there is so much snow that the lodge tops are covered. Men or horses cannot make their way through the deep piles of snow. We would not be able to find any winter game to supplement our dried meat and we would starve. In the hills where we winter camp, the thick trees and many ravines help to keep the snow from becoming so deep. There is some game in the hills where many animals also go to wait out the snow."

"I see." Deseray continued packing.

That night everyone slept under the stars, huddled close together to ward off the early winter winds. Before the sun had risen the next morning, the camp was on the move. It would take many days to reach the hill country and their winter camp.

As the long days of the move proceeded, Deseray grew tired of the cold and wind. It was difficult for her to adjust to such a harsh environment.

Tall Trees noticed her discomfort as he rode beside her.

"I see you have much difficult with the cold."

Deseray smiled.

"We have winter in my time, but I have never spent days and nights in such cold. I am trying to adjust, and I soon will. Do not worry."

Tall Trees still have a concerned look on his face.

"Winters are hard for our people. We have little food, and some may die. I do not want to lose you."

Deseray reached from under her buffalo robe and touched Tall Trees hand.

"You know me, I am a fighter, and I will survive."

The village continued their trek, entering the hill country many days later. Snow covered the ground, making the move more difficult. Once the caravan of people, horses and dogs stopped, Deseray knew they had arrived at the winter camp.

Tipis were nestled in the trees to provide winds breaks. The ample number of trees provided sufficient fuel for their fires. Deseray was pleased to know that she could at least have some comfort in a warm fire throughout the cold months.

The months seemed to pass slowly. Deseray's winter coat consisted of a fur-laden buffalo robe and fur wrapped moccasins for winter boots.

They did most of the cooking within the lodges, serving two purposes, food preparation and warmth. Deseray had lined the lower sides of the tipi with buffalo hides to ward of the cold winds and the covered the floor with hides to keep the cold from seeping up from the earth.

Much visiting took place during the cold months. Deseray spent much of her time at the lodge of Woman Who Sings learning fine art of quillwork. As fortune would have it, porcupines were native to the area Tall Trees people inhabited. She was using the quills she had collected during the summer months for her winter projects.

Woman Who Sings placed water above the fire to boil carefully explaining each step to Deseray. She carefully opened a bladder pouch containing hundreds of quills.

"The quills were stored unclean so the natural oils would keep them for future use. We need to remove the oils so they will take the dye."

Deseray carefully added quills to the hot water.

Women Who Sings continued with her instructions.

"Add a small amount of buffalo tallow soap to the water. Do not boil them too long or they will become soft and unusable." Woman Who Sings laughed as she added. "They will cook!"

After a few short minutes, Deseray carefully removed the quills form the hot water and spread them out to dry.

Woman Who Sings began placing the quills in four distinctive piles.

"You can help me sort the quills. These large, coarse quills, which came from the tail, are perfect for decorating large areas of pattern design or for wrapping pipe stems. The long, thinner ones from the back we will used to do loom quillwork.

The finer ones," she said, as she held some in her hand to show Deseray, "came from the neck and are the best ones for decorating shoes, clothes and pouches and quivers."

Deseray turned the quills over in her hand, making note of the thickness and size.

"The very fine, small ones form the belly we will use for the most delicate quill work."

Deseray had not imagined that quills could vary so much in size and thickness.

Woman Who Sings showed Deseray a pouch that had several smaller pouches within it.

"These," she said as she opened the pouches," are the dried bark, berries, roots and flowers we use to make the colors. These are the colors you used to decorate your parfleches."

"When we return to summer camp, I will take you to learn where and how to gather what is needed for each color. For some of the colors we will have to travel a few suns to find. To get other roots or barks, we will have to trade meat with the southern tribes."

Deseray watched carefully as Woman Who Sings placed a color mixture into a bladder of water.

"The color of red made from buffalo berry or squaw berry. Today I have squaw berry."

She sprinkled the dried and crushed berries into the water as Woman Who Sings continued Deseray's lesson.

"The quills will soak for part of the day until they are the color we choose. When we have the right color, we will add some currents to the color to make the color stay."

Deseray realized that she was using the currents as an acidic mordant used to make colors permanent. How cleaver, she thought.

" When I make the red color I add female dock root to make the color much deeper."

Deseray secretly wished she had her tape recorder or even her notebook so she could remember all the things she was currently learning from Woman Who Sings. She did notice, however, that her memory had sharpened since her arrival and she has learned to pay more attention to details.

Woman Who Sings continued.

"We use only four colors in our quillwork, black, red, yellow and the natural color of white. No other colors."

The next few days Deseray spent her time sorting, cleaning and dyeing of the quills.

As Deseray worked with the quills, she was already planning the design she would put on a new pair of moccasins she was making for Tall Trees.

Because of her past attempts in her own time, she knew her quill techniques were poor. She was overjoyed to know that she would learn these techniques from a true expert.

Tall Trees and Cries In The Wilderness had been out with a hunting party trying to find the buffalo or other fresh game. From Deseray's deductions, she guessed it was February, the month of the popping trees.

She was still quite confused about their calendar and intended to ask Tall Trees more about it once he returned. In the meantime, she concentrated on her quillwork.

A few days later, Deseray could hear a commotion in the village. She jumped to her feet, grabbed her buffalo robe and ran outside.

The hunters had returned. On Tall Trees two ponies, Deseray saw a couple of deer hanging across the pony's backs. Some ponies also held elk and others carried rabbits. The greatest site was several buffalo hides loaded with fresh meat.

Winter hunt for the buffalo was quite different than in the summer. Horses could not be used for the hunt. They would sink into the deep snow. In winter, the buffalo who hadn't migrated further south, grazed on the top and sides of hills where there was the least amount of snow. The fierce winds would blow the snow from the tops of these hills and one side of the ravine, leaving exposed grasses for the buffalo to eat.

The hunters would sneak up on the grazing buffalo who would try to run away. As they ran into the deep snow, they would sink deeply into the snow and unable to move. The hunters would wear snowshoes to keep them on top of the snow and easily kill the buffalo with either an arrow or a lance.

The hunters would strip off the hides and take as much meat as they could pull on the hide. The bladder and skin sacks were nestled in between the layers of meat for later use. The rest of the buffalo was left to feed the wolves.

Deseray was excited and relieved to see that the hunt was successful. She wanted to run up to Tall Tress embrace him in her arms, but that was not good manners. She had to wait until he came to her. Joyous cries rang throughout the camp. The dried meat and most of the pemican had run out and everyone had empty bellies, including Deseray.

She waited in the tipi for Tall Trees' return. As the flap lifted open and Tall Tress rushed in swooped Deseray into his arms.

"The hunt was good," he said as he covered Deseray with warm kisses.

Deseray quickly started water to boil and added dried roots to the water. She went outside to see their share of the fresh meat waiting for her to process and store. She cut a large piece from the deer and quickly placed it into the boiling water. She was so hungry; she was tempted to eat the meat raw. The last time she ate raw meat she became very ill, so she patiently waited for the meat to cook.

Tall Tress walked to the flap and announced to Deseray, "I am going to council and will return by the time our meal is done."

Deseray laughed to herself. She knew that the council meeting was so he could brag about the successful hunt. The people did not see bragging as a bad thing. It was considered strong medicine. The more often a story was told, the stronger the medicine became.

Tall Trees was gone for a long time after the food was cooked. Deseray was so hungry she was tempted to eat without him, but that was bad manners, so she waited. When Tall Trees returned, she quickly began dishing out the food. She had never been so hungry in her life. She truly understood the meaning of the word, starving.

"I am happy the hunt so was successful." Deseray said as she shoved the food into her mouth.

"It was successful.' Tall Trees replied. "We will have enough meat to last until the moon of the red calves being born." Deseray noted that was the first part of May.

She remembered she had wanted to ask him about their calendar, and this seemed like to perfect moment.

"I want to know more about how you count the months of the year. It is different from my time and it confuses me."

Tall Trees finished chewing his food and answered.

"Our moons are counted by the things that are happening in nature. This moon is the moon of the popping trees. The trees make this sound because the cold freezes the sap inside the tree and when the wind moves the tree, the sap breaks and makes a popping sound. It is the same for each moon. We have thirteen moons. Our first moon is hard times, and the second moon is frost in the lodge because the cold is still with us. The third is the moon of the popping trees, and the fourth moon is snow blindness. It snows most of the time in this moon. The fifth moon is red calves are born followed by the moon when horses lose their hair."

"The sixth moon is ripening berries. The seventh moon of our year is Sun Stands in the middle. There are the same numbers of moons before this moon as there is after this moon."

As Deseray listened, she decided the moon when the sun stands in the middle, was June or July. She remained confused. She just nodded her head as Tall Trees talked. She would just accept his answer since she did not want to confuse him about the differences of her own calendar.

Tall Trees continued, "The eighth moon is the moon when all things ripen, followed by when calves turn dark. The tenth moon is the moon of leaves turning brown, followed by when leaves fall. The twelfth one is the moon of winter and the last moon is the moon of midwinter."

When he finished, he asked, "The way we describe the moons may be different each year because we describe the moon by what is happening in nature. Does this help?"

"Yes, it does, but I know I will understand better as the moons come and go."

With a full stomach and her husband next to her to warm her body, Deseray slept the best she had in weeks.

The days that followed were used to dry the meat the hunters had just brought to the village. Deseray found it difficult to get the winter meat as dry as during the summer.

She asked Woman Who Sings what she was doing wrong.

"I cannot seem to get the meat to dry as fully as during the summer. Am I doing something wrong?" she asked.

Woman Who Sings smiled.

"Because of the moist and cold winter conditions, the meat will never be as dry as summer. We do the best we can. "

As Deseray continued to preserve the meat she felt confident that their food supple would last until spring.

The hides and some of the meat from the hunt were given to the families without a hunter to provide for them.

Soon the days turned into weeks and it was the month "when calves turn brown", which to Deseray was April.

The sound of spring songbirds, the longer days and the rush of the melting streams presented all the signs that spring had arrived.

Deseray stood motionless as she absorbed the first warmth of the new season. She followed her well-worn trail to a large snowpack where she had placed sticks to mark the snow depth. It had decreased several inches in just the past few days, soon, it would be time to move the winter camp back to the prairie.

Deseray had grown thin and weak during the bleak days of little food and the harsh cold. As she recalled the long days of blowing snow, sub-zero temperatures, and days with little or no food, she shivered. Many days she was ashamed of herself as she longed for her heated house, a refrigerator full of food and her soft mattress.

The life she was living was the reality of these people. They accepted it and never complained. Yet, she realized, they knew no other way. It was only she, who had ever known the luxuries of her own time. It was only she, who missed them.

Chapter Twelve - The One Before You

The move from the winter camp was full of joy and anticipation. It meant fresh meat, fresh roots, berries, and warmth. The return to summer camp seemed to go much faster. The absence of snow was a contributing factor in the ease of the move.

Once summer camp was set up, Deseray was anxious to visit Woman Who Sings. She wanted to finish the moccasins she had been working on for Tall Trees.

Deseray secretly kept the moccasins tucked away in a leather pouch so Tall Trees would not see them until she had them completed.

Upon arriving at Woman Who Sings' lodge, she found her working on her quillwork as well.

Deseray smiled at her as she approached.

"I am glad to see you are doing quillwork this day. I want to work on the moccasins have made for Tall Trees."

The moccasins were simple in design as were much of the Sioux clothing. The sole was heavily tanned rawhide while the uppers were soft hide with a tongue and a flap coming up around the ankle.

"I have brought my dyed quills and sinew."

Deseray secretly dreaded putting the sinew in her mouth.

As Deseray sat next to Woman Who Sings, she carefully followed her instructions.

"The quills are easier to work with if they are moist. As you work on your pattern, put a few of the quill colors you need into your mouth until they are supple."

I knew it, thought Deseray; I am never going to get away from having to put things other than food into my mouth.

Deseray politely smiled at Woman Who Sings and she listened.

"As you take a quill out of your mouth, pull it between your teeth to flatten it. Get it as flat as you can," she continued. "All but the end of the sinew is cleaned of the natural glue so it will be easy to work with. Before you begin, put the sinew in your mouth and wet the end."

Deseray reluctantly obeyed.

"Now let the end dry. It will be hard when it is dry and you can pierce the very top layer of the leather on the upper sole, sewing the quills in place you go."

After Deseray's sinew end was dry and hardened, she discovered how easily it did pierce just the top of the leather. Picking up a small section of the hide, she ran the sinew under it just enough to make a very small stitch. About an inch from that, she made another stitch. With the moistened quills in her mouth, she flattened them one at a time as she weaved them under and over the stitches, she had made.

Woman Who Sings smiled, "You are very good at quill-work. Have you done it before?"

Deseray also smiled, "Yes, not much, but some."

Woman Who Sings went into the tipi and returned with a small pouch, called a pocket bag. Women worn these on their belts and served the same purpose as a pocket, of which they had none in their clothing.

"I see that you have no pocket bag for your tools. I have made this one for you."

Deseray took the pouch.

"Thank you. I have been meaning to make one for myself."

Deseray attached the pouch to her belt. Woman Who Sings once again joined Deseray on the ground to continue the quillwork.

"How do you like married life?" she asked.

"I am truly happy. Tall Trees is a good husband and provider, and we have a good life."

Woman Who Sings gently squeezed her hand. Deseray understand that she shared her joy.

After lunch, Deseray continued to work on the moccasins. She remained at Woman Who Sings' lodge to make sure Tall Trees did not see them before they were complete. As luck would have it, she saw Tall Trees walking toward her. She quickly bundled up her project and laid it next to the tipi. Tall Tress did not notice.

His voice was very somber as he spoke.

"There is someone who wishes to speak to you." Tall Trees told her. "It is Spirit Walker. He is our medicine man. Come."

He motioned Deseray in the direction of a medium sized tipi nestled neatly amongst several larger ones. The outside of the tipi was adorned and beautifully painted with many stories. She wanted to linger longer and read the stories the pictures told, but Tall Tress seemed uneasy about her audience with the Medicine Man.

Tall Trees lifted the flap of the tipi and motioned Deseray to pass through. He quietly followed her.

Once inside, the old Medicine Man motioned for them to sit. Deseray thought the Medicine Man must be the oldest person in the village. His face and eyes indicated that he had seen many years.

His voice was commanding but gentle. He looked tenderly at Deseray as he spoke.

"You are a visitor to my people. The Spirits have guided you here." His words made a statement and not a question.

Deseray was not sure how much he knew of where she came from, so she answered briefly.

"Yes, I am a visitor."

"You are a visitor guided here by the Spirits?" This time it was a question.

"Why do you ask me this?" she replied.

Spirit Walker's eyes were peaceful as he glanced at the pouch that hung from Deseray's waist.

"You carry a medicine pouch," he said as he waved his wrinkled hand in the direction of her waist.

Deseray's hand went immediately to the medicine pouch she had gotten from Jingles.

"It was a gift from a friend," she replied.

"This friend," asked Spirit Walker, "Is he one called Jingles?"

Deseray's eyes and mouth opened wide with surprise.

"How did you know that?"

The old man slowly and gently waved his aged hand in front of him to assure Deseray not to feel alarm.

"Your friend, Jingles," said Spirit Walker, "He is my friend too. It was I who made the medicine pouch you now carry. It was I, who gave it to Jingles as a gift of friendship. My heart is joyous to know he is well."

His words confused Deseray.

"How could you know Jingles? He's from my time."

Suddenly Deseray wished she could take back her words. She used "my time". Something she worked every day not to use.

The old Medicine Man smiled peacefully at Deseray. His face offered her a sense of reassurance.

"I do not pretend to understand the ways of the Spirits," he said gently, "I am just a mere man and the Spirits have powers that a mere man can never understand."

"I know that many years ago, a young man came to my people, much like you have come, and he lived with us and learned our ways."

Deseray listened carefully to each word as he spoke.

"The Spirits showed me that I should be his protector and teacher, much like Tall Trees is your protector and teacher. Jingles came to be a great warrior and rode beside me in many battles. He decided that the spirits would not mind if he did not return to his own world. I never understood where his people were or about the world he came from. I trusted the Spirits. Jingles said he had no family. He told me his parents had entered the afterlife and he had no one. Among my people, he had family. He decided to stay, and he was accepted."

Spirit Walker paused as he remembered the days of his friendship with Jingles. He drifted back to the time when he was young, and Jingles lived among his people.

"One day, with no warning, our village was attacked by our enemies. There was much confusion. The children were frightened. There were so many. Men and women both fought our enemy that day."

He paused once again remembering the sadness and pain of that day.

"We fought long and hard and soon drove the enemy from our village. Many were dead and many more wounded. My friend Jingles lay on the ground with many wounds. His face covered with blood and body filled with many arrows, a lance through his leg. A short distance from his wounded body laid the body of his wife and a girl child."

Tears formed in Deseray's eyes to think that Jingles was married, and she and their child were killed.

"As I walked up to my friend, I could see that there wasn't much left of his leg. I feared that my friend would die. I did not want my friend to die in a world that was not his own. I prayed to the Spirits to return him to his own world. I was not certain if this would save his life or not, but I knew he would not live if he stayed in mine."

Deseray felt overwhelmed by what she just heard. Jingles had gone back in time. He had lived among the same American Indians she was now living with.

"Jingles is my friend." Deseray told Spirit Walker. "He lives with my family and he is doing well."

Spirit Walker sat quietly for a moment. He rose slowly, showing the years he had lived. He reached over to a small pouch and carefully opened it. He removed a small bundle of rabbit fur. Returning to his sitting position, he solemnly opened the bundle. Lifting an object from within the bundle, Deseray could see and hear the necklace as Spirit Walker handed it to Deseray.

"This totem necklace belongs to my friend Jingles. I

know it has great value and powerful medicine. He lost it during his last battle. I wish you to return it to him."

As Deseray took the necklace from him, she thought of the words he had used. "I wish you to return it to him."

Before she could speak, Spirit Walker spoke.

"You must prepare yourself for your journey back to your own people. I am not certain, but I believe that the Spirits, like with Jingles, desired you to be a visitor only, and that we each belong to our own worlds. You must soon return to yours."

"May the Spirits guide you safely on your journey."

Before Deseray could speak, Tall Trees rose quietly and motioned to Deseray that it was time to leave the Medicine Man. He held the flap open for her and she stepped into the bright sunlight. When she turned to speak to Tall Trees, he disappeared behind the closed flap, remaining with Spirit Walker.

Deseray looked at the necklace she held in her hand. The necklace held many symbols and objects. These were Jingles' totems. The objects brought him comfort and strength. Lined along the leather thong were silver feathers, coins, a variety of stones and small little bells. Jingles' totems, the things he had collected throughout his life. Each item held a story and an importance.

Deseray put the necklace into the medicine pouch with the eagle feather. She stepped outside as she waited for Tall Trees to finish his council with the Medicine Man. Upon joining Deseray in the bright sunlight, Tall Trees gently placed his fingers over Deseray's lips. She knew this meant that he did not wish to speak.

Silently they returned to their lodge.

Instead of entering the tipi with her, Tall Trees looked at Deseray, a saddened expression upon his face.

"I must be alone. I will return and then we will speak."

He turned from her and walked in the direction of the river. Instead of entering the tipi, Deseray sat against the backrest that sat on the ground in front of their lodge. Her mind swarming with so many thoughts, that she could not sort them all out.

My journey, she recalled Spirit Walker say. My journey home to my own time. She felt numb except for the ache she felt within her chest. All she could feel was a sense of loneliness and pain at the idea of leaving her present life and of leaving Tall Trees behind.

From across the village, she could see Women Who Sings preparing the afternoon meal. Her daughter had grown so much during the winter months. It was fun to watch her in her efforts to learn how to walk. She would take a few steps, fall flat on her butt, stand up and repeat the same process all over again.

Watching Little Dry Sands soften Deseray's aching heart. Her little life was just beginning and full of wonderful hope. Deseray rose from her backrest chair and walked over to the little girl. She could not resist picking her up and giving an affectionate hug.

Little Dry Sands giggled and tried to put her fingers into Deseray's mouth as she tried to speak.

"You little silly, how can I talk with your little fingers in my mouth?"

Women Who Sings laughed.

"She is trying to figure out how our mouths work. She's been putting her fingers into everyone's mouth these past few days."

Deseray could see that Women Who Sings was busy scraping winter stored hides for summer clothes.

"Would you like some help?" she asked.

"That would be nice, if you have the time."

"Tall Trees has gone off by himself and I do not know when he will return."

Sadness cloaked Deseray's face. Women Who Sings stopped her work and placed a hand on Deseray's shoulder.

"Is there trouble between you and my brother?"

Deseray softly smiled.

"No, there is no trouble between us. We had council with the Medicine Man this day." Deseray paused.

Women Who Sings became alarmed.

"Do you have sickness?"

"No, I am not sick," replied Deseray, "I am troubled about what he has said and the things that may come to pass."

Woman Who Sings put her arm around Deseray's shoulder.

"Becoming a woman is a difficult thing. There are many decisions to make, but you are wise for your age. You are a good worker and have many talents. You are a good wife to my brother. I have never seen him so happy."

Deseray eyes filled with tears and she began to cry. She ran to a quiet place by the river where she sat and cried long and hard.

I do not want to leave this place, she thought. I will miss everyone, and I will miss Tall Trees. Nevertheless, she knew the Medicine Man was right. She belonged in her own time with her own family. As she wiped the tears from her cheeks, she looked up and saw White One standing faithfully near her. She rose and walked over to him.

From his mannerism, she sensed it was not yet her time to leave. She was grateful for this. She needed to speak with Tall Trees before she left. She placed her hand on White Ones side and stroked him gently.

"How can joy have so much pain?" She whispered.

"I am grateful I was allowed to come to this place," she continued, "but I am sad that I must leave."

White One gently nudged Deseray to indicate that he understood.

"Of course, you understand," she said, "you understand the future of your kind and the future of the people. You have seen the future and felt the pain that it will bring."

Deseray hugged White One. She stood there for a long time.

"If I've got only a short time left here," she said, "I'd better learn all I can and make peace with the things I must."

It was difficult for Deseray to think about going back

home to her own time.

Upon Tall Trees' return, no words were spoken between them. The silence was painful. Deseray began to prepare the evening meal.

Finally, Tall Trees spoke.

"We must honor the wishes of the Spirits. I have battled with these thoughts all day. My heart is full of pain while it is full of respect for the Spirits."

He wrapped his arms around Deseray.

"I will love you forever even when you are gone from me. I cannot change what the Spirits have decided, but I can still love you."

Deseray began to cry.

"I will also love you forever. I do not want to go. I miss my family, but I have a new one here with the people and with you. We will enjoy our time together as long as the Spirits are willing and speak of this saddens no more."

Tall Trees nodded in agreement.

Upon waking the next morning, Deseray was compelled to go to the river. She wanted to wake Tall Trees, but something told her not to do so. As she neared the river, she saw Otter Tail filling bladders with fresh water.

She smiled as Deseray approached.

"I knew you would come," she said.

Deseray returned the smile.

"Yes." She replied. "We must talk. Soon the spirits will take me from this place."

Otter Tail was surprised by her words.

"What do you mean? You are going away?"

"Yes. It will be soon."

Otter Tail hugged Deseray. "I do not want you to leave us. You are my friend and I will miss you. Tall Trees will miss you."

"It is not my choice to leave. The Spirits brought me here and now they wish me to leave."

"Will you die?"

Deseray smiled, "No I will not die. I will return to the

place I came from. I cannot tell you of this as it is not for you to understand. I do not understand. I wish to tell you that I know you will make a good wife for Tall Trees. He will be in sorrow because of my leaving and you will have to help to heal his heart."

Otter Tail cried as she continued to listen to Deseray.

"If I could stay, I would. I know you will be good to him."

Deseray hugged her and turned to leave.

She left Otter Tail as she tearfully continued filling the bladders.

Before she reached the village, Tall Tress met her on the path. An expression of relief covered his face.

"I woke and you were gone. I feared the Spirits had taken you in our sleep."

"No, but soon. I have dreamed this. Soon, my love, too soon."

They embraced, speaking no words.

Instead of returning to the village, they continued walking along the fast-moving river. The rising sun kissed the small ripples as the river traveled along its way.

They paused next to the rushing river, now swelled with the melting from the hills.

As Deseray stood looking up at her husband, the words she needed to say were difficult.

"I have dreamed that I will be leaving soon. I do not know why I must go, but I must." She paused. "I do not know why I was sent here, but I think it is as you said when I first came. The spirits fulfilled my desire. Now that I have learned much, it is time to go."

Tall Trees spoke no words.

She continued.

"I will always remember you and my time here."

Tall Trees took her in his arms as he whispered, "I will always remember you."

He gently released her and quickly walked away.

Deseray knew he needed time to think. She decided it was

time for her to say her goodbyes to the ones she loved. She decided to have a giveaway after the evening meal with Woman Who Sings and Cries In The wilderness. Give away ceremonies occurred for various reason. Deseray knew that the people valued generosity more the possessions they gave away. She had gotten permission from Woman Who Sings to invite Otter Tail.

Since it was not polite to prey into one's personal life, she knew she would not be asked the reason why she was having a giveaway. After she was gone, they would understand. She had completed the moccasins for Tall Trees and had enough hide left to make a strike-a-light bag for Cries In The Wilderness to carry his flints.

Tall Trees returned to their lodge to announce that were invited to eat with his sister and her husband.

"This is good," said "Deseray.

"I will have a giveaway after the meal. I cannot take my things with and I do not want you to have to take care of it after I am gone."

Tall Trees looked concerned.

"Why now? How do you know when you will leave?"

Deseray softly touched his face. "I had a dream. I will leave tomorrow."

At the giveaway, she made a gift to Woman Who Sings one of the two pouches they had made together. One pouch to Cries In the wilderness, the strike-a-light pouch. To Otter Tail, she gave a quilled rosette she had made just for her. She decided to give Tall Trees his moccasins later that night in their own home.

Woman Who Sings was grateful for the gift but had a look of concern on her face. After the meal when the men went out to smoke and Otter tail took her leave, Woman Who Sings spoke.

"I do not want to be rude, but there something you want to tell me?" she asked.

Deseray was reluctant to tell of her leaving, but her love for her was so great, she was aching to tell her.

"The Spirits have told me I will be leaving the people

soon."

Woman Who Sings raised her eyebrows, "Ah," she said. "I thought it was my imagination, but I have been seeing the white buffalo these past few days. It is he who will take you away?"

"Yes." Deseray answered. "With the power of the Spirits, it was he who brought me here."

Deseray hugged Woman Who Sings.

"I can't say anymore. Remember I will always love you and Little Dry Sands."

She quickly left before the tears she had been holding back found their ways to her cheeks.

That night as they lay in their tipi and the love, they felt for each filled the air.

Tall Trees spoke, "Do you remember the story of the White Buffalo Calf Woman?'

Deseray replied, "Yes."

"The people were sad to see her go but she left something special for my people as she departed. I feel the same about you as you leave. As you depart, you will take the knowledge of my people to your time and leave us hope. You will leave us with a hope that all we are and all will become, will not be forgotten by the ones you call the white men."

"I must tell you what the Spirits have told me. It is your purpose. The reason you were guided here. The white buffalo is your power totem. The white buffalo does not appear too many. For those who receive their power from the buffalo it is their purpose to teach about our people and to teach our People's ways. It is to teach respect for the mother earth. Respect for all those who live on it. This is a great task."

Tall Trees continued, "You were brought here so you could bring this message of our people back to the people of your time. It is not too late for all two-leggeds to live together. I have seen the future of my people when I was in your time. It made my heart sad, but you are hope for that future. You will carry the message for our people with you. You will teach the whites and the American Indians who may have forgotten or who were never told of how our people lived."

They lay in each other's arms, taking in the love from each other that they would miss.

Deseray and Tall Trees rose early the next morning, even earlier then the dogs.

They sat quietly beside the river, remembering there times together.

Suddenly, out of the silence Deseray asked.

"Will you take Otter Tail for your wife?"

"Would that please you?" he asked.

"Yes. She will make a good wife and a good mother," she replied.

"Then I will take her for my wife," He said. "Before you came, I was prepared to take her as my wife, but you captured my heart and I no longer saw her for a while. She is special and I know she will please me. I will marry her, but I will often think of you."

Tall Trees stood to his feet. He then helped Deseray to her feet.

"We must go now," he said, "it is time. White One wishes you to return the feather."

They stood silently looking at each other for a moment.

"I will miss you Tall Trees," said Deseray.

He gently kisses her on the lips.

"And I will miss you."

Deseray spoke softly, "We won't see each other again, will we?" she said.

"If the Sprits are willing," he smiled.

Standing near a bend, across the river, White One stood, waiting.

White One's presence conveyed the message to them that it was time. Deseray's heart was breaking. Not so soon, she thought.

Tall Trees also knew it was time. Sadness filled his eyes.

"White One wants the feather back." Gently holding Deseray for the last time, he said, "I will always love you."

Deseray smiled. "I will always love you. Otter Tail loves you and will heal your heart. It will please me."

Tears filled Tall Trees' eyes without shame.

Deseray gently kissed his lips. "I will find a way to return to you this is my promise."

Their final kiss created a connection between them that would never be broken.

Deseray slowly walked to the river. She stood next to White One for a moment, allowing her gaze to linger upon Tall Trees a while longer.

Deseray carefully tied the feather to One White's right horn where the beaded ornament once hung. White One lowered his massive body to the ground, allowing Deseray to climb upon his back. She was tempted to look once again at Tall Trees, but she knew her heart could not stand the pain.

Instead, she sat proudly upon White One as he quickly made his way to the open prairies, joining a small herd of buffalo grazing nearby. Quickly, the herd hastened their pace, moving faster and faster, forming the great circle. They ran freely, just as they had done many times in her dreams, only this time they were taking her somewhere special. They were taking her home.

Deseray's world became surreal as they ran faster and faster, becoming engulfed in the dust and movement of the many bodies that surrounded her. Her thoughts were that of Tall Trees and she looked toward the river where Tall Trees once stood.

"Goodbye my love. I will love you forever."

Chapter Thirteen – Home

Deseray's head swirled with nothingness as she clung to White One's fur, she was over-come with a powerful weariness and was no longer conscious of what was happening.

When Deseray opened her eyes, tiny droplets of water caused her to blink. The sky over head was cloudy and dark. Light rain filled the air.

She shivered for a moment. She felt cold and wet. As she gazed about her, she realized she was sitting at the bottom of a ground-soaked ravine. As she attempted to stand, her ankle gave out and she plopped down onto the soggy ground. Pain radiated from her ankle.

Pondering about her situation, she wondered, where am I? Actually, she wondered, when am I. Attempting to stand proved to be difficult, her throbbing ankle barley supporting her.

Scanning the edge of the ravine, she realized that with a hurt ankle, it would be nearly impossible for her to climb up the embankment.

"Help, can anyone hear me?"

There was no answer. As she stood at the bottom of the ravine, the rain began to pour on her. She refused to allow herself to cry. After all, if her fate was to die in the bottom of a ravine, in the pouring rain, who was she to question fate.

She managed to limp along the bottom of the ravine. She gazed upward, following the edges of the embankment hoping to discover a way out. She found none.

She was weak, tired, and cold. She felt helpless. She simply sat down in the sticky mud and gave into her tears.

Even through the fine mist that had replaced the heavy

droplets, a silent figure caught her eye. Standing in his full majesty was White One.

"Why did you put me in this ravine?" she asked of him. Suddenly there was a figure standing next to White One. The misty rain prevented her from identifying person standing next to him. Then she heard a familiar voice.

"Are ya all right little lady?"

It was Jingles. Deseray's heart felt sadness and joy at the same time, sadness because it was not Tall Trees. Joy because it was Jingles and she knew she was home.

"Here I am." She cried, "Down here." As she spoke, she noticed that she was wearing her original clothes.

"Ya hold on there and I'll be done shortly," Jingles yelled to her.

Her overwhelming exhaustion suddenly disappeared. Excitement at the sound of Jingles' voice filled her with reassurance and hope.

Jingles attached one end of the rope to the four-wheeler he'd been driving. As he slowly lowered himself down the ravine on a length of rope, Deseray could tell it was a struggle for him to accomplish. His bad leg would not support him as he tried to get a foothold in the slippery mud. He seemed to slide most of the way down.

Jingles made his way over to where Deseray sat.

"Thank Goodness we found ya. We ben lookin' fer ya fer days. "

"Days?" exclaimed Deseray. "Is that all?"

"Well, that's how long ya ben gone."

The Spirits had not allowed time to pass the same as it had while she was with the people. In the past, over a year had passed for her, but for her family it had only been a few days.

"I hurt my ankle."

Jingles carefully lifted Deseray's ankle into his hand as he examined it.

"I think it's a sprain, doesn't look to bad."

Suddenly Deseray reached to her side checking for the

medicine bag. It was still hanging from her waist. She carefully opened it. To her surprise the feather was still inside as was the necklace that belonged to Jingles.

I'm gonna call yer uncle and tell him I found ya. Gotta let him know where we are."

As Jingles spoke to Uncle John, Deseray could hear the excitement in his voice.

She couldn't make out his voice, but he spoke quickly and loudly.

Jingles spoke to John, "She is fine. Doesn't seem ta be hurt. We're in the southwest corner of my search area. In a big ravine."

Jingles listened for a moment and the call ended.

"Yer uncle is on the way."

"How'd ya end up down here?' he asked.

"Don't know, but here I am." Deseray replied.

Deseray looked at Jingles, anxious to talk to him about his visit to the past.

"I met an old friend of yours." She said. "His name is Spirit Walker."

Deseray expected Jingles to be surprised, but he was not. He calmly asked, "How is my old friend these days."

"He is good. His heart is joyful that you have survived the injury from the battle."

Jingles smiled. "He told you everything then, I suppose."

"Yes, he did. Why didn't you tell me this? I get the feeling that you already knew about the feather even though I did not tell you."

"I had my suspicions, but I was not certain."

Deseray removed the necklace from the bag and handed it to Jingles. His eyes lit up as he took it from her hand.

"He wanted me to return this to you. He said it is your good medicine."

Jingles took the necklace from Deseray, holding it in his hand as he carefully touched each totem.

"I thought it was gone forever."

To Deseray's surprise, Jingles southern drawl had disappeared.

"Who are you?" She asked. "I suspect you are more than just a cook."

Jingles sat next to Deseray as he carefully placed the necklace around his neck. As he had said, it jingled as he moved.

"It's a long story."

"That's OK," replied Deseray, "I have time."

"One day I found myself in much the same situation as you have. One day, a white buffalo found its way to me in my dreams. Unlike you, I did not meet a real one, only in my dreams. My parents were dead, and I had no other family except my grandmother. Like you, I have always had a fascination about early American Indians since it is my heritage. I spent my time and money learning as much as I could."

"I have a Harvard degree and my parents were wealthy. Even with all this, I felt empty and unaccomplished. One day I found myself transported back in time, coming to live with the people that you did. I lived there many years and had no desire to return to my time."

"After my life-threatening injury, Spirit Walker spoke with the Spirits and asked them to return me to my own time that my life may be spared."

Deseray sat silently as Jingles spoke.

"When I returned to my own time, I received the medical care that saved my life. My leg did not do so well, but I was alive, as my friend had wanted. I was full of anger and resentment that I had to leave, but I remembered that my wife and one of my daughters died in the battle. I had a son and another daughter, and often wonder if they survived."

"I realized that I had lost this necklace." Jingles' hand touched it as it hung from his neck, "The totems are from my entire life when my parents were still alive and my life after they died."

"I knew I had lost it in the past, but I still wanted to find it. The only way that was possible was to sponsor an expedition in this area and hope it survived some degree from time."

Deseray interrupted his conversation.

"You're the anonymous sponsor?"

"Yes, I told you I am rich."

"Did you make sure the arrow heads Carl found, were found by someone who cared?"

Jingles nodded, "Yes, I did."

"Why so secretive?" she asked.

"If I had told you my story would you have believed it?"

Deseray laughed. "No, you are right. I believe it now since I too, have had a similar experience."

"Please do not share any of this with anyone."

"Who would believe me?" Deseray laughed.

Jingles paused for a moment.

"Did Spirit Walker say anything about my young son?"

"No, he did not, but you know if he died, they never speak of the dead."

Jingles nodded, "that is true, but I had hope."

"What was your son's name?" she asked.

He answered, "Tall Trees."

Before Deseray could tell him about Tall Trees, voices came booming from the top of the ravine.

"Jingles are you down there?" It was Uncle John.

"Down here with the little lady" he replied.

Deseray smiled as Jingles southern drawl had once again returned.

The edge of the ravine was full of activity and Uncle John's burly body quickly and expertly descending the side of the ravine.

He swopped Deseray up in his arms and cried.

"I thought we lost you forever."

"I am fine, Uncle John. I just got lost for a while."

Deep inside she knew she had not been lost, only away."

John hugged Deseray so tightly she could hardly breathe.

"Let's get you to the hospital."

"I am fine, I don't need a hospital."

"Yes, you do. You have been lost for days and your mother

would tan my hide if I didn't make sure you were in good health."

Deseray knew she could not win this argument and allowed her uncle to take her to the nearest hospital.

To her surprise, when they reached the top of a ravine, emergency medical team with a helicopter was waiting.

"I don't need to go to the hospital in a helicopter!" Deseray protested.

"You might have internal injuries from the fall. Don't argue." John's voice was stern.

Deseray decided not to argue with him any further.

While the medical team was putting Deseray in the helicopter, Uncle John assured Deseray that all would be fine.

"There is a truck waiting for us and we will meet you at the hospital. It will be a while before we can get there, but you are in good hands."

Deseray smiled at her uncle.

"I'm fine. Don't worry. I will see you at the hospital."

As the helicopter took off, Deseray recalled when she and Tall Trees had watched the geese flying north early that spring. Now, here she was, flying the same northern pattern as the geese had taken. Her heart ached as she realized that she truly returned to her own time.

Upon admission to the hospital, she underwent multiple tests assessing her injuries and general health.

As she lay in her hospital bed waiting for any information about her health and for her Uncle John to arrive, the doctor entered the room.

"You're a lucky young lady. Besides the sprained ankle, dehydration and some malnourishment, you are in fine heath. No other broken bones and injuries."

"Thank you," Deseray replied.

"The really good news," the doctor continued, "Is that the baby is doing fine."

"The baby!?" Deseray was shocked. "What baby?"

"I am sorry. I thought you knew. You are pregnant, about

six weeks."

As Deseray thought back, she knew she had missed her menstrual cycle, but she thought it was the result of the rough winter.

"No, I did not know." Deseray replied. "Please do not tell anyone."

The doctor gently squeezed her hand. "I won't. That is for you to tell."

As the doctor left the room, Deseray's head began to swirl. I am pregnant. I am pregnant with Tall Trees' baby.

Before she could comprehend what was happening, Uncle John came into the room. The relief he felt showed on his face as he smiled at her.

"I called your mother and told her not to come to Montana. She wanted to come to help to find you. She is relieved to know you are safe. We all are."

The room soon filled with familiar faces, as Kachina, Jake, Curtis and Jingles arrived. Kachina gave Deseray an affectionate hug.

"We're so happy you are safe. How are you feeling?"

"I feel fine. Just a little tired. The doctor said I could leave after I get more IV fluids to fight my dehydration. He said early tomorrow morning."

John's voice interrupted the visiting, "We had better let her rest."

As everyone was saying their goodbyes, Deseray spoke to Jingles.

"Can you stay for a minute?'

"Sure, little lady."

When it was just Deseray and Jingles in the room, Deseray asked, "Since you now have the necklace, is the expedition over."

"It doesn't have to be. There are enough funds left to continue for a few more weeks. My main reason was to not only find the necklace, but also prove to myself the whole time travel happened. You bringing me the necklace from your travel convinced me that it did happen."

"When I get out of here, I want to go back to the dig. The rest of the team would be disappointed if we quit now."

Jingles agreed. "That is fine with me. I can continue the charade a little longer. It is nice to spend time with your family and I have been enjoying myself."

"Good."

Deseray moved closer to Jingles.

"I have something to tell you. When I was in the past, it seemed like a year and a half, not a few days."

The same for me," Jingles answered, "but I was gone much longer."

"As you did," Deseray continued, "I got married. The man I married was called Tall Trees."

Tears filled Jingles' eyes.

"My son?"

"I am sure it was. Your daughter, Women Who Sings also survived."

The tears of happiness covered Jingles cheeks. He could not speak.

When he finally was able to speak, he asked, "Are they well?'

"Yes, as I said, Tall Trees and I were married. I wanted to stay with the people, but the Spirits would not let me."

"I have something else to tell you." Deseray paused. "I am going to have Tall Trees' baby. Your grandchild."

"A baby? My grandchild," Jingles was overwhelmed.

"Yes. It is sad that Tall Trees will never know his child, but it makes me joyful to know that I will always have a part of him."

"Tall Trees was troubled about your death, but more troubled because the enemy took his father's body," Deseray told Jingles. "But they never took his father's body because you are his father. When the Spirits returned you, it only seemed like they took your body. I wish I could tell him this, but I know he will never know that you lived."

"I would have stayed if I could, even if it meant that I died. At least my son and daughter could have found peace that I went peacefully to the afterlife."

They sat quietly for a moment.

Jingles rose to his feet.

"You get some rest now. We will talk some more when you are rested."

As Jingles went out of the room, Deseray pondered on her situation.

What now? She placed her hand on her stomach and thought about Tall Trees and the baby she now carried. What now, she wondered.

Early the next day, the doctor released Deseray from the hospital. John arrived early to pick her up from the hospital. When he entered the room, he handed Deseray some clean clothes.

"Kachina picked these out for you. Your old clothes were pretty dirty and torn."

Deseray took the clothes from her uncle.

"Thank you. I am anxious to get back to the dig."

An expression of surprise covered John's face.

"What do you mean? You just had a traumatic experience. Don't you think you need to rest?"

"No. I am fine. The doctor said so. I just want to continue the dig. I need it for my thesis, and I have looked forward to it for such a long time."

"Your mother doesn't think it is a good idea." John replied.

"But it's what I want."

John knew that the expedition was important to Deseray but was concerned about her health.

"When we get out of here, we will go back to Carl's and discuss it with the rest of the team. Does that sound fair?"

"Yes, it does," agreed Deseray. "Could you leave so I can dress?"

"Of course," Uncle John replied. "I'll be outside. Just let me know when you are ready."

As they drove back to Carl's, Deseray was trying to think of a way to convince her Uncle that they should continue the dig.

"I am sorry that I got lost. I didn't want to ruin it for everyone."

"You didn't ruin it."

"Yes, I did. Now you want to abandon the whole thing because of me."

Uncle John didn't want Deseray to carry such a burden of guilt, so he decided that if the rest of the group wanted to continue the dig, that they would.

"OK, you win. If the rest of the group wants to continue, then we will."

Deseray smiled brightly, "Thank you, Uncle John!"

Donna's kind and warm smile greeted them as they entered the house.

"You poor dear, we were so worried!"

"Thank you, but I am fine, it's just a sprained ankle."

Jake and Jingles were in the barn tending to the horses and mules while Curtis and Kachina were at the rock shop with Carl.

"I am just getting lunch. I hope you are hungry!'

"Yes, I am. The food at the hospital wasn't very appetizing."

After Deseray settled at the table, Uncle John walked over to the door.

"I am going to check on everyone and let them know we are going to discuss whether we will continue the expedition or not."

With that, he was out the door.

The kitchen smelled of wonderful cooking smells.

"It smells delicious in here."

Donna wiped her hands on a towel.

"I am cooking a fantastic potato and beef casserole, homemade biscuits and chocolate cake for dessert."

"Smells wonderful."

Deseray thought of the camas roots and buffalo meat she lived on during the winter months.

"So how are you doing?" Donna asked with great concern.

"I am good."

"Well, I guess everyone is going to want to hear your story, so we can wait until they are all here. That way you won't have to repeat yourself."

Deseray immediately became worried. What am I going to tell them? I can't tell them I was in the past for over a year. To them, it was only a few days. She knew she had to make up a convincing story, and fast.

As everyone gathered around the table, Deseray knew they all were expecting to hear your story.

Deseray decided she would be the first to speak.

"I don't remember a lot about the three days I was gone. All I know is that the wind came up and the next thing I remember was laying at the bottom of a ravine. I tried to walk but I knew I had hurt my ankle. I called out until my throat became too sore to call anymore. I guess I slept a lot of the time because I was so tired."

"I was afraid that no one would find me. By the third day I was so thirsty I couldn't call anymore. Then, suddenly, I saw Jingles and I knew I was saved."

The story seemed believable. It was only Deseray and Jingles who knew the truth. Deseray knew that everyone accepted her story. What other explanation could there have been.

Uncle John placed his hand on hers.

"We are just grateful that Jingles found you. We were sick with worry."

"Thank you. I am grateful too that I was found."

As everyone continued to eat, Deseray decided to bring up the discussion about the expedition.

"My ankle will be fine in a week or so. I want to go back to the dig."

No one seemed surprised by her request. Deseray suspected that Uncle John had already spoken to them about it.

Curtis spoke first.

"I think that would be fun. I was really getting into the dig. You know, though, if you are not up to it, we will understand."

Deseray smiled.

"I had been looking forward to this for so long. I really want to finish what we started."

Uncle John piped in.

"I am sure Carl and Donna won't mind the company or the extra help around here."

"It would be great to have you stay," Carl said.

"It is settled then," announce Uncle John. "As soon as your ankle if strong enough, we will go back."

Chapter Fourteen - Discoveries

"We're too close to the river." Deseray explained.

John was curious.

"What is your reasoning in that conclusion?"

"In the spring when the tribes moved from their winter camp, the river would have been high with water from the spring runoff. The high waters would make it difficult to put camp too close. Another reason why the village wouldn't have been so close may have been the wildlife."

Deseray continued.

"If the village were far enough away, the animals would feel safe to come and drink. That way, the hunters could sneak up on the animals and have fresh meat."

As Deseray spoke, she was recalling what Tall Trees had told about the village placement.

John smiled.

"That is very perceptive. Where would you put a village?"

Since Deseray had actually been a member of the village in her time travels, she knew exactly where it would have been.

"Let me think," she said, as she appeared to be thoughtful.

She walked on the seemingly virgin ground that had once been a well wore path many years ago. As she passed through some bushes and reached the top of the small hill, she pointed.

"There," she said. "I would put a village there."

Everyone followed behind Deseray. When they came to a stop and she pointed. Uncle John smiled.

"OK. It's settled. We will search in this area."

Once again, the camp was set up and everyone was ready to start a new search.

While everyone slept, Deseray took some paper and carefully drew the village the way she remembered it in the past.

The key to their discovery would be the central fires of each tipi. Another feature they could discover, which would be conclusive, would be the burial scaffolding.

Post mold or postholes would verify the existence of the structures and of course, the bones and artifacts now embedded within the earth would finalize the discovery.

Deseray slept peacefully as she thought about her plan.

Early the next morning Uncle John took out the transit.

"OK, Deseray, where to you want to start the dig?"

Deseray memorized her crude map. She already knew the general area where she wanted to start. The terrain was different than it had been in the past, due to winds and erosion, but she knew the general idea where tipis once stood.

She stopped in a location where she thought Women Who Sings tipi once stood.

"We can start one grid here," she said, "and another about 50 feet away."

Uncle John seemed confused. "Why fifty feet away/"

If I had a village here, I would place the tipis that far apart. This will increase our chances of finding something. Two teams, two sites."

After setting up the first dig site, John said, "Curtis and I will begin with this one. After we have the other site ready, Deseray, you and Kachina will work that one."

Everyone agreed.

Deseray constructed the simple frame for the screens her and Kachina would use. Taking out her small shovel, she began carefully removing the dirt in her first grid.

Kachina gently shook the screen, hoping to find a treasure. By evening, the tired teams stopped for the day and returned to camp.

Jingles had coffee and supper cooking on the fire.

"It smells good, Jingles," said Uncle John.

Curtis added, "And we are very hungry."

The digging continued for the next five days without any discoveries.

Sometime in the early afternoon, Curtis's voice boomed throughout the dig.

"John, I found something. Come quick and see!"

John carefully put down the screen he had been shaking and stepped into the grid Curtis was working.

Curtis pointed to the spot where he was digging.

"Look here. It is a circular stain. I believe it is ash from a fire pit."

Bending down, John carefully scoped some of the dirt into his hand. As he examined it, he said, "I believe you are right. I will get a test kit."

John walked over to his supplies and removed an empty test tube and another jar of Ph testing liquid.

He carefully put some of the soil in the test tube. To this, he added the testing solution. After shaking the tube, he placed it on a tube stand.

"If the Ph is high in this sample than there is a good chance it is ash," he said. "It will take about an hour for the results. In the meantime, we can all work to uncover more soil to see the size of the stain."

Deseray got her camera.

"I want to take pictures as we uncover the stain," she said. "I will take notes as we go."

Uncle John and Curtis carefully removed small shovels of dirt while Kachina worked the screens. Deseray took periodic pictures and made notes to go with the pictures.

When an hour had passed, John picked up the test tube, smiling.

"The color indicates that the Ph of this soil is close to nine. That is very alkaline and a good indicator of its ash content. I will package some of the soil for more detailed tests in a lab."

Uncle John continued. "Next we need to take a measurement of the depth of the discovery."

With Deseray's help, Uncle John used the transit to get an accurate depth measurement.

She added the measurements to her notes.

The reward of discovery spurred the diggers to continue with their task.

They concentrated on the grid of the discovery, gently shoveling dirt into the shaker screens looking for other sign of historic human habitation. As the days past, the fire pit stain became larger.

Suddenly Kachina stopped shaking her screen.

"John, "she said, "I think there are some tiny bones on the screen."

As excitement escalated, the digging stopped to look at the screen.

"Sure enough," Uncle John announced. "These appear to be tiny bone fragments, maybe from a cooking instrument or bones that fell into the fire."

Deseray took picture of the fragments.

"Deseray," Uncle John said, "go to my supplies and get some small jars."

When she returned, John carefully placed the fragments in a jar.

"Now," he said, "make a label with a reference number and place it on the jar."

"Documentation is extremely important," he explained.

Deseray did as he asked.

By late afternoon, the edges of the ash stain became apparent. The circle was a little over two feet in diameter.

"We should take a brake and eat lunch," Uncle John announced.

Even though Deseray was high on excitement, she agreed.

"I am so happy we are finding artifacts to support my theory," she said.

Uncle John took a sip of coffee.

"Our find may show that some early American Indians had a village here, but nothing so far indicates the tribe."

"This is true," Deseray agreed. "But it is a start."

After lunch, Deseray made a suggestion.

"Uncle John?" She said, "If a village was here, wouldn't the burial location be near as well?"

"It would," he agreed. "But finding it would be near impossible with the vastness of this area."

Even though Deseray had a general idea where the burial grounds were, she needed a creative way to lead them in the correct direction. She decided to think about it for a while.

"We should concentrate on the grid we are in and hopefully will find other artifacts."

Following lunch, the team returned to their tasks.

Deseray put loosened dirt from around the circle on the screens as Kachina continued to shake.

As she dug deeper into the area, Deseray decided to change her tool to a large brush. Uncle John had been using a brush for over an hour.

Shortly before they decided to stop for the day, Deseray squealed. Uncle John," she exclaimed. "I think I found a fleshing tool". Just a small edge was showing.

"How can you tell? You barely have it uncovered."

Deseray could not tell her uncle that she knew what it was right away since she had used one for several months while in the past.

"Wishful thinking, I guess," she said.

"Now is the time to take another measurement for documentation," Uncle John said.

Once the measurements were complete, Deseray continued to unearth the object she discovered. Within an hour, there was enough of it showing to verify that it was indeed a flashing tool.

Very soon after, there was enough dirt removed for her to pick it up.

As she and Uncle John examined the tool, Uncle John proclaimed, "Yes, I do believe it is a Sioux tool."

"I agree," said Deseray, as she took pictures of the tool.

"That is enough for one day. A great day," John said. "I think Jingles has some food for us."

As John carefully put the artifacts in a small box, he said, "What is next Deseray?"

"Reference label and documentation," she replied.

Deseray made the label, placed it on the box. She made notations in her book.

Dusty and tired, the food was a welcoming smell.

"How did it go?' asked Jingles.

Deseray replied, "It went very well."

She shared their findings with Jingles and Jake as they enjoyed the fresh stew Jingles had made.

"Uncle John," Deseray announced, "I would like to see if we can find the burial grounds."

"Let's work the other grid we have set up and see if there is another fire pit. If there is, then we can be confident that there was a village here and not just one tipi."

Jake offered some suggestions, "I've seen a lot of this country and visited other burial sites. They seem to have similar characteristic. While you continue to dig, I can explore the area and see if I find a promising location."

Deseray was relieved that Jake offered her expertise and hoped she would find the area for them.

She offered her own suggestion.

"From my studies, the Sioux used scaffolds for burial. They chose an area far enough from the village to prevent the ghosts of the dead from entering the village. Since trees are the main construction of the scaffolds, the area should have trees available to use."

Jake agreed. "That makes sense. Once time starts to disintegrate the trees and the bodies of the dead, there should be indications of variations of the ground. I will look for these signs."

"Good plan," Uncle John confirmed. "It will be another long day; we should get some sleep."

Sleep came easily that night. Deseray missed her white buffalo dreams, but knew they no longer served a purpose.

She rose early the next morning. She was starting to experience morning sickness. She remembered that Woman Who Sings told her that spearmint and peppermint were good for this. Earlier the day before, Deseray had noticed both peppermint and spearmint growing near the campsite.

She gathered a large pouch full of both spearmint and peppermint leaves. By the time she returned to camp, everyone was awake and waiting for Jingles to get breakfast ready.

"I was hungry for some tea," she explained.

She laid the leaves out on a tarp to dry. Secretly, she put some leaves into her pocket. Woman Who Sings had told her the leaves would work as well as the drink.

After yet another fantastic breakfast, the explorers return to the dig site. By evening, it was evident that they were in the wrong spot. Deseray suggested they move over a few feet and start again.

"We can do that," agreed Uncle John.

Before they went back to camp, a new grid was complete and ready for digging.

Jake spent the day searching the area around the dig for a possible burial site, but had no luck either.

Supper consisted of beans, roasted beef and baked bread.

"This is great Jingles," Curtis said. "I am still impressed by the way you manage to bake and roast while in a base camp."

"That's my job!" he replied.

One by one, the weary explorers made their way to the tents.

The next morning, the breakfast conversation centered on the new dig site.

"We can work the new site for a day or two and then we will have re-evaluated our plans." John announced.

"What if we don't find anything more?" asked Deseray.

Uncle John replied, "Unfortunately, the expedition will come to an end,"

Jingles piped in, "I guess ya have ta find somethin then."

"We still have time," said Uncle John.

"I am going to explore around the Medicine Rock area for the possible burial grounds," Jake said. "It is a sacred place and maybe it was chosen for that purpose."

Deseray was excited that Jake choose the area, for indeed, the burial grounds are near Medicine rock. She hoped Jake would find some promising signs. It would be a good excuse for Deseray to get near the rock formations where she and Tall Trees had hidden their treasured items.

"I think that is perfect," Deseray agreed with Jake.

Jake headed northeast of the dig. The team continued to work the new site.

"Uncle John," Deseray asked. "What will happen if we find a burial site?"

"At that point, we will no longer be able to explore it. The Bureau of Indian Affairs will take over. Burial sites are a very delicate issue. They are sacred and we would be considered intruders."

"I understand," said Deseray. "But it would be a great discovery, wouldn't it?"

"Yes, it would," Uncle John said.

"I will work the screens with Kachina," Curtis said to John. "You and Deseray can dig."

The new location proved to be productive.

"Uncle John." said Deseray. "Look, I found an ash stain!"

John examined the spot where Deseray dug.

"Yes, you did!"

Just as Deseray was taking pictures and writing in her book, Jake rode into the dig site.

As she dismounted, she seemed excited.

"I think I found the burial grounds," she said. "The terrain is extremely uneven with small mounds protruding from the dirt. The area surrounding it has smooth variations and gently rolling hills."

She took out a map, spread it on the ground, and pointed.

"This area here," she explained, "Is the best place to look."

As Deseray looked at the map, she noted that Jake had found the burial site. She wanted to tell everyone Jake was right, but of course, she could not.

"We have good news here as well," Deseray told Jake. "We found another fire pit. The odds of your discovery of the burial grounds have just increased in probability."

"We will document this area for future excavation for an advance archeological dig and move to the possible burial grounds," Uncle John announced.

Deseray felt sadden at abandoning their present site, but the burial grounds would offer concrete artifacts that would prove that a Sioux tribe lived in this area.

"We can move the camp closer to the possible burial site," Jake said. "I have already found the best location for a new camp."

Horses, mules and riders followed Jake to the new location.

The small caravan went three miles northeast of the old site.

When they arrived, Jake brought the caravan to a halt.

"I think this area will make a good spot for our camp," she said. "The possible burial site is about a mile from here."

"We can set up camp and get an early start in the morning." John said.

Deseray and Kachina put their tent up in record time.

"You guys are getting pretty good at that." Curtis complemented. "I guess practice makes perfect," he added.

When Curtis returned with a fresh supply of firewood, Jingles started the campfire.

"I think I'll make some cake," announced Jingles, "to celebrate."

Curtis rose to his feet and walked over to Jingles.

"Can I watch? I would really like to see how you make cake in a camp kettle."

As Jingles and Curtis made the cake, John and Jake looked at the map. Deseray and Kachina decided to rearrange their packs preparing for the next day.

At the end of supper, everyone dined on fresh baked cake.

"This sure was good cake, Curtis," John said, "as he put the last morsel into his mouth.

"I had a great teacher," Curtis replied.

While sitting in her tent, Deseray organized her notes. Upon reviewing all her digital pictures, she felt pleased with herself. As she thought about her return to college, she realized that the baby would be born before her graduation.

Suddenly panic swept over her. She placed her hand on her slightly bulging abdomen. To cover her weight gain, she began wearing her loosest fitting clothes.

How am I going to explain this to my parents? She wondered.

Kachina's voice interrupted her thoughts.

"Are you excited about tomorrow?" she asked.

"I am. If we find the burial grounds, we will be done with our part of the expedition though," she answered.

Kachina settled into her sleeping bag.

"But we will have accomplished what you set out to do. That is pretty great, isn't it?"

Deseray put her notes and camera into her pack.

"Yes, you are right, and summer is about over. I have enough material to write my thesis."

She said. "We had better get some sleep, tomorrow hopefully will results in some interesting finds."

Deseray was the first to rise, even before Jingles, which was unusual.

She gathered some wood in her arms and placed it in the fire pit. By the time she lit the match for the fire, she heard a voice.

"Yer up perty early, little lady."

"Good morning Jingles. I couldn't sleep anymore. To excited I guess."

"How ya feelin?' Jingles was concerned for both Deseray and the baby.

"Very good, better than I thought I would."

"Well, I'll make ya some tea and git some coffee goin. I can hear stirrin in the tents."

Sure enough, one by one, everyone gathered around the now roaring campfire.

Kachina stretched, "That fire feels nice in this chilly air," she said.

Eggs sizzled and coffee brewed, tantalizing the appetites for the hungry explorers.

Jingles finished the dishes and turned to John, "Mind if I come along today?"

"Sure, you're more than welcome to tag along," John replied.

"Since this here expedition is bout done, I figered I should see what the fuss is all bout." Jingles continued to clean up the breakfast dishes.

Upon arrival to the proposed dig site, everyone did his or her share to set up the grid.

"We'll concentrate on the unusual dirt formations and work outward from them." John instructed.

Deseray and Uncle John carefully removed shovels of dirt as Curtis and Kachina shook the screens.

By late afternoon, Deseray motioned to Uncle John.

"Look here," she said, "I think this is a carved stone."

John kneeled next to her and she carefully ran his finger along the protruding edge of the object.

"I think you are right." He said, as he switched from his small shovel to a large brush. He carefully swept the dirt away, revealing more of the stone object.

As each inch of dirt disappeared it become evident that the object was carved of stone.

"I think it is a pipe made from stone."

Leaving the object in place, Uncle John and Deseray continued to unearth the carved stone.

Within a few hours, the soil along the side of the carved stone indicated pieces of decayed wood.

"This is the stem," Deseray said.

She took pictures as John continued the remove more dirt.

Once the carved part of the object was completely unearthed, John carefully removed it from its resting ground.

"The stone is nicely preserved." Uncle John said. "The style of the pipe bowl is defiantly Sioux."

Deseray smiled with excitement.

"We did it Uncle John. We proved that a Sioux tribe lived here. This pipe must be part of the burial ceremony. Relatives put the dead one's personal possessions with them at the burial."

"It is a good start, but this does not prove it is a burial site." John explained. "We still have a lot of work to do. We can continue early in the morning. It's getting to dark to do a decent job of looking."

The reluctant explorers agreed with Uncle John as they headed back to camp. No one needed encouragement to go to sleep early. They all were anxious to start digging as early as possible.

Deseray found it difficult to sleep due to her excitement over the discovery of the burial grounds.

Finally, she did sleep but the clatter of Jingles' cooking pots awakened her.

As breakfast ended, Jingles asked, "I like ta tag along agin, if I kin."

"Of course," Uncle John said. "Today is going to be a great day."

Once at the dig site, Jingles piped in "Why don't ya have Kachina and Curtis help ya dig. I can work the screens."

"Great suggestion," answered Deseray.

"I'll work the other screen," said Jake.

While Jingles and Jake worked the screens, Deseray, John, Curtis and Kachina worked the grids. They each worked different grids in order to make quicker progress.

As two days passed, there were no new discoveries. Early on the third day, a high-pitched squeal came out of Kachina.

"Oh, I think I found a finger!" she screamed. She jumped up and away from the spot she was working.

Deseray was the first one to reach Kachina's grid. She bent down and carefully examined the object Kachina had unearthed.

Uncle John was soon kneeling next to Deseray.

He took his brush and continued to uncover the possible bone. Upon removing additional dirt, the appearance of several much-diminished hand bones became apparent.

Deseray took pictures and wrote notes as Uncle John continued to uncover the bones.

A stone object soon began to appear near the small bone fragments.

"I think this is a bowl to a pipe.' Uncle John commented.

Within an hour, remnants of a human hand and part of a pipe lay before them in the dirt.

"Yes, John said, "this is a burial site. By the pipe bowl design, it is also Sioux origin. Unfortunately, we have to stop our dig."

John stood up and took out his cell phone." I have to call the Bureau of Indian Affairs and report out findings. This belongs to them now," he explained.

Deseray was both excited and disappointed at the same time.

After John finished his conversation on the phone, he could sense Deseray's disappointment.

"I wouldn't be so sad, Deseray. You not only have the information for your thesis, but you also have an archeological finding to add you to list of accomplishments."

"I hadn't thought it that way," she said.

"Besides," Uncle John added. "Since you are one of the discoverers of this site, I am sure they will let you be part of the team to work this site."

Deseray's smile returned.

"I never thought of it that way. What do we do now?"

"We will hang around here for a few days and keep the site secured. When the proper authorities arrive, they will take over. They will put their own security team in place and make decisions about future excavation of this site."

"Wow," Kachina said, "this is really exciting."

"What will we do for the next few days?" Deseray asked.

"We can work the village site, or we can just enjoy being out in nature," Uncle John said.

"We can just relax," he added.

That night was full of excitement and conversation about their great find.

Over the next few days, everyone went on their own adventures.

While Deseray was sitting next to Kachina, she got an idea on what adventure they could share.

"Kachina?" she said, "do you want to ride to Medicine Rock with me?" She was thinking about the items she and Tall Trees had placed with the formations of Medicine Rock when she was in the past. She was curious if they had survived.

"That sounds like great fun!" said Kachina. "Ok, then, to Medicine Rock we go!"

When Deseray and Kachina arrived at the Medicine Rock area, Deseray was surprised at how much the formations had changed.

Since the formations were sandstone, she realized those three hundred years of wind, rain and time would change the formations.

Deseray and Kachina tethered the horses.

"Let's take a closer look at the formations." Deseray said.

As they walk around the formations, Deseray feared she would not be able to find the particular one that housed the items they had hid.

"I am going to go this way," Kachina announced to Deseray.

"Ok," she replied, "I will go this way."

She was relieved that Kachina decided to separate. Since the discovery of the burial grounds, the items she and Tall Trees hid were no longer as significant. Deseray just wanted to see if they survived.

Just about when Deseray wanted to give up, a formation caught her eye. After careful examination, she realized that she was in the correct area. She carefully climbed to the spot where she believed the items should be.

The rock that she used to cover the hole in the formation was much smaller than when she first placed it there.

She removed the rock and cautiously put her hand inside. Sand had formed into the hole, but she could tell that there was something below the sand. She grasped the bundle and pulled it through the hole. The deterioration of the leather was evident as it crumbled in her hands. Parts of it remained as she carefully un-wrapped the bundle.

The quiver had not survived well but she could tell what it had been. The fleshing stone was quite well preserved. The feathers on the end of the arrows were completely gone, but the shafts, though very fragile and thin were identifiable. The arrowheads, like the fleshing tool were well preserved.

To her surprise, there was a flat stone also wrapped in the bundle. A stone she had never seen before.

As she turned the stone over, she noticed carvings on one side.

The carving on the flat stone was an I M and a happy smile carved into the stone. Below these letters, were small, barely distinguishable letters. Deseray had difficulty making out the small letters.

"Is this a message from Tall Trees?" she wondered. She thought about how much time and effort it must have taken to carve the letters.

I am happy, she thought. That is what it means. She smiled at the thought that Tall Trees was happy. She secretly put the stone in her pocket. She would study it later. She placed the other artifacts in her pack. Since she discovered them on public land, she was obligated to turn them into the authorities. She decided to think about whether she would mention them to Uncle John.

Just as Deseray's feet touched the ground, Kachina came

into view.

"Are you ready to go?" she asked Deseray.

"Yes, I am. I've had enough exploring," Deseray replied.

When they arrived back at camp, Uncle John had news for everyone.

"The representatives for the Indians affairs will arrive early tomorrow morning. After we discuss our discoveries with them, we can be on our way back to the ranch."

"This has been fun," said Kachina, "but I am ready to go home and sleep in my own bed."

Deseray decided not to mention the artifacts she had found. She justified her actions because technically they were hers, only from the past.

Deseray was excited to have some possessions that she and Tall Trees had shared.

The next morning came early. Several trucks arrived, waking everyone from their sleep.

Jingles quickly started coffee, eggs, and bacon for breakfast.

The small circle of logs around the campfire quickly filled with guests.

Deseray and John shared their notes, discussed their findings and pictures with the representatives.

"After breakfast," said John "We will take you to the site of the burial grounds."

Only Deseray and John rode in the trucks to the burial grounds.

After walking around and seeing what they had discovered, an older American Indian man spoke.

"Thank you for discovering this sacred place," he said. "It is important to honor the dead by honoring their resting place."

Deseray said, "You are most welcome."

"I would be interested," she continued, "to be part of the expedition that will excavate this area, if you would let me."

"We owe the discovery to you and your team. We would like to include you when we begin. Of course, we must hold many rituals and keep the ground holy before we can do any-thing more," he explained. "We will be in contact with you and let you know of our progress."

After the tour and information sharing, it was evident to Deseray that the expedition had ended.

Chapter Fifteen - The Future

Once the equipment, horses and mules settled quietly in the trailers, the journey home was underway.

"Uncle John," asked Deseray, "do you mind if Jingles and I ride together?"

"That would be fine," he replied.

She and Jingles had not been able to talk alone since the hospital. She was anxious to share information about his past family with him.

"I am happy to finally be able to talk to you about my experiences in the past." she told Jingles.

"I would like to hear about my surviving children," Jingles said.

Deseray once again noticed the disappearance of his southern drawl.

"I met Tall Trees in our time and also the white buffalo. The white buffalo gave me the feather that transported me back in time. When I met him, he said his name was Regional but said to call him Reg."

"Regional was my father's name," Jingles said. "Funny how things seemed connected."

"Tall Trees is a great warrior. Women Who Sings was my best friend." Tears came to her eyes. "I miss them all so much."

"I am overwhelmed that two of my children survived." Jingles said, "I am even happier that you were a part of their lives. I wish I had known my son though."

Deseray smiled, "You can know your grandchild. The baby is part of your son. The baby is part of you."

"I am worried about telling my family about the baby. I am having a baby by a man who has been dead for 300 years.

How can that be? I want to finish college, but I don't know how I can do that. The baby will be born halfway through my last semester and my parents will want to know who the father is," she said.

"We'll figure it out together," Jingles said. "I am going to rent a car and drive back east." He added. "Would you like to drive back with me? We can work out a plan. After all, it is my grandchild."

"I would like that," Deseray replied. The ranch house was a welcoming site as the small caravan stopped in the driveway near the porch.

Elisha followed by little Louis greeted the travelers as they gathered on the porch.

John gave Elisha a hug and a kiss as they embraced.

"I have coffee brewing and fresh huckleberry pie almost baked," she announced.

"That is a good idea. We will all meet back here for fresh baked pie as soon as we bed down the horses and mules," John announced.

Jake shook John's hand. "I am going to a hotel, but I will be leaving in the morning," Jake said, "I already have another guide job."

"We will be sorry to see you leave," John said.

Elisha placed her hand on Jake's shoulder.

"You will not go to a hotel," she insisted. "You get your horses settled and we have plenty of room here. You will stay."

"OK," Jake agreed. "I'll stay the night."

After putting the horses and mules in the stables, one by one, everyone found a seat at the kitchen table.

"Maybe Jingles can learn to make huckleberry pie in a kettle," Curtis said as everyone enjoyed the pie.

"I kin give it a try," Jingles replied.

Deseray interrupted as she spoke to Jake, "Can I get copies of your artwork to add to my report?"

"Sure, I am flattered," Jake said.

Deseray reached for her pack, which contained the notes

and images from the expedition.

"Uncle John, can I use your computer and scanner?"

"Sure, I will get you set up." Deseray followed John to his office.

Jake stood up as John and Deseray started to leave the kitchen.

"I'll go get the sketches," Jake said.

A few minutes later, she was back. Elisha showed her to John's office.

Jake handed the sketches to Deseray.

"Can I get a copy of your report when you complete it?" Jake asked.

"Sure. Leave me your address and I send you a copy when I am done."

Jake wrote her address on a sheet of paper and handed it to Deseray. After completing the copies of the sketches, Deseray handed the originals back to Jake.

"These will add a lot of validity to my report," Deseray told her.

"My pleasure," Jake replied.

Uncle John ran his fingers through his beard.

"It's been a busy day," he said, "we should all turn in. I will bid you all a good night."

As the house settled into a restful quiet, Deseray thought sleep would be difficult, but sometime during her thoughts, she fell asleep.

Deseray rose early. She grabbed the pouch with the feather and walked outside. She found an inviting spot near a tree. As Deseray sat and rested against the tree, the early sun began to warm her face.

The sound of an eagle's cry lifted her eyes upward. She watched as it soared seemingly above the mountains. When she lowered her eyes, she held a baby in her arms. It was a boy baby, Tall Tree's son.

Deseray suddenly felt a hand on her shoulder. She looked

up and saw Uncle John's face.

"You ok?" he asked.

"I'm fine," she said. When she looked at her arms, the baby was gone.

"I must have fallen asleep," she replied.

"I just wanted to tell you that Jake is leaving. I thought you would want to say goodbye."

"I do," she said and rose to her feet.

As Jake latched the door on her trailer, a smile formed on her face.

"I was hoping to see you before I left," she said to Deseray.

"I was hoping to see you too." She embraced Jake affectionately.

"It has been so much fun getting to know you," she said.

Jake returned the hug.

"It has been nice getting to know you too. We should keep in touch."

"We will," Deseray, answered.

Waving and chants of farewell followed Jake as she drove down the road.

Shortly after Jake had left, Jingles announced that he was also leaving.

"I got some friends ta visit," he said. "But I will be back next week ta take the little lady back home."

After Jingles left, activates of the ranch starting to resume as usual.

Deseray spent her last week at the ranch working on her paper. John, Curtis and Kachina settled back into their daily chores. When she completed her report, Deseray decided to take a break and to help Kachina.

She found Kachina in the barn mucking stalls.

"Want some help?" Deseray asked.

"I thought you were working on your report?" she replied.

"All done," Deseray smiled.

"Really? I can't wait to read it."

"I will share it at supper tonight. I am really happy with

it."

Deseray grabbed a shovel and began helping Kachina.

Shovel after shovel of soiled hay found its way into a small trailer.

Kachina showed Deseray where the new bedding was located. Together they open bales of bedding and tossed it on the nearly cleaned floors.

"All done," announced Kachina. "We should take showers before supper. We smell pretty ripe."

They laughed about how they smelled all the way to the house.

As they stepped onto the porch, Curtis began waving his hand in front of his face.

"Phew, you guys stink."

Kachina slapped Curtis on the shoulder. "Brat."

At the end of supper, Deseray handed out copies of her report.

As John turned the pages, he commented, "This is a great report. I like how you added the personal aspect of the explorers throughout your report."

Deseray smiled. "Jake's artwork helped to personalize the report. I felt it was important to include the frustration, disappointments and excitement of the excavators."

"You will get a good grade," John added.

"I would like to include a copy of your report with the report that I am sending to the Bureau of Indian Affairs," Uncle John said.

"I can send it to them after I submit it to my professor. I hope you don't mind," said Deseray.

"I can see your point. I will let you know where to send it when you are ready."

"So, you are heading home in a few days?' John asked.

"Yes. As you know I will be driving back with Jingles." Deseray added. "We get along well and he thought I might like to see some of this country on my way home."

Uncle John smiled. "I like him as well. A little reserved,

but he has a great personality."

Deseray realized how quickly the next two days passed, when she saw Jingles coming up the driveway in a car.

Once Jingles exited the car, John met him with a warm handshake.

"Good to see you again, Jingles," he said.

"Good ta see you agin too, John," he said. "Is the little lady ready ta go?" he asked.

Curtis was bringing Deseray's luggage onto the porch.

"Hope you have a big trunk," he laughed, as he set the luggage onto the porch.

Jingles opened the trunk, "Prety big I guess."

Once the luggage was in the trunk, Uncle John's family gathered around Deseray.

Elisha gave her an affectionate hug.

"It's been wonderful having you visit. You have to come back soon."

Curtis gave her a quick hug. "The dig was fun. Maybe we can do it again sometime", he said.

"I would like that. It was great getting to know you."

Deseray and Kachina embraced as tears formed in their eyes.

"I am going to miss you," said Kachina. "It was like having a sister for the summer."

"I am going to miss you too," said Deseray. "We can write and email all the time. Heck, we can talk whenever we want. It is modern times with cells phones and all."

They both laughed.

Deseray patted Louis on the head then bent down and gave him a little hug.

"Bye, Louis it was nice meeting you.

Louis just smiled.

Last, but not least was Uncle John.

"Thank you for letting me be part of the dig. It was more exciting and more fulfilling than you will ever know."

They embraced for a while.

"You come back for visits now, you hear?" Uncle John said.

"I definitely will. I would like to follow the progress of the burial site. Maybe they might let me join them after I graduate."

"I am sure they will," Uncle John proclaimed.

Jingles and Deseray got in the car and drove down the driveway.

"It's hard to say goodbye to everyone," said Deseray. "But it isn't like it will be forever."

"We can go as far as Miles City before we drop down to Wyoming. We can get a hotel there."

"That sounds good." Deseray paused. "So, what is your real story? The stuff I don't already know."

"As I told you, my parents were killed when I was young. They were wealthy. My father was a successful businessman. When they died, I inherited all their wealth. I used some of the money to attend college. I ran my father's business but felt unaccomplished. Little by little I began to delegate so I could have more free time."

"My heritage is through my mother, who is full blooded Sioux. She met my father at college. After my parents were married, we visited the reservation from time to time, but I wanted to spend more time there so I could learn about my people.

"My mother let me visit my grandmother whenever I wanted."

"After they died, I stayed on the reservation until I was eighteen and left to go to college. After college, I took over the business operations. I go back to the reservation whenever I can to see my grandmother and take part in ceremonies."

"So that is my life," he concluded.

Deseray sat quietly for a while. It was a lot for her to understand all at once.

"So, your heritage is why you have a strong interest in your culture?" she asked.

"Yes. The necklace you returned to me held all the totems from my childhood up to the day I lost it. It was important to me since some of the totems were from the time I spent with my parents."

"Why were you so secretive about the expedition?" Deseray asked. "You had the money for it, why didn't you just sponsor one openly?"

"I could have, but my reason for it was unbelievable and I also wanted to keep that part of my life private. As I told you, I wasn't sure it all happened. When you return the necklace to me and after hearing your story, I was certain it did happen."

"We should stop for lunch," he said.

After the lunch stop, they continued to Miles City.

"Jingles?" asked Deseray, "When you returned from the past, didn't people wonder how you injured your leg?"

"I don't remember my return, the doctor said I was hit by a car and believed that the impact caused the leg damaged. Of course, I don't remember a car and I know how my leg got damaged. Of course, I couldn't tell the doctor, so I just let it go as a car accident."

Deseray wondered at the way things were working out.

"I was just thinking about a conversation I had with Elisha," Deseray said. "I told her about how informative a nice man had been on the train. When you arrived at the ranch, I told her I was surprised that you were the man from the train and how strange it was that we were going to the same place but didn't know it."

"Elisha answer seemed so relevant, even more so now. She said, "It's funny how things work out sometimes, even without us realizing that they are working out for the best."

Jingles laughed, "It really is, isn't it?"

"I got two hotel rooms for us in Miles city," he continued. "We will be there soon."

The rest of the ride was quiet. Deseray sat in the car as Jingles got the motel key cards. The rooms were side by side.

As Jingles handed Deseray the key he said, "We can get cleaned up and go to the restaurant for dinner. How does that sound?'

"That sound good to me," replied Deseray. She took her

pack from the car.

As Deseray opened the motel room door, the room had a pleasantly fresh smell and astonishing cleanliness.

About twenty minutes later, the knock on her door made Deseray aware that Jingles was ready for supper.

Upon opening the door, Deseray had to prevent her mouth from dropping open in surprise as she gazed at Jingles.

He was clean-shaven, hair nicely combed, and his shirt was quite fashionable. Deseray just smiled.

Jingles laughed.

"I clean up pretty good, don't you think?"

"Very good," replied Deseray, who was still trying to comprehend the "new" Jingles.

With the beard gone, Deseray was right when she had thought he might be a handsome looking man. He reminded her of Tall Trees.

They were silent as they walked across the parking lot to the restaurant.

After they had ordered their food, Deseray had to ask, "What is your real name? As you told me, you were not born Jingles."

"To honor my mother's heritage, my first name is Chaska, which means, eldest son. To honor my father's heritage, my middle name is Regional, like my grandfather."

"It is a good name," Deseray commented.

"I did end up being the oldest son, but my two brothers died with my parents," Jingles told her.

"I am so sorry," she said.

They sat in silence for a while as they ate their food.

When they were done, Deseray asked, "Why do you let people think you are a seemingly uneducated, semi poor southerner?"

Jingles smiled, "I wanted my life to be simple. The business is complicated and time consuming. I had to deal with so many people day after day. I just wanted to take a break from my reality."

Jingles continued.

"Lately, the only time I am myself is when I visit my grandmother on the reservation, but I haven't seen her for a while."

Deseray piped in, "Let's do that!"

"Do what?' asked Jingles.

"Let's go visit your grandmother. We could stop on our way through the Dakotas."

"Are you sure?"

"Yes!" replied Deseray. "I would like that."

"My grandmother lives on the reservation in the southern part South Dakota. The reservation consists of Dakota, Lakota and Nakota. She is Lakota," Jingles told her.

"We can go to see her. I would like you to meet each other. She has great knowledge of the Spirit world. She may be able to give us some advice."

By mid-morning two days later, Deseray and Jingles arrived at the reservation.

"I let my grandmother know we are coming for a visit. She is excited to meet you," Jingles told Deseray.

As they entered the reservation, Deseray was surprised at how much poverty existed.

"Don't they have a casino here? Doesn't that help them?" she asked.

"The casino is small. Not enough visitors go to the casino to impact the poverty here," Jingles replied.

Many of the houses were old, small and some even falling down. Dotted here and there were a few houses that seemed newer and more inhabitable than most of them.

Jingles stopped in front of a ranch style house.

"I build my grandmother's house but kept it modest so she would not be ridiculed by other tribe members. She has several of her close friends live with her. It is her way of helping to make life better for some. She does not want to leave the reservation because she feels it is her home."

After Jingles knocked on the door, a very elderly woman

answered. Tears came to her eyes as she embraced Jingles.

"Chaska," she said.

"Grandmother, I have missed you," Jingles replied.

As soon as Deseray entered the house, grandmother smiled.

"Dry Sands," grandmother said as she took Deseray's hand. "I have been waiting for you."

It surprised Deseray to hear her past American Indian name. How did she know?

Jingles just smiled.

"Please come in," grandmother said. "I have lunch ready for you. My friends have gone visiting so we will have time to visit undisturbed," she added."

"My grandson has told me of his journey to the past people," grandmother began, "I have had visions that you have also taken this journey and returned."

Deseray sat quietly as grandmother spoke.

"This is a special gift for both of you. You have much knowledge of our past people that you can share with others. It makes my heart happy to know that the people and their ways will not be forgotten."

Deseray smiled.

"I am honored that the Spirits chose me to take this journey," she said. "I have learned so many things about their ways and I will find a way to tell all that I have learned."

She looked at Jingles.

"Chaska and I will find a way together."

"This is good," grandmother replied.

She slowly left the room and returned with a bundle wrapped in fur.

She handed the bundle to Deseray.

"This is for the baby," she said.

Before Deseray could comment, grandmother simply said, "The Spirits have told me."

Deseray un-wrapped the bundle to discovery traditionally made children's moccasins.

She reached over and squeezed grandmother's frail hand.

"Thank you," she said.

"My grandmother makes items in the traditional way," Jingles said, "and sells them at the tourist gift shops."

Grandmother smiled.

"I remember some of the old ways," she said. "My mother and grandmother told me stories and thought me how to make many things that were used before our way of life was taken from us."

She continued, "I taught these things to my daughter, but the Spirits have taken her. I think you learned these things on your journey and hope you will teach others about them."

"I will," Deseray said.

As she ate the lunch grandmother had made, the buffalo they ate reminded Deseray of the importance of this meat when she lived in the past.

"Are their very many buffalo around here?" she asked grandmother.

"Some of the community members raise buffalo. They provide some for the people and sell some the visitors."

"The baby," grandmother continued," is from you joining to a brave from your journey," she stated.

"Yes," Deseray answered. "He was my husband."

"The father is my grandson's son?" she asked.

"Yes," Deseray answered.

Grandmother was silent for a moment.

"A child needs a heritage, and my family is your child's heritage. My grandson is your child's grandfather. You should tell everyone this is true. His son is the father, and his son has gone before us. This is true. This is what you tell."

Deseray thought about what grandmother said.

"This is true," Deseray replied.

Grandmother smile as she touched Deseray's hand.

"You will have a son."

Deseray smiled.

After saying their farewells to grandmother Deseray and

Jingles began the last leg for Deseray to Wisconsin.

"I really like your grandmother," commented Deseray. "She is really wise."

Jingles smiled.

"Yes, she is. She is the only other one that I have ever told of my journey. She has great connections with the Spirit world, and she understands."

"She told us to be truthful about the baby," he said. "I am the grandfather no matter how that came about. My son is dead, many years now. If you tell your family that the father is dead and I am the grandfather, it will all be true."

Tears came to Deseray's eyes as she thought about Tall Trees being long dead, hundreds of years ago. Yet she carried his child.

Jingles continued. "It is the way of my people, if the father is dead, the grandfather becomes the father. If you are more comfortable with that, we can tell them I am the father."

"Why would you do that," she asked.

"We have something in common that no one else has. We have traveled in time. I am the only one who really understands. I want to be part of raising my grandchild, even if I have to pretend that I am the father."

"I think what your grandmother said is best," Deseray replied. "I will tell my family that I was in love with the baby's father, Reg, and he died. I will tell them that I had not met you yet, so I did not realize you were Reg's father."

"I think that is the best," Jingles said. "I can be a part of both you and my grandchild's life and it will all be true."

"Your grandchild is a grandson," Deseray said.

"A boy?" Jingles asked. Tears came to his eyes.

Deseray was relieved that she finally had a way to explain the baby and a way that was true. She would leave out the time travel. It would be unbelievable and complicated.

"We can stay in a nearby hotel," Jingles told Deseray," and continue in the morning,"

"I would like that," Deseray said.

That night, Deseray dreamt of Tall Trees.

He held their son in his arms. The sun cast warmth upon them as they sat near the river. Deseray was cooking lunch as they had what modern times would refer to as a picnic.

Deseray's heart filled with love and overwhelming joy.

The knock on her hotel door woke her from her dream.

Tears filled her eyes and she realized it was just that, a dream.

"I have something to show you," she said as she invited Jingles into the room.

She opened her pack and removed the artifacts she found at Medicine Rock.

"Tall Trees and I placed these in a cavern at Medicine Rock so someone from my time could find them. I didn't tell my uncle because I knew I would have to turn them in. I decided to keep them because they are possessions that Tall Trees and I owed together."

Jingles looked at the artifacts.

"I don't think it is a problem," he said. "They became insignificant when you discovered the burial grounds."

Deseray agreed.

"I have something else to show you." She took out the stone with the carvings on it.

Jingles read the words on the stone.

"Do you think it is from my son?" he asked.

"I do," said Deseray. "Somehow the Spirits made it possible for him to send a message to me in English."

As Jingles touched the stone he asked, "What are these small letters at the bottom. I can't read them."

Deseray took the stone from Jingles.

"I think the first one is an R, but I can't make out the rest. I think it is REG."

"You are probably right," Jingles said. "'Tall Trees' would have taken him forever to carve."

As Deseray was about to return the stone to the medicine pouch, she remembered that it belonged to Jingles.

"I guess I should return your medicine pouch," she said, "It was a gift from Spirit Walker."

Jingles smiled.

It has been through your journey, so it is yours now. You should keep it."

"Thank you," she replied, as she returned the stone to the medicine where it rested with the eagle feather.

"So, we have a plan," Jingles said. "I will take over my duties as grandfather. Financially I can take good care of you both. You can finish this semester and after the baby is born, you can continue where you left off and finish your degree."

"That would be wonderful," Deseray said.

Jingles continued, "I will be moving closer to you after I make arrangements when I get home. I want to be a big part of my grandson's life. I want to take him to the reservation so he can participate in the rituals that he should undertake to become a man."

"I would like that," she said. "It will honor his father if he learns the ways of his people."

"Speaking of college," Jingles added, "I am going to set up a scholarship for Kachina to become a Taxidermist and another scholarship to pay the balance of Curtis' tuition."

"That is very kind of you, but why would you do that?"

"Because," Jingles said, "they are now my family. Each year I give scholarships to my grandmother's community so some of the young people there can have a chance to make a better life for themselves and their families. I just wanted to do the same for my new family."

Deseray smiled.

Deseray and Jingles continued to discuss their futures as they drove toward Wisconsin.

"Do you want to stay for a while and meet my family?" Deseray asked. "I won't tell them about the baby until I am ready, but I would like you to meet them, so you aren't a total surprise when the time comes to tell them the whole story."

"We can give them bits and pieces for now," Jingles said.

Deseray was nervous as they drove down they long driveway. Jingles stopped the car and opened the trunk as he unloaded Deseray's luggage.

Deseray's mom came to greet them.

She gave her daughter an affectionate hug.

"Mom," she said, "I would like you to meet Jingles. He was on the expedition with us."

Jingles shook her mom's hand, "Nice to meet you."

Deseray noticed the southern drawl was gone.

"Oh, my," she replied, "you're the one who found my daughter."

She immediately gave Jingles a tight hug.

"Yes, I did," he replied.

"Come in for some coffee and something to eat, won't you?"

"I would be happy to," he said as he carried some of Deseray's luggage into the house.

Deseray's mother was excited as she prepared lunch.

Jingles left and soon returned with the rest of Deseray's luggage.

As they sat down to eat, Deseray's mother was full of questions.

"Did you have fun on the expedition? Did you make lots of discoveries?"

"Yes, we did," Deseray replied. "The biggest discovery I made is that Jingles is the father to my boyfriend, Reg. I know you haven't met Reg yet, but we have been together for a while now. We met in Menomonie. I was going to have you meet him once I got home."

Deseray knew this was partially true, as she had hoped that the Reg from her time and she would have gotten close enough to meet her family.

"What a surprise," her mother commented. "So, you had no idea he was your boyfriend's father."

"No, I didn't." Deseray answered.

After lunch, Jingles rose from his chair.

"I hate to eat and run, but I have a long way to drive yet. It was nice meeting you."

"It was nice meeting you too," her mother said.

After Jingles disappeared down the driveway, Deseray was anxious to visit the animal refuge, just in case Reg and the White buffalo might happen to be there.

"Deseray, her mother said, "I didn't realize you would be home today, and I have a meeting to go to. Is it ok if I leave for a while?"

"That's fine, mom. I want to go to Menomonie to see if I can find Reg. You know how it is."

"Young love," she replied, "Of course I know how it is."

As Deseray approached the buffalo yard, her hearted ached with anticipation. Upon scanning the yard, she realized that White Buffalo was nowhere to be seen.

She sat under the tree where she and Reg had sat. She sat and waited. As the sun lowered in the sky, she knew he would not return. She opened her medicine pouch and gently stoked the feather.

She placed her hand on her stomach, talking to the baby.

"Don't give up hope," she said. "We do not know what the Spirits may have in mind for us. After all," she continued, "we still have the buffalo's feather."

About The Author

Rita K. Kasinskas

Rita was born Rita Kaye Miller and married Tom Kasinskas in May of 1979. She is a mother of three children and two grand-children. She is an artist and journalist.

She has been an entrepreneur having undertaken a variety of business adventures. Her true passion has been writing, art, and jewelry making.

Another of her passions has been the study of American Indian art and history. Writing The White Buffalo's Feather is her way of sharing her passion with others.